the Retreat

the

Retreat

DAVID BERGEN

NAKUSP LIBRARY

McCLELLAND & STEWART

Library and Archives Canada Cataloguing in Publication

Bergen, David, 1957-
The retreat / David Bergen.

ISBN 978-0-7710-1253-2

I. Title.

PS8553.E665R48 2008   C813'.54   C2008-900775-1

We acknowledge the financial support of the Government of Canada through the Book
Publishing Industry Development Program and that of the Government of Ontario
through the Ontario Media Development Corporation's Ontario Book Initiative. We
further acknowledge the support of the Canada Council for the Arts and the Ontario Arts
Council for our publishing program.

Typeset in Centaur by M&S, Toronto
Printed and bound in Canada

ANCIENT FOREST
FRIENDLY

This book was produced using ancient-forest friendly papers.

McClelland & Stewart Ltd.
75 Sherbourne Street
Toronto, Ontario
M5A 2P9
www.mcclelland.com

1 2 3 4 5   12 11 10 09 08

To Mary

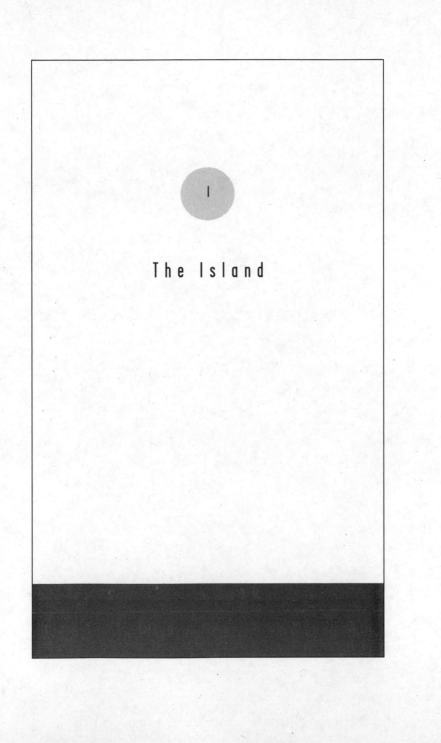

1

The Island

In early summer of 1973 he left his grandmother's house and moved his belongings off the reserve to a small cabin near Bare Point where his existence was rigorous in its simplicity. The unpainted rooms, the coop that held the chickens, the furniture of castoffs from the dump, the evenings around the small table upon which several candles burned. He had just turned eighteen, had dropped out of high school the previous spring, and he liked the freedom of his sparse solitary life. He worked at the local golf course and in the evenings drove to town where he met Alice Hart, the daughter of a local businessman who owned the town lumberyard. At the Paramount on Second Street, beneath the marquee, Alice leaned against the wall and waited. She sucked mints and when she kissed him her mouth held the scent of his grandmother's peppermint tea. Her tongue was quick. She told him to grow a moustache and what he produced was an uneven failure. Because her father had forbidden her to spend time with him, they usually drove the back roads outside Kenora, heading north and then circling back to his cabin where they played cards and drank and undressed each other and Alice promised him eternal love. "Ray," she said. Her fingers were slight and the part in her hair revealed a white scalp. Her ears turned bright red after sex.

He had an eighteen-foot aluminum Lund with a twenty-horse Johnson and one evening at dusk Raymond took Alice out onto the lake and they watched a thunderstorm approach from the west. The lightning was high and moved sideways across the sky and it was as if someone were striking matches and failing to light them. Alice wore an orange lifejacket. She was drinking beer and sitting looking back at Raymond and he saw his future and it did not include her. She smiled. Raised her beer and drank. The sky lit up behind her head.

Earl Hart, one of the constables on the town police force and an uncle to Alice, paid Raymond a visit at the golf course on a Tuesday night, just at closing. He was parked beside Raymond's pickup, and as Raymond approached, Hart rolled down his window and said, "Mr. Seymour." Raymond nodded and opened the passenger side door to his pickup. He threw in his jacket and lunch bucket and then shut the door and looked at Hart, who said he should get in the cruiser.

"I'd like a word."

Raymond looked out over the roof of the cruiser to the clubhouse. He put his hands in his pockets and then walked around to the passenger door and got in.

"You golf?" Hart asked.

Raymond said that he didn't. He just looked after the course, cut the greens and the fairways. He did play basketball though, he said. Point guard. He offered the faintest grin.

"Yeah? You good?"

Raymond shrugged. He said it wasn't up to him to know that. His coach, Roger, would be able to say.

"So, you're modest."

"Might be," Raymond said.

"You're not sure."

"I guess not."

"Huh. He guesses he's not sure. Jesus Christ." He shifted and tapped the steering wheel with a thick finger. "And about golf, you know nothing. Funny. That'd be like me cleaning someone's gun so's they could use it, but me never having fired one." He patted the gun at his right hip. "Don't you think that's odd?" Then, without waiting for an answer, he said that he used to golf, but he was a poor player, especially the long distances. "Give me a hundred yards and I'm fine. But off the tee I land out of bounds. Terrible thing to hit out of bounds, don't you think? Lose a stroke, lose the ball, lose your pride. Big losses all around." He chuckled, but it wasn't truly a laugh, more the simulacrum of a laugh, as if he had spent much time as an unhappy man learning how to imitate happiness.

He said, "Alice Hart, my niece. She's seventeen. You know her."

Raymond said that he did.

"My brother, Alice's father, he wanted to talk to you, but I suggested he let me handle it. You see, my brother is impulsive. He gets protective of Alice. She's his only daughter. You know? Anyway, Alice is impulsive like her father, nut doesn't fall far from the tree, and the simple fact is Alice isn't going to see you any more. It's finished. No more evenings and whatnot with Alice. As far as you're concerned, she doesn't exist. As far as she's concerned, you don't exist. Raymond Seymour no longer exists. Got it?"

There were falcons nesting in the spruce trees just next to the clubhouse. They lifted and settled and one circled high in the air, a black dot barely visible against the darkening sky. A mother bear with her cubs had been spotted the day before, ranging the bush between the fifth and sixth fairway. A family of deer came and went on the ninth green; every morning he found their fine hoofprints on the soft green. This was the order of the world. No one had asked Raymond Seymour to chase these animals from their place. Raymond asked Hart if Alice agreed. Did she know that he no longer existed?

Hart shifted and with his right hand cupped his crotch as if to signal the utter insolence of the question. He was a short man with a large stomach and his hand disappeared under his stomach and then reappeared. He said that Alice had no say in the matter. The girl was naive. "She will not be bait for a boy like you." He lifted a hand and pointed a short finger into the air. "You're an Indian. Stick with what you know. Rumour has it you're smart. Prove it." He waved his hand in dismissal and said, "Go."

Raymond climbed from the car and stood and watched Hart drive away. Darkness had fallen. The tail lights of the cruiser blinked and then disappeared. Raymond drove into town and bought a Coke at the Shell station and then parked near the Paramount. He went inside and asked for a ticket for the late show of *Live and Let Die*. The girl at the wicket said it had started an hour ago. He could just go in. He bought popcorn and went inside and sat near the back. The theatre was half full. A collection of couples, a few solitary heads outlined by the screen. He put his feet up against the seat in front of him and watched James Bond save the world. Later, he stood on the sidewalk beneath the marquee and waited for Alice to appear. He imagined that she would walk up in sandals and jeans and a flower-print sleeveless top and say his name and take his hand. She'd be wearing hoop earrings. He would take her to the Kenricia. They would eat steak. Then they'd go back to his house and drink a nightcap and crawl into bed and in the morning they'd sit across from each other and eat toast.

Instead, Raymond drove up the 71 to his turnoff and then down the gravel road to his cabin where he lit candles and sat at his only table and ate ravioli from a tin can. Then he fed the chickens and he sat on the swing that he had rigged from the front seat of a Studebaker. Four chains and a steel frame. A mosquito landed on his forearm. He killed it. Lit a cigarette.

In the morning, he washed and dressed for Mrs. Kennedy. Clean jeans, a button-down shirt. Nine holes at nine a.m. every Wednesday, Raymond as her caddy, though he knew little about golf and no other golfers used caddies. Still, the management wanted Lisa Kennedy happy, and she was happiest with Raymond at her side. She golfed alone. This morning she wore a pink pleated skirt that fell to her knees and a white short-sleeved blouse. A white sweater with the arms tied around her waist. Raymond carried her clubs and her coffee. She drove off the first tee neatly, though not getting much distance. They walked side by side, the bag of clubs banging against Raymond's left leg. The morning sun had burned the dew off the grass. Mrs. Kennedy held out her hand for the coffee and Raymond passed it to her. She drank and walked and said that she was flying down to Texas the next day to meet a man who wanted to marry her. "He made his money in oil," she said. "You have to wonder about a man who gets rich from pumping black stuff from the ground." She asked for a three iron. Raymond slipped it from the bag and put it into her hand. She set up and took a practice swing, then turned to Raymond and asked if he planned on getting married some day. Raymond grinned and shrugged. "Don't do it for money," she said. "You'll be unhappy. A couple can be happier if there aren't the distractions of riches. Making it. Spending it. Keeping it." She stopped talking, looked down at the ball, and swung.

At the third tee, waiting for a foursome to proceed, she sat on a bench, crossed her tanned legs, and said that the Texan wanted her to become an American citizen. "It's a wild place. They elect their presidents and then throw them out like garbage. I told him that. He said that freedom had its problems sometimes. Still, I'm thinking about it. He wants to go to Egypt for the honeymoon. Where the Pyramids are."

Raymond said that he knew about the Pyramids.

"Of course you do. You're not stupid."

She four-putted the sixth green, letting loose a soft curse as she overran the hole on the second putt. When she was finished, Raymond replaced the flag and together they walked up to the seventh tee. She was shorter than him and he looked down at her. The whorl of her ear, sculpted marble.

Her small soft head. She lived alone in a large house on Coney Island. Her husband had given it to her after an amicable divorce. Her words. He sometimes came over in the evenings for sex. Her words. She had told Raymond this just after the divorce had gone through. She said, "I never thought that sex with my ex-husband would be so good." She did not look at Raymond when she said these words. She looked past him, and so it seemed that she was talking to someone else, someone just beyond Raymond, someone who actually existed.

A week passed and he did not hear from Alice. He drove by her house one night but it was dark. He waited for her to phone him at the clubhouse, which was her habit, but no calls came. One evening he visited his grandmother and watched TV with her. Then they played crib and he let her win. On the wall behind his grandmother was a picture of Jesus bending to touch a man with a crippled leg. On a cabinet nearby there were graduation photos of Raymond's brothers and sisters. The table they sat at was covered with an orange plastic cloth that was printed with green flowers set in brown pots. His grandmother's hands rested on top of one of the pots. Her hands were dark and lined and the small left finger was crooked, the result of a broken bone years earlier that had never been properly fixed. His grandmother stood and went into the kitchen and came back with a grilled cheese sandwich on a pink plate and she handed him tea.

His sister Reenie and her four kids returned from the evangelistic crusade at the town arena. A preacher from Kansas was in Kenora for the week and Reenie loved the music, the preaching, the plea for sinners to come forward, and inevitably she went forward because she considered herself a sinner. She loved the physical contact of the preacher laying hands on her. Lee, Reenie's fourteen-year-old, walked in the door and sat down beside Raymond and put her head against his shoulder. "Uncle Ray," she said.

Reenie went into the kitchen and came back with a peanut butter sandwich. She said that Pastor Rudy was the most amazing man. "He's on a higher plane," she said. "When he touched my shoulder, right here, it was like electricity was flowing from him to me." She looked at her daughter and said she should have come forward too.

Lee shook her head.

"Nobody's special," Reenie said. "Shoulda come too, Ray. You could use some God talk. Look, I got a New Testament."

The Bible was small and blue and Reenie's large hand smothered it. She handed it to Lee. "It's yours now," Reenie said. Lee held it lightly, with some misgiving.

Reenie told Raymond that she'd gone up to look for him at the cabin about a week ago. He wasn't there, but Alice Hart was. "She was sitting in her father's car, pretending to be sure of herself, and when she saw me she asked about you. Where were you? As if because she was there, so should you. Her eyes are too close together. Don't you think?"

Raymond took the New Testament from Lee and fanned the pages, smelled the newness. Handed it back and imagined Alice's eyes. He felt an ache in his stomach.

Reenie said that any girl who drove a Cadillac at that age would expect far too much in life. "She got holda your pecker?" Reenie laughed. Lee giggled. In fall, Lee would be attending the school Raymond had just left, a monstrous building that swallowed children unformed and then spat them out again four years later, bigger and sadder and sometimes wiser. Lee was already wise. She held the New Testament with a degree of doubt. Raymond stood and went out to his pickup and drove up to his place. His windows were open and air blew in and above him the sky was vast and stars fell and it smelled of autumn.

The following evening Alice came up to the cabin in her father's Cadillac and parked with her lights shining through his front door. At first he did not know who it was, and he might have shot out the headlights with his .22, but Alice's voice floated through the darkness, calling his name. He went to her and leaned in through the driver's window and put his hands like a loose necklace around her small neck. It rained that night, a heavy downpour accompanied by thunder and lightning, and out on Highway 17, when a streak of lightning swept from left to right, they saw a moose standing smack on the centre line. He did not speak of what had transpired with her uncle, even when she said, out of the blue, that her uncle Hart could be an asshole. The statement seemed an admission of something; approval perhaps, or the understanding that this was a secret and thrilling game. When she dropped him off he told her there would be mud on the tires and wheel wells, his mud, and she should wash the car down. And this is what she did. Headed over to the wand wash, where she wiped the car clean, in and out, ridding the car of all proof of Raymond Seymour.

In October his brother Marcel stayed a night at the cabin on his way through from Vancouver to Montreal, where he was planning to work for a law firm that specialized in land claims. Marcel brought with him a twelve of beer and the brothers sat on the glider swing and drank while Marcel told him once again how his eight months in prison had informed his choice to go into law. "Better to get buggered on the outside," he said. "At least there's the possibility of escape." He said that the odds were stacked against them. "I'm not whining here, but the fact is, Ray, you can choose to lie down and let the man drive back and forth over you, or you can do the driving. That's what I'm doing, the driving." He paused, opened another beer. "I met this girl in Vancouver, studied law together. Her father is a bigwig in the court system there. Lives in a large house overlooking the harbour, except the neighbour's tree, a huge fucking cedar, was blocking the view, so he hired someone to poison the tree. His daughter, Naomi, my girlfriend for a while, told me this. She told it as if this were perfectly acceptable. Our problem, you know, is we're too nice. You see. Too fucking nice. Most people when they want something, they go out and get it. There's a lesson to be learned here."

Marcel was wearing a dark blue suit jacket and the collar of his shirt was folded over the jacket's collar. The shirt's top three buttons were open and he wore a gold chain with a fat pendant. His watch, quite expensive looking, moved back and forth over his wrist whenever he lifted his arm. He said that he loved coming home. "You should leave, Ray. Then you'd appreciate this more."

"I'm fine," Raymond said. "I don't need to leave."

"Tell you what. I'm twelve years older than you. You plan on doing something stupid, give me a call and I'll talk you out of it." He pointed at his chest. "I'm thirty. Lot of wisdom to impart to my baby brother. I'll walk you through so you don't end up before some asshole judge like Nottingham, who'd happily lock you up and swallow the key. Man is so fat it takes him years to shit it out. Know what he said to me? He says, 'Mice deserve better than what you're getting, Mr. Seymour.' And then he bangs his gavel and goes for steak dinner."

In the sky, stars fell. In bed, before sleeping, Raymond listened to his brother tossing on the nearby mattress. "Marcel?" he said.

Out of the darkness: "Hnnnh."

"I could come up with you. To Montreal. I'd find work. Take care of your place, cook and clean. Stay out of your way."

"You could be my wife, in other words."

"Other words?"

"That's what you're saying."

"I ain't saying that. I'm just asking."

"I thought you liked it here."

"I do. Most of the time."

"Reenie said you've got a girl."

"Reenie's got a big mouth."

"What's her name?"

"Alice. Hart."

There was a silence that extended and stretched and then fell into itself.

A grunt and then: "As in related to Hart the constable, his daughter?"

"Niece."

"She's the niece."

"That's what I said."

"Oh, boy. Who do you think you are? Jesus, Ray. This isn't heaven."

"She likes me."

A laugh, derisive and disbelieving. "*She likes me.* Whoop-de-do. Listen, little brother. Hart's in Nottingham's pocket and this Alice is in her father's pocket, and even if it seems like she's jumped out of her father's pocket into your pocket, your pocket isn't big enough to hold her. Or keep her. Or whatever it is you want. Maybe you want to marry her."

"Forget it."

Marcel laughed. A slight snort and then a bark and the sound moved around the room. When he spoke his voice was softer, cajoling, and maternal. "What would you cook?"

"Noodles. With cheese. Hamburgers." Then he talked about Mrs. Kennedy and how she told him about the husband she used to have and the man she would soon be marrying and how she wore pink skirts just above her knee and he said that she smelled really good. "The wind comes from behind her and passes my way and I smell soap. She leaves me ten dollars every time."

"She wants to marry you."

"I said that?"

"You think that. You imagine it. It's all pretend, Ray, like with Alice."

"That's not pretend."

"Yeah?"

Quiet then. The plastic in the windows popped in and then out. Marcel said that clams and beer was fine. He could live on that. "You know how to prepare clams?" Then he said that a blow job was a good thing. "Nothing better in life." He said that he hadn't been laid in weeks.

Raymond said he spoke some French. He'd taken it in high school.

"*Parlez-vous?*" Marcel said, and he laughed.

In the morning Marcel shaved outside by the pump. Then he washed his hair and under his arms and he towelled himself dry with a T-shirt. He stood and put on a clean shirt and buttoned it, looking out towards the sun in the east. He was wearing dark brown pants and black wing-tipped shoes. His duffle bag was in the back seat. His face was flat in the morning light. He punched Raymond on the chest and climbed into his car and drove away. The sun blinked off the top of the Monte Carlo just as it crested the hill. Then it was gone.

In late October, payday in his pocket, Raymond went to the Kenricia and sat at a back table and ordered a beer and a whisky straight-up. The whisky went down hard and hot and the beer followed slowly. His feet rested on the chair beside him. He was wearing his best boots, the ones Alice liked, dark leather with yellow stitching. The warmth of everything good; work finished, the straw laid out across the greens, the clubs stored, "Closed for the Season" in the clubhouse window, a harsh wind coming off the lake, the anticipation of Alice and her thin arms. Leona brought another whisky. She set it on the coaster and Raymond flashed his bank, peeling off a bill and waving away the change. "Careful, big boy," Leona said. She wiped the table. The sharp scent of her perfume, the whisper of a cue ball. Raymond was excellent at pool. He was gifted. Mr. Knight, his math teacher at Lakewood High, had told him that he was gifted. He could do whatever he wanted. "You can be a doctor," Mr. Knight had said. For now, he was a greenskeeper. Still eighteen. Years to go.

Alice blew in. A short dark coat with double-breasted buttons, hair straight and long, cheeks red from the wind. She sat and took off her coat. She was wearing a tartan jumper, white shirt, black knee-highs, and short boots with fat heels. The straps of the jumper criss-crossed her back. She wrinkled her nose and lit a cigarette. "What you buying me?" She called out for the same, waggling her fingers at Leona, pointing at the table. She swivelled and aimed her cigarette at Raymond's nose. "I'm at Jenny's for the night, so you have to take care of me. Okay?" She crossed her legs. The black socks reached to the top of her calves. Her knees were bony and bare and dry.

They played a game of pool and Raymond let her win. At one point he stood behind her, his crotch against her bum, and he showed her the angle of the shot. "See?" She laughed and the vibration of her voice passed through her back into his chest. A man with oily hair watched from the bar. "Hey, Chief," he called. Raymond didn't answer. The eight ball dropped, Alice squealed and gave him a hug. They went back to the table and drank.

"He worries," Alice said. She was talking about her father. Raymond studied her bare arms. She liked to push her small breasts against his mouth. The pink of her nipples. Where he might be ashamed, she was proud. Laid out like the fallen branch of a birch, she peeled back the bark. Her lack of shame made him shy.

Leona came over and said that Ed Farber was drunk and he was making threatening noises and because she was alone tonight she didn't want trouble and she'd appreciate it if Raymond and Alice left. Maybe they could take a six-pack to go. Okay?

Alice said she wanted another whisky, just one more, and that Farber could go fuck himself.

"I don't think so. Anyway, Alice, you're underage, and if trouble starts, I don't want your father running in here, you see, so just pick yourselves up and walk out and I'll take care of Farber."

Raymond stood. He reached into his pocket but Leona waved him away. "It'll be a long winter," she said.

Alice put on her coat, picked up her cigarettes and purse, and then clacked in her fat heels towards the door. Raymond followed her, past a man and a woman playing pool and, beyond that, Farber's wide face, and then through the door and into a hard sleet falling. They took shelter under an awning, where a pale yellow light reflected off the wet sidewalk. Alice reached into her purse and took out a joint and lit up. She held out the joint. Raymond put his back to the wind and swayed and smoked. Alice slipped an arm into his, pushed her small face against his chest and said that her father's float plane was down at the wharf and they could go hang out there, if he liked. At least it would be out of the wind. She tugged at him and he followed. The simplicity of being led, the pressure of her hand, the anticipation of her warmth, her voice at that moment announcing that Farber's problem was he had a small dick, and this was why he went after Raymond. And then a sweep of light and a police car pulled up alongside them and together they halted.

"Run," Raymond said. He stepped backwards and turned. Waited for Alice to follow.

She moved towards him and then looked back and said, her voice uncertain, "Uncle Earl?" She pulled away from Raymond and stepped towards the police car.

Hart moved around the front of the car, his hip brushing the grill. "Got a call from Leona," he said. He nodded back at the hotel. "You okay?" He reached out and touched Alice, as if laying some sort of claim on her. He didn't look at Raymond.

"Yeah, I'm fine. Cold maybe." Her voice trembled.

Raymond was two steps away, hands in his pockets. He looked down and saw that the sidewalk had a thin layer of wet snow.

Hart opened the passenger door and told Alice to get in. She looked back at Raymond with her sorry face, and then climbed in. Hart opened the cruiser's rear door and motioned at Raymond, who said that he didn't need a ride.

"Nobody's asking." Hart held the door and waited. The shoulders of Alice's coat, her too-small head. The heat of the interior. Raymond climbed in and the door shut.

"Hey, I'm sorry." Alice didn't turn to look at him, she just talked to the windshield. "At least it's a ride home." Raymond didn't answer. He was on the other side of a wire grating, looking at the back of her. The radio talked. Someone talked back. Hart climbed in and drove in silence. Alice didn't say anything more to Raymond, and when they pulled up to her house she climbed from the cruiser and she didn't look at him, just followed her uncle up the sidewalk, hips moving back and forth. Tiptoeing, like she was trying to creep back into the place she should never have left.

The house was large, with many windows, and some of the windows had lights on, and in Alice's room on the second floor, there was an orange lamp hanging in the window. And then Alice's mother was standing behind the lamp and she looked out at the driveway. She reached up and a curtain was drawn across the window. Last June Raymond had been in that room. He had walked Alice home from school and they had gone inside the empty house and he had removed his shoes at the entrance and followed Alice up the stairs and then down the soft carpet of the hallway that led to her room. On that day after school, when they were alone in her house, she had lain down on her bed and she had invited him to lie down with her. Somewhere, in the house, the air conditioning had clicked on. Alice had gasped, a sharp, short intake of breath as he entered her, and she had cried out, "Yes, go," and on he had gone, deep into her, and her head was sideways against the yellow slip of her pillow, her eyes closed, and he had finished quickly. She slid out from under him and walked to the bathroom adjoining her room and he watched as she sat naked on the toilet and grinned sleepily at him through the open door.

The curtain was drawn now, and on the roof there were two chimneys, and smoke rose from one. In the driveway was a brand new car. A dark brown Cutlass. Alice's father was a pilot. He flew rich Americans into remote fishing camps around the Lake of the Woods in his twin-engine float plane. It was from hearing about him that Raymond learned how luck fell down on certain people. Someone like Alice smelled of luck and when Raymond was with her she gave him the confidence that he might have some of that luck.

Alice's father stepped outside. He lit a cigarette and stood talking to Hart under the protection of the front porch. He never once looked over at the cruiser. He dropped his cigarette and crushed it with his shoe, patted Hart on the back, and went inside.

Hart came slowly down the walk and climbed into the car and backed out of the driveway. It was midnight. Nothing was said for a long time. Hart drove east past the prison and then a right turn up towards Bare Point. When they passed Raymond's grandmother's house on the right, the light in the main room was on and Raymond imagined that his grandmother would be watching TV. Hart drove on, past Isaac Badboy's house, and into the darkness. Snow dove at the headlights and then fell upwards. Hart spoke. "You like fishing, Raymond?" He looked in the rear-view mirror. "Sure you do.

I can see that. You like fishing for white girls." He paused. Then he said, "You catch 'em, reel 'em in, fuck 'em, and then throw 'em back. No harm done." His voice was easy, as if he was talking to a close friend, or as if he was leaning forward to whisper a special secret. He turned in order for Raymond to hear him better. "And after me telling you to stay away.

"You've got a boat up at Bare Point. That right? What I hear, you go out on the lake by yourself and fish. Sometimes you stay away all night, sleep in the boat, or park on an island so as to not waste time." He nodded. "Good to know.

"Fishing for white girls is dangerous," he said. "'Cause sometimes you catch something that's so big it threatens to pull you in with it. That's what's happening here, Raymond." He sighed. His radio crackled and he reached to turn it off. "Don't need company," he said. Then he said that he'd heard a story once about a man who was fishing off a wharf. "Just sitting on the dock, enjoying the day, probably sunny, warm, feeling a little sleepy, and all of a sudden, *bang*, a big mother-fucker takes the hook and the rod goes skittering along the dock and the man jumps for it and hangs on. Only the fish is a monster, and when the line is all wrung out, the rod along with the man are pulled right into the lake and down under the water. That big. Only the man won't let go. He's hooked this fish and damned if he's going to lose it. He should let go but he can't because the line is caught around his wrist and the fact is the line is cutting his wrist down to the bone and if he could he would cut himself free but he can't, you see, because he got greedy and thought he could pull the fish in. And then the line snaps and the man ascends, up through the dark water, and when he breaks the surface he is far out into the lake with no fish and his hand bloodied and he bobs out there thinking that he almost gave up his life for some impossible thing, something he would never touch or see."

Hart paused and then said that it was pretty obvious to anybody with a brain what a man should not do, but it never failed to astonish him how there was always one more ignorant man out there in the world, and sometimes these men were boys, who jumped foolishly into a place that was not for them. "You see what I'm getting at? I think I'm being pretty obvious here. You shouldn't have touched what wasn't yours. Uh-uh. Even if she asked you to touch. She's a bit of a simpleton, giving her father lots of grief. She can have anything she wants and she spreads her legs for what? Here we are."

The cruiser came to a stop before a marina with two jetties. Hart got out and opened the rear door. Raymond followed the constable's back down to the south jetty. Hart was pointing in the dark, his arm stretched out like half a scarecrow. "Which one's yours?" he asked, and he halted and turned, his face shadowed and dark.

Raymond nodded to the left, pointing with his nose. His hands were shaking. His legs.

"Good stuff. You got gas, I imagine." Hart hopped down into the stern of the boat, lifted the gas tank, and grunted. "Get in. Loose the rope." He gestured at the bow and then released the stern rope. Looked up at Raymond, who hadn't moved. "You can run," he said, "but you won't get far." He motioned again at the bow and watched as Raymond climbed in. Hart pulled the starter, one, two, three times, and then manoeuvred the choke and pulled again. The engine fired and started, a loud whine that gathered and howled until Hart pushed the choke back in. He backed out and then, once clear of the jetty, slipped the engine into forward and pointed the boat at the middle of the lake. He didn't speak. The snow was still falling. It hit Raymond's face, and it fell against the bottom of the boat and melted and collected in small pools. Raymond was wearing a thin shirt and a jacket of nylon that protected him from the wind slightly, but it was cold enough to make his ears ache. There was nothing to see and the prow of the boat banged against the larger waves and the water came up over the gunnels and splashed Raymond's back and neck. He ducked. The hull vibrated against the soles of his runners and up into his shins.

Hart knew the lake and he was clear about this journey. The darkness was no impediment. It was as if he were charging into an obscurity out of which only he could discern the escape. He angled the boat to the left, bulling into the blackness at full throttle, and then he eased off, standing and leaning forward, as if sniffing the wind that would lead him to land. And it did. The island appeared as a wall and then, as the boat entered the leeward shore, trees took shape and the softness of a sandy bay accepted the bow of the boat. Hart cut the engine and leaped from the boat and waded onto shore.

"Get out," he yelled, and Raymond obeyed. He obeyed in the same manner as when he had climbed into the police car and then climbed out again and stood waiting by the boat. Like a dumb animal, he followed the beck of the policeman.

His feet hit the icy water and he wallowed up towards the dark trees. The boat shifted in the waves and hit his thigh, banging him sideways. Hart had him sit on a log. He looked down at Raymond and said that there was only one story to tell. "Understand? You were out fishing and you lost your way and ended up here. Your boat was taken by the waves. That's the story. You're lucky to be alive. What a salvation. Marooned in the Lake of the Woods. Someone'll find you. If not, you're a fucking Indian. Do your thing."

He tipped his hat then, as if this were a cordial goodbye, and he said that when he got back to Bare Point, he would send the empty boat out full throttle into the lake. "Maybe'll it come right back at you. Wouldn't that be a surprise." He turned and went to the boat and climbed in. The waves were large and they tossed the small craft. Hart spent a few good minutes trying to restart the motor. The boat floated away and then came back with the waves. Finally, the whine of the engine lifted into the sky and was picked up by the wind and the boat disappeared, both sight and sound.

Raymond remained on the log. The snow and sleet drove against his back and neck and slid down under his jacket and shirt. He had, in his pockets, his cigarettes and matches. His wallet, which held the cash from his last cheque. His ID, a driver's licence. The keys to his pickup, but this had been incidental, because the pickup was back at his cabin, broken down. He'd hitchhiked to town from the golf club, a fact that Hart had made certain of. He stood and looked out into the darkness to gauge the island's size. He walked away from the wind and came to a rock that descended towards the shore. At the base of the rock was a gully of sorts, out of the wind, but with no protection from the sky. He sat in the dip and pulled his jacket over his head. The wind came down around him. He blew onto his hands and feeling the numbness in his feet he stood and stumbled up the rocks back into the driving wind. He eventually found a stand of spruce and poplar and in that place he dug a shallow hole and attempted to light a collection of small branches and bark. His matches burned briefly and then went out. The branches were wet, the bark would not catch. He scraped together some moss and laid it down in the hole, and then he curled up in the shallow dip and covered himself with more moss. He was shaking severely. He pressed his hands between his thighs and blew warm breath down the inside of his jacket. When dawn arrived the rain had halted but the air was colder. In the grey light he finally started a fire in the hollow that he had slept in, and he stoked the fire with dry moss and dead branches. He warmed his hands and feet and bent towards the flames like a requester who sees the possibility of salvation but is too abject to cry out.

He kept the fire going throughout the day, studying the lake for boats, but it was late fall and most of the boats had already been dry docked and there were no more houseboats or cabin-goers. The water was black and choppy and the shore of the mainland could only be imagined as a thin, dark line many miles away. He was all alone.

On the third day, hungry and weak, he lay on a rock at the edge of the water and studied the shallows for fish. Minnows appeared and disappeared and a crayfish scrabbled away from his grasping hand. He rose, empty-handed, his arms numb, and he sat in the hollow by his fire and watched a chickadee come and go beneath a scrubby bush nearby. He gathered rocks and he waited for the bird to return. When it did, he took aim and threw a rock. The bird flew upwards and did not come back for a long time. When it did return, it sat on the moss of a rock and hopped slightly, again and again, as if there were a blueprint set out before it.

As a young boy, Raymond had hunted chickadees and benddowns with his cousins. Using slingshots and rocks, they would kill several birds and then carry them home where the girls would pluck the birds and boil up a soup and then the whole group would squat and eat. Back then, it had been a game to be played; with great ease and nothing to gain but the satisfaction of the unnecessary hunt. Now, all was necessary.

He killed the small bird in the early evening. The rock he threw was sharp and it caught the bird's wing and the bird went up and then fell. The bird fluttered and called out and Raymond went to it and picked it up and broke its neck. He plucked the chickadee and then impaled it with a stick and roasted it over the fire. The smell of meat filled his head, but when he attempted to eat the bird, he discovered there was little substance. So he opened the bird up and sucked what he could from the carcass. The following day, in a small pool on the windward side of the island, he found three frogs in the mud at the bottom of the pool and he speared the frogs onto a stick in the same manner he had done the bird, and he roasted the frogs over the fire and ate them delicately, one at a time.

That evening, at dusk, a motorboat passed by the island and he ran towards the sound, calling out and waving his arms. As he reached the shore his right foot caught in a small crevasse and he fell hard and his ankle popped. The sound of the motorboat disappeared. He sat up and examined his ankle. The foot sat at an odd angle, and when he tried to stand, his leg could not support him and the pain was severe and he fell sideways onto the rocks, cursing. He crawled back to his fire and spent a sleepless night struggling out into the bush for fuel and then back to the fire, dragging his bad leg and fallen branches behind him. At one point, he must have fainted from the pain and when he woke his back was against the rock. The heavens rose above him, pierced with pricks of light, and much later the moon appeared, fat and yellow on the horizon; it slid upwards into the sky and threw down its glow onto the island and onto Raymond and he held his hands out in order to see them in the brightness, in order to verify his own existence.

He did not consider that rescue would be imminent. He believed that he might be on the island until the ice took hold and he could walk his way back to the mainland, though he was not certain which direction he would take. He would not be missed. He had finished work at the golf club; he lived alone and often went for days without seeing anyone. Alice would not hunt him down until much later, if at all. He did not pity himself nor was he resigned to death, though he imagined that death was possible. He suffered from constant hunger. He dreamed of fried eggs and a chicken roasted on a spit. Great mounds of food marched across his vision: hamburgers, potatoes, slabs of butter, Klik and Velveeta cheese laid out across stacks of bread. By the seventh day he was eating grass and sucking on bark. His leg was badly swollen and he had fixed a splint from two branches and bound them at his ankle with the shoelaces from his runners. Only once did he experience dread, and this was late one night when a storm came out of the west and extinguished his fire and left him shivering and frozen. In the morning, snow covered the island and the trees and the rocks. Seen from above, the land mass upon which he lived would have appeared as a white comma drawn against the dark roiling paper of the lake. And inside that comma he existed. The dread arrived with the image of blankness and the understanding that he could not be seen even if someone were looking. That night, in a dream, his grandmother came to him and called his name and then sat beside him and moaned words that he did not understand into the fire before them. One of her hands was withered and crooked and she held it out over the flames as if to warm it. Then she leaned into him and whispered that he should go home. "Go home," she said. He woke from this dream and looked about, and he thought of his brother Nelson, whom he had not seen in nine years, and he thought of the night he was alone just after Nelson had been taken away, and how his chest had felt hollowed out, and that after a while he could no longer remember what his brother looked like, or the sound of his voice, his shape, or his smell. The wind had stopped and in its place was the sound of his breathing, irregular and thin.

On the ninth day he stood weakly on one leg by the rocks at the edge of the island, peeing into the water, when a barge that carried propane from cabin to cabin along the lake's sinuous interior came out of the light fog. Raymond lifted a hand and lowered it and then lifted it again and tried to call out, but his voice had disappeared. He lifted both hands to the sky, and from the deck of the barge a man in a red coat lifted a hand in return greeting. The man's mouth opened but Raymond did not hear a sound. The barge charged on. It appeared that the greeting was a simple hailing hello from boat to island and back again and that there was nothing unusual about a shrouded figure on a blank island. And then the barge slowed and turned and hovered off the leeward shore while a small boat was lowered from the deck. Two men clambered into the boat and rowed towards shore and it would have appeared to any literate onlooker that this was a re-enactment of the discovery of a new land.

Raymond hobbled across the rocks and then slid on his bum to the water's edge where he leaned forward, his face tilted towards the approaching boat. So logical and wise and right was this rescue that there was nothing to be told. And no one to tell. And so he relayed a fiction, a heroic story of sorts: his boat had capsized nine days earlier and he had swum to shore and survived on a few frogs and a bird, and he had drunk the water from the lake and sung songs to his ancestors, who sent the Canadian shipping barge bearing propane across the water to pull him from this grave.

II

The Retreat

The Byrd family left their home in June and drove east across a country that was flat with fields newly planted. The sky was deep and whitish blue and the towns they passed through were small and isolated. Early that first morning, when everyone was sleeping except for Lizzy and her father, Lizzy bent and smelled the head of the smallest kitten. Her father had just told her what had to be done. He was telling her because she was seventeen. She needed to understand, and if she understood, then she could help the younger children understand. He said that her mother agreed. In fact, it had been her suggestion. The Doctor didn't allow animals at the Retreat and they couldn't leave the little things for two months or more, how would they survive, and this was a humane act, a work of mercy. "Your mother has her heart set on this place. You know that. She believes that she will be happy there."

Lizzy had listened. She hadn't argued. She asked how.

"Painless," her father said. "Don't worry. They won't suffer."

This was near Brooks, just after they had left Calgary. That night, they took a room in a motel by the side of the road, outside of Regina. Using the small hotplate, Mrs. Byrd cooked spaghetti and served it with ketchup. It was raining and the boys sat with the kittens and tossed them from bed to bed and watched them land right-side up. At night, Lizzy woke and lay listening to the radiators bang and she heard the slow breathing of her three brothers and her mother and father. Fish called out. She heard him the first time but willed him away. If he knew she was awake, he would want to sleep beside her. He was barely four and he liked to curl up against her stomach and steal her warmth.

"Lizzy?" he said again.

She waited.

"Lizzy," he whispered. "A dream."

"Go back to sleep."

"A bad dream. With death and God."

"It's okay. Come here, I'll hold you."

He came to her bed and pressed his nose to her neck. His face was hot, his knees clamped her leg.

"Daddy was drowning."

"It's just a dream."

"I'm afraid."

"Here." She placed a hand against his back and rubbed. Went "shhh" and then said, "It's okay. Go back to sleep."

"Uh-uh. I'll dream again."

"Not the same dream. It doesn't happen that way."

"I don't want to dream at all. God had a big hand and was holding Daddy down. God's hand was big and Daddy's head was small."

"God wouldn't do that."

There was silence. Lizzy heard someone move, perhaps her mother.

"I don't want to die," Fish said.

"You won't, silly. You'll live so long."

"Forever?"

"Yes. Go to sleep now."

And he did, finally. His breathing slowed and his chest, narrow beneath Lizzy's hand, moved up and down slightly, and then his hand twitched and finally his foot jumped as he startled. Lizzy slipped out from between his scissored legs and lay at the edge of the bed, away from his heat. The rain fell against the window. Lights from a passing car passed over the wall above Lizzy's head. Her father snored lightly. One of the kittens climbed onto Lizzy's chest and lay down, tapping her face with a paw.

In the morning, the rain had stopped. Mr. Byrd was shaving. While he shaved he sang and then he spoke of omelettes made with special cheeses and how, when he was twenty, he had worked on a farm in the south of France, and he had risen at four every morning to milk the seven special cows. Friesians, he called them, and he said, "*Oui, mes amis*, how *incroyable, ce que le* farmer and his wife prepared for breakfast. Fresh croissants so buttery they melted in your hands before touching the mouth, and whole milk with thick cream, and muesli from the Swiss Alps, and then, after *étouffing* ourselves, we sat by the fire and smoked *une pipe*. Oh, man. That was the life." He paused. Inspected his chin and his nose and said, "I'll go out into this little village we're perched by and I'll forage for a nice breakfast. How about it?"

He left. Half an hour later he returned with tiny cereal boxes and a carton of milk and plastic spoons and he laid everything out on the small table and rubbed his hands and pronounced breakfast prepared. "Not the fare of my youth, but fuel nonetheless."

Fish wanted crescents with butter.

"I looked, son. Believe me. This isn't France, this is Canada. No culture here. Where your treasure is, there will your heart be also. We have white bread and Jiffy Pop. The world would be a sad place if my children stooped to graze on Jiffy Pop. Hey, come along. Here." And he held Fish on his big lap and pulled out a jackknife, opened it and handed it to Fish, and said, "Slaughter the beast." The boy happily stabbed at the small box. William, who was nine, and Everett, fourteen, climbed onto chairs and joined in. When the boxes were gutted and laid open on the table their father poured milk and looked at the two women in his life and said, "Et voilà."

Mr. Byrd was not as cheerful as he appeared. His French farming stories, his singing, his banter, all of this was a form of bravery; he was trying to please his wife. The week before, his foreman had finally agreed to let him take the summer off and he had pulled his children around him and said that the family would be travelling to Kenora, to stay at a place called the Retreat. They would stay the summer. This is what their mother wanted. She had read an article about the place in a liberal Christian magazine, made a point of seeking out the man who ran the Retreat, and in him she discovered the possibility of her own salvation. Ever since Fish's birth, Norma Byrd had suffered deep anxiety and a prevailing sense of her own demise. Lewis was aware that her children floated about her like so many extra limbs, and if she could have, she would have lopped them off. She was searching for the promise of freedom and the Retreat appeared to offer that assurance. It would be a place of harmony and friendship; ideas would be discussed and food would be grown and gathered and collectively shared. No one person would be better than another.

At first, when Lizzy heard of the plans, she refused. She said that she and her boyfriend Cyril were starting a band, and she planned to work, and besides, she hated camping.

"There are comfortable cabins with screens on the windows," Mr. Byrd said. "Work, and Cyril and the band, all of this can wait till fall, when you go back to school. You're young."

Everett, who had been sitting beside Lizzy, was conscious of her silence and of how she bit her lip. The light fell into the room through the large front window onto her hands. She had painted her nails just the day before, and Everett had watched her, and then he had painted his own nails and it had given him a feeling of pleasure.

Their mother said that the trip would be educational. Broadening. A chance to get lost in nature, to let loose their wild side. Mrs. Byrd had spoken softly, her mouth moving quickly. She looked at Everett and said, "You'd like that, wouldn't you, Everett? Go wild for a bit?" And he had lifted his shoulders and then finally nodded, because he loved her and wanted to please her.

Miles further, just on the other side of Winnipeg, where the highway curled through hills and past lakes, Mr. Byrd pulled to the side of the road. While he slept, the children sat on rocks by the edge of a lake and ate peanut butter sandwiches.

Their mother poured water from a glass jar and offered apples and pecans and raw wieners. Fish took off his shoes and socks and waded in the shallow water, trying to catch minnows. He fell forward into the cold water and came up grinning. Mrs. Byrd called out, "Don't go too deep, the lake drops off."

Lizzy was sitting higher up on the rocks, holding one of the kittens, and inspecting her bare legs. She was wearing a short skirt and it hiked up high on her thighs and she kept turning her legs towards the sun, hoping for a tan. She had left a boy behind, a boy who had loved her madly. She tried to imagine a world without disenchantment, but this thought was fleeting. Earlier, in the car, she had written a letter to Cyril, her boyfriend. The looping script, the promises she would never keep, this had induced in Lizzy a brief longing. She had already forgotten the shape of Cyril's mouth. Fish had been at her feet. Everett was sleeping on the back floor. William was in the front between their mother and father. He was prone to carsickness and had already thrown up into a plastic bucket and the car still smelled sour. Trees and rocks passed by. A tractor-trailer shook their car with its backdraft. The kitten in Lizzy's lap woke and stretched. Yawned. Lizzy saw the skeleton of the kitten's pink mouth.

At the edge of the lake now, waiting for their father to wake, Everett was skipping rocks. William had two of the kittens, one in each hand. Mrs. Byrd was lying on her jacket, looking up at the sky. She was wearing sunglasses to fend off her headaches. A green skirt down to her knees. Lizzy had legs like her mother, long and tanned.

Then their father appeared. He stood high above them at the top of the road. He was rubbing his neck and he carried a large gunnysack. He descended towards his family, his feet sliding on the shale. Fish squealed with delight as a small rock bounced down and landed beside him in the lake. "Boom," he cried.

"Careful, Lewis," Mrs. Byrd called. "You're going to kill your children."

Lewis came down towards his wife and laid out the sack on the rock and sat. He took her hand, and talked. Lizzy, from where she sat, couldn't hear his words but she knew they were discussing the fate of the kittens. He talked and talked. Her mother sat up at one point and spoke, her long face turning towards Lizzy, and then away, quickly, as if what she had disagreed with should not be witnessed. Mrs. Byrd shook her head. Lewis took her hand and pressed it to his mouth. He kissed each finger. Then he stood and told his children to go up to the car. It was time.

"Give the kittens over to your mother," he said. "She'll hold them."

William, at first, refused. He held the kittens to his cheeks and climbed towards the car. Lewis caught him and gently took Shadrach and Meshach. Patted him on the bum and sent him upwards. Lizzy descended towards her mother and handed her Bagger. Mrs. Byrd looked at her and said, "Your skirt is too short."

"What are you doing?" Lizzy asked.

"Take up your brother," Mrs. Byrd said.

Lizzy went down to the lake and scooped up Fish, who placed a wet hand in the warm hollow of her neck. She talked to him as she climbed. She said that the lake had a monster and sometimes the monster came up to eat little boys and it was almost lunchtime and it wouldn't be a good thing to offer Fish to the monster.

"Does it eat fish really?" Fish asked.

"Not little fish, just big ones, but if little fish are waiting at the shore, it sometimes eats them as a snack." She had him on her back, and the way she was bent, facing the earth, stooped over, she imagined that she appeared as a figure both ancient and weighted down. William went up last, following Everett. Lizzy deposited Fish in the car and told Everett to watch him. She descended the hill and stood beside her mother. Her dad said, "Take the kittens, Lizzy. Your mother will go up to be with the children."

Lizzy held the kittens and watched her mother wind her way up the rocks towards the highway. Her father could ask anything of her and she would do it. "Please," she said.

Lewis stepped down towards the lake and bent to pick up a large rock. "Don't make a fuss," he said. "It won't help." He put the rock into the sack. "Here," he said, and he held the sack open. She went to him and lowered the kittens into the gunnysack. The kittens clawed at her wrists and hands, and Bagger, believing this was a game, tried to climb up the inside of the sack. There was much mewling. Her father had a thin rope. He put the bag down and looped the rope around the top of the bag and tied it tight. He didn't speak. Then he took the bag and threw it out over the lake and when it hit the surface it floated briefly, and then it filled with water, and it sank.

Half an hour down the road, Everett cried out, "Where are they? Where are the fucking kittens?"

"Your mouth," Lewis said. Both of his hands were on the wheel. His eyes sought out the black strip of road.

And then Fish's voice joined in. "Where are they? Where went Bagger fucking?" This was his favourite, white with a single dot on the left ear. His speech was erratic. Sometimes he stuttered.

"See," Lewis said. "Your words become his words. Care is required."

"You murderer," Everett said.

"Bang, bang," Fish said. "Murder." And he began to whimper. "Bagger," he said. "Bagger."

Lizzy watched a large truck approach. It passed in a swoop. Her father's neck was brown from the sun. He needed a haircut. Her mother had long hair that covered parts of her thin shoulders. She was looking out the window and then she turned to Lewis and Lizzy saw the hollow of her left cheek and the sharpness of her collarbone and the darkness of her eyes. She didn't speak.

And in the tomb of the car, floating above the sobbing of Fish and then William, their father's voice rose, calling out that everything in its time had to die and what would they rather have: three kittens starving and mistreated, or the certainty that Shadrach, Meshach, and Bagger were in a better place. He said that there was a time to be born, a time to die, a time to dance, and a time to mourn. He said, "I have maintained that which is under my control." He said this as if it were something that he had just thought of, with a certain mellifluent surprise, as if to say, listen to these words I have found.

And into that claim, into the buoyancy of his timbred voice, soft and silky, there fell a silence, the stillness of the children, who seemed to hold their breath, as if the words themselves would become proof of a bigger place that only their father could provide. Words and words and words. He must know. But Lizzy knew that he might not know. In fact, she knew it with utter certainty. But she didn't confess her knowledge, because that would make Fish cry. And Everett was silent now, a wall falling down and separating him from the world. Lizzy, in the sticky morning heat, beneath the drone of her father's voice, took Everett's hand, held it, and he let her.

The Retreat was located several miles outside the town of Kenora, on two acres of wooded land. Up the highway and then a left turn and down a winding gravel road, past a collection of houses, and on further towards a small lake and then right again down a narrow road that was really two tracks of mud and a strip of grass and, finally, out of the bush and into a clearing. The main cabin was an old house that had been gutted and opened out with pine beams. This was the dining area and it was also the meeting place and it was called the Hall. Across from the Hall, at the opposite side of the clearing, stood seven cabins in various stages of disrepair, cabins that housed the occupants.

There were sixteen people living there: three families and several younger men and women who found, in the Doctor's vision, their own parallel dreams. The Doctor's goal for the Retreat was both spiritual and practical. A chiropractor by training, he had lived all his life in Duluth, Minnesota, married there, and come to Canada when his wife left him and after the divorce eventually came through. He settled in Thunder Bay where he opened a small chiropractic office and fell in love with his receptionist, Margaret. She became pregnant, they married, and during their first spring together he bought the land for The Retreat. In the following years, each April, they travelled around, giving talks in small school gymnasiums and recreation halls, encouraging people to visit The Retreat, with the notion that a refuge from the hurly-burly of the world for several months of every year would augment peace; not world peace but individual reckoning. If the Doctor wanted this place to be considered a spiritual oasis, it was also sometimes referred to as an artists' colony, though there was very little art happening, except perhaps at the hands of Emma Poole, who was playing with watercolours. Harris, her husband, had money in his pockets that had been made in an earlier stage of his life. Lewis felt that this was the only reason Emma Poole stayed by his side. "That's the problem with money," he announced. "When you have it, you don't know who your true friends are."

Of the families in the group, the Byrds took up two cabins, the children in one, Lewis and Norma Byrd in the other. Doctor Amos lived with his red-headed wife Margaret and their son Billy, who was overweight and breathed noisily through his mouth; the children had taken to calling him Big Billy. Harris and Emma Poole were from the United States. They had arrived with a younger man in tow, a German named Franz, a man fascinated by anything to do with the original people of Canada. These were his words. He was a photographer and a collector. He lived in the smallest cabin, the one with the bowed roof. He spoke with a heavy accent and spent more time with Emma than with Harris. Harris was a novelist who had once been very successful. According to Emma, his achievements had been brilliant but brief; he had not written anything for a long time. She had dropped this into several conversations and in doing so her voice became thinner and her words came out of her mouth more quickly, as if she were talking about a farm animal that had failed to do its job.

Harris had carried part of his library with him and he had opened it up to the rest of the people there. He was in a wheelchair and rumour had it he had come to the camp to be healed by the Doctor, though that hadn't occurred yet. His wife was an entomologist and a painter. She was often seen wandering around in the bush, wearing her wide-brimmed hat, carrying a butterfly net, being trailed by Franz. Emma had a large collection of butterflies pinned up in the Hall and Everett would study it lovingly, conscious of how the Latin names lent a seriousness to the dead insects. Lewis said one day that Emma Poole was like a butterfly herself, frail with gossamer arms. He said that even her clothes were diaphanous, and then he said to Everett, "She's bossy, and she thinks the world owes her something, but she's beautiful. In her way."

Everett was surprised and a little embarrassed by his father's enthusiasm. He didn't find Emma that good-looking, certainly not like his mother, or his sister Lizzy, who spent her afternoons sunbathing down by the pond. Often, Everett joined Lizzy there and she asked him to spread baby oil on her back. Everett did this willingly, aware of the sharp shoulder blades and the small freckles upon her light skin, and how when her long hair was pulled up into a swirl, her slender neck revealed soft patches of hair moistened by her sweat. She smelled warm. She was wise. One time, several days after their arrival, they were down by the pond, watching over Fish and William who were stabbing frogs with sharp sticks at the edge of the water. Lizzy was on her stomach, her chin in her hands. One leg was raised and her bare foot waved at the sky. "It's so nowhere, the Treat, but I kinda like it," she said. This is what Fish called the Retreat, and the other children had picked up the term, though their mother thought they were being disrespectful. She worried about the Doctor's feelings.

Everett looked out across the pond to the other side where there was a forest that extended into more forest, and beyond that, more forest. "It's sort of bleak," he said.

Lizzy rolled onto her back and held a hand up to shade her eyes. She grinned. "Sweet little Ev, always wishing for something else." Everett looked at Lizzy's flat white stomach, her navel, and the sharp edge of her ribs.

"Take off your shirt," she said. "Come." She sat up and pulled at the base of his T-shirt and as he raised his arms she lifted the shirt up over his head. "Lie down," she said, and when he obeyed, she spread oil on his back. "Oooh," she said, "blackheads," and she spent the next while squeezing the blackheads and mounting them on her thumb for Everett to see.

"Mum lied," he said. "There *are* cats."

"She didn't lie. She said there was no room for *more* animals."

"There's lots of room. Look around. Someone was lying."

"Maybe it was Doctor Amos. He talks a lot and sometimes too much talk leads to bullshit. Maybe he wanted some sort of sacrifice."

"What are you talking about?"

"I don't know. Forget it. He talked to you yet?"

"Uh-uh. You?"

"Hmm . . . yesterday."

She said that he had called her over to the Den for nine a.m. and when she showed up he had a fire going and it was hot but she had had no intention in taking off her sweater. "He probably wanted to look at my bare arms or something." She said that the Doctor had brought his chair really close and leaned forward, playing up the closeness, as if they were best friends. He had talked about hope and despair and then he'd asked what she believed in and she told him that she didn't believe in anything, or at least not much. The Doctor had been surprised and said that that was dangerous and she didn't want to fall into solipsism. She didn't know the word, so he stood and went over to a dictionary and pulled it out and had her look it up, like he'd suddenly become a teacher. Then he'd asked if she read at all, and she said some and he said what, and she'd named some really crappy books and he'd raised his eyebrows. He asked if she did drugs, and she said that she was a real addict. Everything: coke, heroin, acid, hashish. And he'd looked surprised and asked if she was joking.

Lizzy stopped talking. Touched her bare feet, rubbed a bit of sand from her toes. She smiled. "I asked him if *he* did drugs and he didn't answer." She said that he'd called her insolent, but he said it so lightly that she thought it might be a compliment. Then he asked about their mother. He wondered if she was aware of how beautiful their mother was. "That was weird, talking about Mum that way," she said. "With him. It felt like I was betraying Dad, only the Doctor made it seem very normal. But it wasn't." She admitted that, strangely, she did

47

find herself liking the Doctor. His voice was soft and what he said was pretty interesting. "He's got the most gorgeous hands," she said. She had moved away from Everett slightly and he was alert to her voice and its elasticity and how she seemed to project her soft certainty onto others. Everett could hear her breathing. Back at the camp someone started up a saw. Fish looked up from the water's edge and called out, "Ainsaw."

Everett said, "Dad isn't very happy here."

"Mum is. She thinks that her life is real now. Everything before was superfluous. I think that's what she said, though I bet she was quoting the Doctor or something. I've never heard her use that word before."

She called out to Fish who was waving a dead frog on a stick. William was up to his waist in the water, looking down as if seeking out a lost object.

"Shakespeare, come out of there," Lizzy yelled, and she got up and walked down to the shore and pulled William in. Everett saw her knees and her long calves and thought about what the Doctor had said about his mother. He wondered if his father wanted to take the chainsaw and cut off the Doctor's hands.

In the mornings, Lizzy took to wheeling Harris down to the edge of the water where he sat and read, or he peered from beneath the bill of his cap and watched the children play. Usually, by mid-morning he fell asleep, his chin dropping to his chest, his hand lying like a small stranded animal on his lap. Emma had approached Lizzy and asked for her help. Her husband needed fresh air and he disliked the adult chatter in the Hall, and when she and Franz went out into the bush, Harris couldn't keep up, obviously. She was wearing a wide-brimmed hat and Lizzy could not see her eyes properly, but Emma hesitated as she said Franz's name. Then her voice rose again and she said that her husband was fond of water and children. Would Lizzy take care of him in the mornings? She would be well paid. Emma raised her head and then stared at Lizzy and Lizzy understood that Emma was betraying her husband for Franz. One day, early into their stay, Emma had called Lizzy up into her cabin to help move a dresser and during that brief visit Lizzy had noted two narrow beds with a bamboo divider between the beds. There had been, in the way Emma talked about her husband, something cold and efficient and intolerant in her tone, as if she were speaking of a difficult child.

49

Harris was little trouble for Lizzy, and when he did ask for something — a drink of water, or for his chair to be turned away from the sun, or for his book to be taken out from the rear carrier — he was almost apologetic, as if he were imposing. He had none of the impatience of the other adults. He sat, a solitary sentry, looking out over the goings-on at the pond. Fish became quite attached to him and treated him as one more receptive container into which he could drop his many questions.

When Harris chose to speak, he addressed Lizzy, who was usually lying on a beach towel off to the side, sunning herself. He spoke offhandedly, as if he were addressing an equal, or as if he had been out walking and stumbled upon something banal yet extraordinary and had to share it with Lizzy. He was not interested in gossip or idle talk. And for Lizzy, this changed the atmosphere at the pond. She found herself looking forward to the mornings with Harris. She had never heard someone talk in this way before. Certainly not her mother, who was more concerned with what the mirror offered her, or her father, a man who had turned inward and appeared lost. Harris had revealed to her that a conversation could be full of surprises.

One morning, he placed the book he had been reading on his lap and he said, "Ahh, I don't believe it."

Lizzy opened her eyes and saw Harris's shoes beside her chair, which she had removed for him earlier when they arrived at the pond. She looked at him, but she said nothing.

He continued, "This author assumes that I will trust what he tells me, but I don't."

"Is it true?" Lizzy asked.

"Not if he can't make me believe it."

"It still might be."

"Doesn't matter. Even a lie has to be convincing."

Lizzy said that she didn't like true stories. Her favourite stories began with "once upon a time" because that meant that the story was made up and made-up stories were always more convincing.

"That so." Harris grunted. He said, "Once upon a time there was a man called the Doctor who claimed he could make lame men walk."

Harris sat looking out across the water. He didn't smile or make any motion to indicate that he had said anything remarkable. Then he said that of all the stories that could be told by him, one in particular came out of Africa, and maybe he would offer it to her. He said the word *offer* slowly, as if it were the most important word in the sentence.

Lizzy was not sure what to make of this, but she nodded. Fish and Big Billy began to fight over a stick at the water's edge. Lizzy called out to Fish, and when he didn't listen, she rose and walked down to him and picked up the stick and gave it to Big Billy, then carried Fish over to the towel and sat him down. "Here," she said, and handed him a cracker. He took it and ate and then looked at Harris, pointed and said, "Your foot."

Harris's left foot turned inward, a small club attached to his ankle.

"Fish," Lizzy said, her voice lifting in a reprimand.

Big Billy dropped the stick and came over and reached for a cracker. He ate quickly and then took another and pushed it into his mouth. Crumbs gathered on his wet lips.

Harris lifted his leg so that Fish could inspect the foot. "It has a mind of its own," he said.

"Why?" Fish asked.

"I'd like to hear that story," Lizzy said.

"Because it's sick," Harris said. He moved his leg up and down slowly, and then pulled it back towards his wheelchair. He looked at Lizzy and said that he would tell the story another day, though, from one day to the next, the facts would be slightly altered. "Everything depends on place and time and mood," he said.

Lizzy wanted to say that she did not understand, but she kept quiet, then finally said, "That's okay. No problem. Whatever."

And then, one morning after breakfast, the boy came with his chickens. He lived up the road and twice a week he arrived in an old pickup and parked at the edge of the clearing and walked to the Hall. Lizzy and Fish had just come back from the pond and were sitting on the stairs to their cabin, hair still wet, when she saw Raymond's truck. She knew his name was Raymond because she had seen him once before, just after her family had arrived at the Retreat. He'd shown up for dinner one evening and had sat beside the Doctor at one end of the long table. Lizzy, several seats down from him, had been

aware that he was younger than she first thought, closer to her
age, and this stirred her interest. He had his hair in a ponytail
and she noticed that he rarely spoke, except when the Doctor
addressed him. He ate with his face close to his plate. No one
else spoke to him. When he was finished eating he said thank
you, stood, and left. The Doctor had asked if he wanted
coffee, but he shook his head and said he had to go. She had
hoped that he would notice her, but he kept his eyes lowered.
Later, she had asked Margaret, the Doctor's wife, who the tall,
dark boy was. Margaret had told her his name, and that he
lived in a cabin not far from the Retreat, and that every
summer he provided them with chickens and rabbits. She said
that her husband thought it was important to reach out to the
community, and inviting boys like Raymond to dinner was
one way to do that.

Raymond sat in the pickup, smoking and looking out the
windshield. Lizzy thought he might be watching Fish and her
on the stairs by the cabin, but it was hard to tell because he
wore sunglasses, and his baseball cap was pulled down low.
The only movement she could discern was that of his hand
lifting the cigarette to his mouth and then dropping again.

Lizzy looked down at her legs. She liked their long slim-
ness, a feature she had inherited from her mother. She had,
according to her father, inherited other attributes from her
mother — a soft vanity, wilfulness, and a heightened sense of
longing — but Lizzy, at seventeen, believed that she was more
hopeful and generous than her mother.

Raymond ducked slightly, shouldered the door, and
climbed out. He stood in the sunlight. His cap said Black Cat.

He reached into the box of the pickup and then walked, with his slight limp, down the path towards the kitchen, carrying several dead chickens. One pigeon toe, Lizzy thought. She could see that the chickens were headless and they'd been plucked. When Raymond passed by, Fish said, "What's that?" and Lizzy said, "Chickens."

"Naked chickens?"

Raymond looked at them both briefly and then continued on.

The Doctor stepped out of his door and stood on the porch, then walked out across the clearing and disappeared into the bush. When Raymond came back a few minutes later he was empty-handed.

Lizzy stood and said, "I'm Lizzy, Lizzy Byrd, and this is Fish, my brother. I saw you at dinner one night last week. Remember? We had scalloped potatoes. So, you the chicken guy?"

"Guess I am." He gave his first name and then, after a pause, his last. Seymour.

Lizzy looked at him and said, "Can't see your eyes to know if that's true or not."

The side of his mouth went up a little. He lifted his glasses.

"They're normal," she said.

"I know that," he said. "And I can see you're not a bird."

Lizzy wondered if he was trying to tell her something. His voice was soft but somehow coded. Maybe he thought she was fat. She lifted Fish up onto her hip and said, "Funny guy, eh? Not a bird."

"Why?" Fish asked.

Raymond nodded, and then set his sunglasses back into place and went to his pickup, got in, and drove away.

That afternoon she sat on her bed and wrote a letter to Cyril, though by the time she had finished, she knew that it would never be sent. In it she described the Retreat as desolate, and she said that she was surrounded by old people and children, and that she had become a nanny, a kitten killer, and a nursemaid. Her mother had promised that all this would be great fun, but it turned out that this was not true; fun was hard to come by, as was illicit pleasure. There was nothing to do all day while the adults gathered in their silly discussion groups or listened to the Doctor talk about the compartments of the soul. She didn't know how she was going to stand it here for the next two months. She had tried on her miniskirt the other day, the mauve silk one, and she had walked around inside her cabin, because there was nowhere to go here, nothing to dress up for. She had been alone, which was a rare thing, and she had stood with her back against the cabin wall and imagined hands sliding up under her skirt. She wrote, however, that the hands did not belong to him; they were disembodied hands, with skilful and knowing fingers. She said that he was rarely in her thoughts now, and that she had discovered here a man called Harris. He asked lots of questions. He was not embarrassed by candour. She said that she had been a child and now she was putting off childish things. Harris had a wife who appeared to have a lover, though this didn't seem to disturb him, and she wondered if *she* could ever live that way. Could she ever be so uninvolved in the world, so cold, that betrayal would mean nothing? Then she wrote that this was sort of humorous, because even as she was writing these words she was betraying him. Cyril. Though it wasn't really a betrayal, she was simply stepping through a door from one room into another. She wasn't lonely; she didn't think that loneliness would ever plague her. Speaking of which, she had been reading a novel Harris had handed to her, *The Plague*, and though the story was weird and somewhat difficult, she was winding her way through it. She wrote that there was a boy who brought chickens to the Retreat. He wore cowboy boots with yellow stitching and he was quiet. He held his fork with his fist. Maybe more shy than quiet, she wrote. Or were they the same? She might, she thought, write a poem titled "Basic Problems," or some such thing.

She studied her handwriting and the words and how the words, to a foreigner with a different language, would appear as beautiful nonsense. She tore the letter from her notebook, folded it, and pushed it into the drawer of the bureau next to her bed. Outside, in the clearing, she heard the voices of her mother and William. Her mother was talking and William was interjecting, asking questions, and though nothing was clear, and no words were understood, the familiar sounds were consoling.

Raymond came back four days later bearing skinned rabbits that resembled chickens, only they were smaller and shinier. It had been raining and Lizzy was lying on her bed, reading to Fish. When she heard a truck, she got up and went out onto the porch and watched Raymond pass by. Fish stood behind her, holding her right leg.

Raymond nodded as he limped by. It was still drizzling slightly, and the bill of his cap was pulled down low.

"Chickens?" Fish asked.

Lizzy said, "Yeah, chickens," because she knew that Fish was in love with rabbits.

When Raymond came back she asked him where he was going and he said, "Town."

She asked if she and Fish could come along. "It's raining," she said.

Raymond looked up at the sky and then at the ground. "True." He kept walking and got into the truck.

Lizzy waited, not sure. Then she picked up Fish and said, "Come on." She ran to the pickup. She was wearing yellow shorts and she was barefoot and the path was slippery, and when she almost fell, Fish called out, "Ohh." She climbed in the passenger's side. Her feet were muddy and her legs were slick and wet and she thought of the shiny rabbits. She put Fish in the middle seat and said, "Here we go."

Raymond started the engine and backed up and then pulled out onto the driveway. When they were on the highway, the rain began to fall more heavily. Only the wiper on the driver's side worked. Lizzy felt a heaviness and wondered what she was doing, how could she have gotten in the truck. And with Fish. She thought she might ask Raymond to bring them back and then he turned and said, "Fish."

Fish looked up at him.

"That your real name?"

Fish nodded.

"Huh." He reached into a front jacket pocket and pulled out a cigarette and lit it, exhaling out the half-open window. "Last year there was a different girl with your name. Liz, though."

Lizzy was surprised that Raymond should talk about the Retreat so casually, as if it was a permanent and normal place, and she was curious about this other girl called Liz. She wondered how well Raymond knew her, if perhaps she too had climbed into his pickup. She felt jealous and then felt embarrassed that she was jealous. She could smell Raymond, a slightly wet musky scent, and she saw his hands on the wheel and the shape of his forearms. She said, "How old was this other Liz?"

Raymond shrugged. "Old enough. Maybe twenty. Closer to twenty-five."

"How old are you?" Fish asked, looking up at the underside of Raymond's chin.

"How old are *you*?" Raymond dropped his spent cigarette to the floor of the pickup and ground it with his boot.

"Four," Fish said.

"Well, Fish, add fifteen onto four."

Fish closed his eyes and opened them again. Looked down at his fingers and began to count.

It had stopped raining so they went to an outdoor hamburger stand, on Second Street, and sat at a picnic table under a green umbrella. Fish was beside Lizzy, across from Raymond, who asked why his name was Fish.

"Because," Fish said. He lifted his shoulders and let them drop. He appeared to be pondering the question.

"It's a nickname," Lizzy said. "His name's Jack and then my dad started calling him Jackfish and then it became Fish. Now it's just Fish. And I have a brother called Everett, who's weird and three years younger than me. He's fourteen. And then there's William, who is really Will, but my dad loves Shakespeare and so he's sometimes William Shakespeare or just Shakespeare. He's nine."

Fish's mouth was full of fries. He looked at Lizzy and then back at Raymond. He said, "Lizzy and I are getting married."

"That so?" Raymond grinned.

In the pickup later, Fish wanted to sit by the window. Lizzy said it would be cozier if he was in the middle but Fish insisted. Raymond said, "Let him," and she said, "Okay, for a bit." Fish fell asleep, pushed against Lizzy's hip. It was raining again, the one wiper slapped at the windshield. The pickup had a floor shift and she sat with her left thigh pressed against the stick, which had a dark worn knob with numbers on a grid, 1, 2, 3, and an "R" that was closest to her hip. When Raymond shifted, his palm covered the knob, and his wrist brushed her bare thigh.

Lizzy felt like she did sometimes at the beach or the pool back in Calgary where the boys would stare at her. She felt almost naked. Raymond's face was right beside her and she knew what he looked like because she had studied him at the hamburger stand. He had a small scar on his upper lip, in the middle, and she liked how it broke up his face, which was smooth all over, perfect. He had small ears. His jeans had a hole at the knee. She put an index finger there and traced the cloth. She said that a colourful patch would look good and that she knew how to sew. He looked down at her hand and back at the road. It appeared he might say something, but he didn't.

They were still sitting like that as they passed the turnoff to the Retreat. Lizzy made note of the road but she said nothing. She experienced a slight moment of panic, until Raymond lifted a finger and pointed into the distance and said, "My place is right up there." He drove fast, the palm of his left hand on the wheel. A few minutes later they turned off the main highway and drove up a gravel road, past houses that had signs with numbers on them, all the way up to sixteen. In the yards, there were trailers with boats, pickups on blocks, bicycles lying down as if in wait for something or someone. The gravel road fell into a tunnel of trees and the further they wound into the backcountry, the more Lizzy felt a sinking, a falling away.

When Raymond slowed, she held her breath and looked around, but there were just trees and trees. Raymond shifted, his hand pushing up against the stick, away from her. He turned onto a narrow trail and followed the tracks, which were muddy and slippery and full of holes that held the rainwater. He kept the pickup in low gear and reached with one hand into his jacket pocket, pulled out a pack of cigarettes, and handed it to her. "Light me one."

Lizzy removed a cigarette and put it in her mouth. Fish stirred beside her, and slept on. She slipped the pack between her thighs and took the book of matches from the dash. She lit the cigarette and inhaled as his hand reached up and asked for the cigarette.

He said, "You're okay," and at first Lizzy thought this might be a question, but it wasn't. He was proclaiming something, or laying out an assessment of sorts, and she knew she was supposed to be pleased.

"Better than," he said, and he grinned and flicked the cigarette ash out the window.

They came to a stop before a small cabin with a sagging roof and a faded blue door and windows that had plastic taped over a few broken panes. The door was open. Fish sat up and said, "Where?" and he rubbed his eyes and then lay down again, eyes open, staring at the dashboard. Lizzy stroked his forehead, which was sweaty and hot.

Raymond said, "Here we are. My brother's here. He came back home a month ago. He has a cat." He got out and stood beside the pickup, looking out across the tops of the trees. Then he walked towards the cabin and disappeared inside. Lizzy sat and waited. There was a black cat in the sun near the side of the house and just over to the side of the cat was a swing made from thick chains and the seat of a car. When Raymond reappeared he was with a boy who looked like him, only his hair was shorter and he was heavier. Raymond's head moved slightly as if to indicate something and then the other boy said her name, "Lizzy." He walked over to the pickup and leaned into the passenger door. He said that his name was

Nelson and that his brother was too shy to be polite and they should come into the house. It had sounded like he'd said *hose*, and at first Lizzy was confused. She gathered up Fish and said, "Okay," then climbed out and stood on the muddy ground in her bare feet.

"Lizzy and Fish," Nelson said. He led them into the cabin and offered them two chairs, one covered in blue plastic and the other wood, painted red. He sat on the corner of the table and asked if she wanted a beer.

"Sure," she said. There was a propane tank in the corner with a gas burner beside it. A few pots and plates and cups in a wooden box. Some tins, beans and corn, beside the box. And beside the box a large green garbage pail that held water. There was a dipper floating in the water. The walls of the cabin were rough and unpainted. Beyond the makeshift kitchen was a door that led somewhere, perhaps to a bedroom. The light in the room they were standing in was muted by the plastic on the windows.

Raymond stood in the doorway, smoking. Lizzy took a beer from Nelson and went over to Raymond and stood beside him and because she didn't know what else to say, she said, "So, this is where you live."

"In the summer," Raymond said. He gestured towards Nelson and said that his brother had just moved in. Nelson was the cook and the cleaning lady. He grinned and said, "Not doing a very good job."

"That's right," Nelson said. In the dusty light he raised his bottle as if proposing a toast. He drank. "No electricity, so warm beer."

Lizzy asked Raymond if he wanted to share her beer, and she offered it up for him to take. He shook his head and said that he was fine. He wasn't thirsty. Fish, who was still dazed from sleep, slipped off his chair and went to Lizzy and wrapped his arms around her bare leg.

"Funny thing," Nelson said. "Ray said there was this girl down at that place who was pretty good-looking. That'd be you, I guess."

"Or someone."

"It's you," Raymond said. He seemed embarrassed; he made a slight grimace as he leaned back out the doorway and spun his cigarette towards the pickup.

Fish pulled at Lizzy. "Swing?"

She looked at Raymond and said, "He wants to swing. That okay?"

"Course it is. Come on, Fish." He held out a hand and Fish let go of Lizzy's leg and went outside. Raymond turned to look at Lizzy as he stepped out the door. "My brother was taken away to live with a perfect family in Manitoba and now he comes back full of bullshit." He nodded gravely at Lizzy and then he grinned.

Nelson lifted his beer in a salute and told Raymond to fuck off. His hand was big on the bottle and his wrists were thick. He seemed to be much stronger than Raymond. From where she sat, she could see the swing and Raymond's back as he faced Fish, who was talking, and she felt a sudden affection for Raymond. The sound of the swing came in through the open door. Lizzy said, "We gotta get back. I didn't tell anyone where we were going."

"Raymond told me about the Retreat," Nelson said. "Every year the Doctor arrives, and every year there's this new group of followers."

"We're not followers," Lizzy said.

"Ray manages to make money there selling chickens to city people who think chickens don't have to be raised and then killed. You don't look like that kind of person. What do you do down there?"

"The Doctor who runs it says that it's a place to gather and make sense of the world," Lizzy said. She shrugged, looked about at her surroundings, and then said that she shouldn't have to defend it. "Maybe it doesn't have to have a purpose. It just is. People live there for the summer and then go home."

Nelson's skin was slightly mottled, like he'd had acne when he was younger. He wasn't as handsome as Raymond but he seemed surer of himself, with his bigger vocabulary, his wider mouth. He was a little too sure of himself, as if he had some secret he was hiding. He asked why Lizzy had gone there anyway.

She didn't answer right away. Outside, by the swing, Fish called and Raymond said something, but she couldn't hear him properly. She finished her beer and put it down on the floor. Her parents were there, she said, her brothers were there, and so she was there too. "Where else should I be?"

"I don't know. You're old enough to have a kid, you're old enough to be somewhere else. The Retreat sounds like this church I went to as a teenager. Where one man has a vision and throws it out for others to lap up. Don't you think?"

"I dunno. Maybe."

"I was raised by a white family. Did Raymond tell you that when I was ten, I was taken away to live with a white family in a place called Lesser? You remind me of my stepsister."

Lizzy looked away.

"The family I lived with was religious and I went to a Mennonite church for a while and then I went to the Pentecostal Church where people spoke in tongues and moved their hands through the air and one night Pastor Phil tried to raise a cat from the dead. There were good things, though, living in Lesser. We had linoleum on the kitchen floor and I learned to play viola. You play an instrument?"

"No," Lizzy said. "My brother Everett does."

"'Nother beer?" Nelson asked again.

"No, thanks, we have to get back." She rose and stepped out the door and said to Raymond that they had to go. "Okay?"

Raymond grabbed one of the chains on the swing and slowed it and as he did so he said, "Whoa," as if he were talking to a horse. Fish said, "Don't want to go." He was looking at the cat and he went over to it and took it into his arms. He scrubbed at the cat's ears and then held his head close to the cat's chest and listened to her purr. "Bull," he said, looking up at Lizzy.

Raymond was standing by the open door to the pickup. He slipped behind the wheel. Lizzy walked to the pickup and got in. Looked back at Fish who was taking his time. She said, "Nelson thinks that Fish is my kid? Did you tell him that?"

Raymond was looking through the windshield at the sky. "Nope, that wasn't me. I didn't say anything about Fish, or you, or you being a mother." He seemed pleased with himself.

"Well, that's what he thinks."

"Like I said, Nelson can be full of shit. Anyway, you know what's true and what isn't."

Lizzy called for Fish. Then she opened the door and went and took Fish by the arm and hauled him back to the pickup. Bull, suddenly out of Fish's arms and on the ground, went over and rubbed the side of its face against the corner of the cabin. Fish started to whimper. Then he said he was hungry. And thirsty. Lizzy put him in the middle of the seat, so his feet were touching the stick shift. Fish began to cry.

Raymond started the truck and said, "He's thirsty."

"That's okay. He can drink at home."

Raymond put the pickup in gear and crawled down onto the trail. She looked out the window at the trees and the sky and thought about Nelson. She wondered what he had done wrong to be taken away, but didn't want to ask. The sun had finally come out and the puddles reflected the trees. Above them, as if drawn against the sky, a falcon hovered.

When they got back to the Retreat, the only person visible was Emma Poole, standing at the edge of the treeline in her butterfly-catching outfit. She was leaning forward, peering into the bush. It turned out that no one had known Lizzy and Fish were gone; they hadn't been missed.

Everett was not happy. He yearned for where he had come from, the city, and he yearned for his clarinet lessons, taking the bus downtown to the apartment of his music teacher, Miss Douceur. She lived in a high-rise in downtown Calgary and her apartment overlooked the Bow River. There were large windows and from the balcony on the seventeenth floor you could see the river below and the streets and on the streets there were the small dark slashes that were people. Once, Miss Douceur had asked him out onto the balcony for a drink. They had sat on padded chairs around a glass-topped table and sipped at lemonade. The sun was falling onto their shoulders and their heads. Everett was facing the sun and he had to squint to see Miss Douceur, who was wearing a pale green dress that fell just above her knees. The dress was sleeveless and Everett snuck looks at Miss Douceur's thin, tanned arms. She always wore shoes with heels, even in her apartment. She was married, he thought, because there were signs of a man in the apartment — suit jackets, loafers, a tie thrown over the back of a chair — though Everett had never met her husband and she did not speak of him. He loved her carriage and confidence. He loved her straight posture and the way she sat and kept time, tapping her hand against her thigh. He loved her apartment with the shelves filled with many different kinds of books and the wineglasses that hung from under the cabinet, as if in wait for a party. He imagined dinners in the apartment. A group of men and women, all well-dressed, all rich. And Miss Douceur would be the prettiest and the smartest.

Once, when he had arrived a little too early for his lesson, she had invited him in and asked him to wait on the couch in the den. He had heard voices, hers and another voice, lower, that of a man, he thought, and then the front door had opened and then closed and she had appeared and asked him to come, please. That day she had worn a yellow skirt and a white blouse with black swirls. Her legs had been bare and her feet were bare. This was the first time he had seen her feet and he could not stop himself from glancing at her toes and ankles.

For hours during the day, Everett read. Both Harris and the Doctor had collections of books that were kept in the Hall, though most of these books were strange and unapproachable, especially the Doctor's. Lewis called them philosophical and theological tomes, and not very good ones at that. Everett discovered several short novels by John Steinbeck and he also read *The Old Man and the Sea*. He found a slim book on knots and so now he knew all about knots. He had not read any of Harris's novels, though they were available; it was too strange to think of reading Harris's words while the man was living next door.

Down by the pond, in the afternoons, Lizzy and Harris talked while Everett lay nearby and listened. Harris spoke of his life as a writer and he spoke of trips he had taken by himself and trips he had taken with Emma. One time he spoke of a month that he had spent in the south of Italy, and he said that if he were a wealthier man, and if Emma would follow him, he would live out his life in that place, close to the cliffs that fell down to the Mediterranean Sea. Everett, listening, but pretending not to, imagined a world of villas and late-evening meals with the sound of laughter and the ocean crashing on the rocks below. He recognized, perhaps for the first time in a real way, that the family he had been born into was poor and not very sophisticated and he wished that it weren't so. Lately, he had been aware of his parents' battles, of quarrels that upset his father more than his mother. His mother seemed to slip around the fights; she would smile and turn her back on Mr. Byrd, or later in the Hall she would be leaning in towards the Doctor and enjoying herself as if everything was normal and good.

One time, he had been asked to join some members of the Retreat as they drove into town to gather stale food – day-old bread and cast-off cinnamon buns – from the Dumpsters behind the Safeway. This was a regular event but Everett, curious at first, quickly found that he did not like the smell of the garbage. He was also uncomfortable with behaving in this way. He went once, and then decided to stay back at the camp and read, or to go down to the pond, where he lay, chest down, chin resting on his hands, conscious of Harris's faint voice offering stories of lives that had been lived in other places.

Visitors often passed through, staying at the Retreat for several days, and the Doctor entertained these people, sitting with them in the Hall and talking to them. The room was full of light and smelled of cooking. Everett sometimes went back to the Hall in the late morning after breakfast, or on several occasions after lunch, when the conversation had carried through the meal and into the long afternoon, and he stood and listened to the adults talking, aware of a tightness in his throat, the cause of which he could not locate. When he heard the Doctor speak on some topic — one time he had been talking about space and time, and he kept using the name Hider — Everett felt a twinge of excitement, and then loneliness. He felt the possibility that he might grasp in a small way what was being said, followed by the realization that he did not, nor would he ever, match up to the people gathered around the long table. A circle, like a fence, surrounded the Doctor, and it remained a mystery to Everett how a person might enter that place. Perhaps an invitation was necessary, or humour, or intelligence, or maybe there was a password. If there was, Everett did not know it. His mother must have known the way in, because she was often there, sitting close to the Doctor, and he wished that she would call him over and ask him to sit beside her, but she never did. Once, he heard her speak, but he did not catch what she said, only the Doctor's response as he said, "Good question, Norma." At that moment, Everett's chest began to ache, and he stepped out of the room.

Everett's father rarely went to the Hall, because he said that the atmosphere was stultifying. "You know the word," Lewis said to Everett one afternoon. "That's what it is. Stultifying. The air is heavy with minds roiling in their own crap." Everett was helping cut stringers for a new set of stairs, the same stairs that his mother had lost her footing on during the family's second week there and broken her wrist. His mother and father had just had an argument. Everett had been sitting on the stairs of their cabin and he had heard his father's voice as he said, "That may be, but he's got a pecker, you know, Norma," and his mother had laughed and said, "Lewis, Lewis." And then his father came outside and he walked past Everett, got into the car and slammed the door, and then he was gone. Everett heard his mother behind him, on the porch, and she said his name as if surprised to see him there. Then she came down onto the first step and it gave way. She fell forward with a small "ohh" and put out her arms to stop her fall and as she landed her right wrist snapped backwards. Everett heard the sound that came out of her mouth. It was a sharp cry, and he felt embarrassed and looked away; his mother's legs were spread and he could see her panties. He felt humiliation and willed his mother to close her legs. His help-lessness kept him from moving. And then the Doctor appeared and bent over Mrs. Byrd and put his face very near hers and it seemed he would kiss her, but he didn't. He helped her up, placing his hands under her arms so that he touched her breasts. Everett turned his head away and then back again. The Doctor's mouth was close to his mother's neck. He told her that her wrist might be broken. She shook her head and studied her arm. She looked at Everett, her face very white. She moaned then, and the sound was intimate and sexual. Her cheek rested against the Doctor's chest. The Doctor asked for help and Everett finally stepped forward and gripped his mother's arm. The three of them hobbled towards the pickup. His mother was muttering. She said, "Fuck," and then laughed and she turned her face towards the Doctor and said, "Sorry." Everett's forearm was under her bare armpit and there was a slickness of sweat. This was her good arm, round at the shoulder and clean and straight, and Everett had been surprised at the strength in her bicep. Her dress, sleeveless and soft, had smelled of soap. "Tell your father," she said. "Okay? Tell him I'm fine."

The Doctor drove his mother to the hospital, and when Everett's father came back he had told him about the fall and he said that his mother's wrist might be broken. He described the fall, the colour of his mother's face, her bravery. He said nothing about the Doctor almost kissing her, or the tilt of his mother's body as she whispered *sorry* to the Doctor. He wanted his mother and father to be happy, and he imagined that this accident might soften his father in some way. When his mother returned from the hospital, she had made her way onto her porch where the family gathered. She called out to Fish and put him on her lap and showed off her cast. When she saw Everett standing off to the side, she motioned for him to come, and she allowed him to write his name on her cast. As he did so, he caught his mother's scent, a mix of leaves and sweat and soap, and overlying that, a slightly wet odour that reminded Everett of the sculptures he had created in his junior-high art class.

It was Lewis's job to fix the stair, and Everett asked if he could help, which really meant that he wanted to watch. In Calgary, when his father had worked Saturdays, Everett would walk over to the glass-blowing factory, sit on a crate, and watch. He liked the tools, the rubber tubing, the lapping wheel, the pastorale. His father would make him wear special glasses. He'd put them on and watch the liquid glass pulled from the furnace. The movements of his father's hands, and the shapes and colours that suddenly appeared. He made vases, birds with long necks, butterflies, and fancy ashtrays. Sometimes, when a piece didn't turn out, his father would set it aside, let it cool, and then hand it to Everett. "You can take it home," he'd say.

On this day, Lewis intended to rebuild the stairs completely. He held a pencil, eyed the square, and said that it was absolutely essential to measure the stringer at least three times so as not to waste a good piece of board. "Care must be taken." And then he nodded in the direction of the Hall and said, "Like I was saying, it is not a pretty thing to watch men stew in their own crap. Or women. You know?" He seemed to want to say more, but then he shook his head and said, "Ach, I sound bitter." Then he said that Norma was content at the Retreat, and if she loved dipping into those dull conversations in the Hall, who was he to complain about their mother's happiness. "Eh?"

Above them a V of geese was flying north.

"Here," Lewis said, handing Everett the hammer and some nails. "Drive in a few spikes." The hammer was twenty-two ounces and Everett had trouble holding it. He tapped lightly at a nail and it went spinning off into the grass. He tried again and this time managed to put the nail in halfway before it bent. Lewis took the hammer back and said that he shouldn't be timid. The hammer was a simple object really. "The less you stare at it, the more you seize and hold it, the more real it becomes. If you try too hard, you will either bend the nail or miss completely, or hit your own thumb. Sort of like life. Oh, listen to the wise man." And with three swings, Lewis drove in a nail.

Everett tried again and managed to put home a nail with many hits.

"There you go," his father said. "Feels good, doesn't it? Sometimes too much thinking can get in the way."

One night, Everett woke and heard Lizzy and William talking. William was telling her about a dream, something to do with a cave and an animal inside the cave. Then Everett slept, and when he woke again the light from the moon was falling across Lizzy's bed. He could see her hands resting on her chest, and he watched them to see if she was sleeping or not. She looked childlike, soft and innocent, though he knew she wasn't innocent. When Lizzy and Lewis had drowned the kittens, Everett had been sad not because the kittens were dead but because his father had seen that Everett was incapable of helping. And, it was true. He might have failed. Choosing Lizzy made sense. She was efficient and she could be cruel. Lately, she had seemed to him distracted and restless, and one time she had asked him what he thought of Raymond, the boy who delivered chickens. When she asked the question, Everett felt as if she were turning away from him to look in another direction, and he did not like this feeling.

The cabin began to open up and reveal its shape as dawn arrived. Everett crawled out of bed and dressed and went outside, and instead of walking up to the outhouse, he went into the bush and peed. He pulled up his zipper and stood in the grey light, listening. Everything alive in the bush seemed to be moving, crawling through the leaves, flying in the air, calling and screeching. "A cacophony," his father had said late one night, cocking an ear towards the forest. His father didn't like the forest, and neither did he. He missed hot water, television. He missed streets, sidewalks, pavement.

The sky was getting brighter now, rosy. A door slammed and he heard footsteps approaching. Then he saw the Doctor step out of the far cabin. He walked right up the path, past Everett who was still standing, out of sight, at the edge of the treeline. The Doctor was wearing only red shorts and he had a towel draped over his neck. He was talking to himself, something about declaring the facts. Everett went down onto the path and followed him at a distance. The Doctor turned towards the pond, and when he arrived at the pond's edge, he folded the towel and laid it down, then he slipped off his shorts and looked up at the pink sky and walked into the water.

Everett had cut around the pond and was standing in the trees off to the side, quite close to the Doctor. When the Doctor bent forward and removed his shorts and then straightened, Everett saw the Doctor's penis. Then the Doctor walked into the water and Everett saw only his mouth moving. He was talking to himself again, nothing Everett could understand, and then he was singing. He had a deep voice and he sang so loudly that his voice probably carried back to the cabins. He came up out of the water and bent to retrieve something from his towel. A bottle of shampoo. He soaped his hair and his armpits and he soaped between his legs.

The Doctor's legs were thin and ropey. He was very blond and did not have much hair, except under his arms and at his groin, and even this blended in with the whiteness of his body. Everett turned away, and then looked back. The Doctor had gone into the water again and he was knee-deep and rinsing himself. Then he dove in with a soft splash and his head resurfaced far out into the pond. When he finally came back on shore and towelled himself dry, Everett's legs were shaking and his mouth was dry and hot.

For the next two mornings, Everett woke early and walked out to the pond and waited in the trees. The Doctor came. He undressed and he bathed. He towelled himself dry, put on his shorts, and walked back to his cabin. Everett did this for several more mornings and always it was the same. And always, standing there hidden in the bushes and watching the Doctor bathing, Everett felt a strange thrill and then shame. When he returned to the cabin that last morning, Lizzy lifted her head and looked at him.

"Where are you *going* every morning?" she said.

"To pee," he said. He sat on his bed and removed his runners.

"You're gone a long time, Everett," she said.

Everett didn't answer. The image of the Doctor's ropey legs appeared and disappeared. He said, "I couldn't sleep. I was walking."

Lizzy seemed to consider this, then she lay back down and said, "Oh."

Later, at breakfast, the Doctor asked Everett if he wanted to come by the Den. "Just a little meeting," he said. "I like to get to know everyone here."

Everett looked around at the rest of the group. His father wasn't present, he'd gone into town for building supplies. His mother smiled encouragingly. She said, "Of course he'd love to. Right, Everett?"

Everett shrugged. He believed that the Doctor had seen him down at the pond, spying, and this was why he was to join him in the Den. He searched for a reason why he wouldn't be able to go, but his mind was empty.

His mother said, "You'd think he was going to his death. Don't look so glum, Ev."

And so, after breakfast, Everett knocked on the door to the Den, and when the Doctor called out, he entered. The room was cool and dark. There was no fire, as Lizzy had said there was when she had come here. The Doctor was sitting in a canvas chair, holding a book. He put the book down and got up and pulled a chair over for Everett. There was a large desk in the corner of the room with papers and magazines scattered across the surface. The shelves on the walls held books and there were framed photographs, many of which were of the Doctor posing with people, both men and women, and always the Doctor appeared to be on the verge of a smile. There was a white owl mounted on the far wall and it was looking right at Everett, and though Everett knew that the owl was dead, the eyes disturbed him.

The Doctor explained that there was nothing to fear, everyone in the camp had already sat, or would in the future sit, in the chair Everett now found himself in. "Not to worry. We are not bullies here, nor are we black-and-white thinkers. This place exists as a harbour from the world, a place to find the courage to affirm one's own reasonable nature over what is accidental in us. I'm interested in the accidental. I'm also curious about how society works. Take a group of people and plunk them down in a village, a village that is created from scratch, and make those people live together. What happens? That's what interests me. I'm not a social scientist. Neither am I a hippie who believes in free love or self-abasement or the willy-nilly taking of drugs for pleasure. Don't get me wrong, I'm interested in pleasure as well as in denial and sub-limation, but all these things are much easier to measure in this place than in the chaos of the city. And, I'm interested in communism. Not the communism of a centrally controlled government, but the machinations of a community. How do I take what I have that is special and share it with others? Take your father, for instance. His gift lies in his hands and in his ability to build things, to imagine a water system that will provide a shower for the community, and then to build it. One has to be clean, no? Or, my wife Margaret. Her gift is garden-ing. The tomato you had for breakfast was provided by her hands. You see?"

"I didn't eat a tomato."

"Maybe not, but you see my point. One gift is no better than another."

On the wall, behind the Doctor, was a barometer. And beside it was a photo of the Doctor on a sailboat. The Doctor was standing with his arms crossed and he was wearing a blue hat, and beside him was Margaret and she was holding a baby, possibly Big Billy. Everett had always wanted to sail.

"What about you, Everett? What do you bring to this place?"

Everett said he wasn't sure. "I help my dad," he said.

"You admire him?"

Everett said that he did.

"Good. That's important." The Doctor paused and then he said that he too admired Lewis. "Your father is a fine, fine man. He is an independent thinker and he doesn't like to be boxed in, and believe me, this camp is a kind of boxing in, isn't it? But your father bears it because he loves your mother and that is what I admire. His ability to sacrifice his own wishes for the desires of your mother. You must notice this. And that, that is the biggest thing someone can do for another. Lay down his life, as it were. God knows, this community has its failings. We are not self-sufficient. We still have to buy milk in town. And flour. And when your mother breaks her wrist, we have to drive her over to the local hospital. We don't live on the moon, and we can't exist as if we lived on the moon. We have to be in the world. Do you like films?"

Everett looked up. The question had dropped in as if from the moon. "You mean movies?" he asked.

"Yes, movies."

Everett said that he liked watching movies.

"Good. We want to have a movie night. As soon as we find a projector. I was saying to someone, perhaps your mother, that we needed more entertainment. And film is a great place to start. I would love to see a small orchestra as well. Your mother tells me that you play clarinet. You see what I mean?"

Everett had begun to understand that there was no response required. He simply nodded. The Doctor continued. "We are travellers on this earth. Isn't it curious that truth doesn't fall from heaven to earth? At least, I don't believe this. We have to beat our way through the bushes to find it, and what better place to do that than right here, where we are surrounded by actual bush. Don't get me wrong, I'm not saying you must go out there into the forest and hatchet your way to truth, but it's a great metaphor for what we are trying to do here." At this point he thumped his chest with a fist. Everett startled. He had no idea what the Doctor was saying, though he assumed there was a deep wisdom that he might some day understand. The Doctor's eyes were bright blue and Everett, who wasn't always good at gauging the age of people over eighteen, could see that the man before him was not as old as his father or mother. A clear light came from his eyes. He bent towards Everett and whispered confidentially, "And what do you believe?"

Everett was trembling. He didn't know if it was from the cool air in the room, or because Doctor Amos frightened him in some new way. The Doctor continued to whisper. He said that belief was not anachronistic. Belief took tremendous courage. He said, "I was considering shame the other day. Something we have failed to sustain in our lives. Shame is what makes us different from the dog or the cat or the cow. When we go to the bathroom, we close the door behind us. When we make love, we do it in the privacy of our bedroom. When we masturbate, we might feel shame, but it is only because we imagine being caught. Being seen. Do *you* masturbate?"

Everett looked down at his hands, aware that there was a right answer, but he did not know it.

"*I* do," the Doctor said. "This might surprise you. Does it surprise you?"

Everett was perspiring. He knew what the Doctor's penis looked like but he could not imagine it hard and in the Doctor's own hand. He wanted to talk of something else, or to have this meeting finished, but he did not know how to accomplish either thing.

"Of course it does. Because I'm a married man. I'm an old man in your eyes. Though not that old, truly. Thirty-five is still young. The fact is, talking about this embarrasses you. You feel shame. Perhaps it is shame for yourself, or even some shame for me, because you like me and yet here I am talking about onanism. You should know the story of Onan, as you've been reading the Bible. It's a tale of caution, though not necessarily true. Isn't it interesting that this works this way? You're looking at me as if I'm mad."

Everett found his voice and said, "No."

The Doctor nodded. He said that Everett should save himself because no one else could do that for him. Not Jesus Christ, nor Allah, nor Buddha, nor any other human who claimed to be God. "There is no theology or God to save us. There is no thing that will save us, save ourselves. These are things that may not concern you yet, but they will, and if they don't, they should. Even as we speak, they should." He paused and became thoughtful. He said, "Last night I dreamed that all the people left on earth were on a raft on a vast ocean. There was not enough room on the raft and survival depended upon throwing someone else off the raft before *you* were thrown off. There was much wailing and violence. Babies were hurled into the water. Mothers. Fathers. Children. In the end the strongest were left, or those who found themselves by some chance in the middle of the raft. I knew I wouldn't last, because I wasn't strong enough, and so I took a rope and tied it to my wrist and fashioned a knot around part of the raft, and when someone attempted to throw me off, it was not possible. This is how I survived. And then I woke up." The Doctor paused and then he said, "The wise man's eyes are in his head, but the fool walks in darkness. And yet I know that one fate befalls them both. As is the fate of the fool, it will also befall me. We have only one life. Isn't that right?"

He looked at Everett with eyes that had been glowing minutes earlier but now seemed darker. "Do you trust?" he asked and Everett said, without thinking, that he did. The Doctor smiled and said that he could leave now. That was all. Everett got up and he stepped outside and stood on the porch in the bright sunlight. In the distance, beyond the Hall, he saw his mother hanging laundry, and she was singing. It was the same song the Doctor sang every morning as he bathed in the pond.

And then, some days later, during the aimless hours before dinner, the Moll family arrived. They pulled up in a bus that was painted blue with various types of fish swimming on its sides. There were two daughters, Shanti and Dee Dee, and Everett immediately liked Shanti, the oldest, whose voice was smooth and barely audible. She was haughty and distant and Everett was pleased; he felt that he and she might have the same opinions on many different subjects. She called her father by his first name, Geoffrey, and said right off that she would not be sleeping in the cabin that the Doctor had offered the family. Geoffrey ignored her and said that they had heard of the Retreat from a gas-station attendant in town. He said that the possibility of a commune interested them and so here they were. He was standing in the shadow of the bus, swivelling his bald head to take in the layout of his surroundings. The Doctor had welcomed them; offered them the cabin, and then offered them dinner. Geoffrey said that the family had been travelling North America — they were from England — and they were making stops in various towns and villages along the way, where they put on plays in the evenings, like a touring troupe from Elizabethan times. He chuckled, looked about, and said, "This wild and wayward world." Everett thought then that he resembled his daughter Shanti;

they both lifted their noses slightly, as if they had smelled something unpleasant.

In the afternoons, the girls managed to escape their parents' grasp and join the Byrd children at the pond. Dee Dee wore a blue bathing suit, Shanti, black. They were one-piece suits, not at all like Lizzy's bikini. Both of the girls were at first frightened by the water, which had weeds growing in it, close to the shore.

"Is it safe?" Dee Dee asked one afternoon, and William ran in up to his waist and then back out again. "See?" he said, looking directly at Dee Dee. Shanti touched the water delicately with a toe. She made a face and said that she was used to swimming pools where the water was clear and you could see the bottom.

"Just a bit of algae and weeds," Lizzy explained. "Because it's a pond and there's no fresh water flowing in. It's not dirty."

Shanti ventured out further so that her ankles were covered and she turned and motioned for Dee Dee to follow. All of them waded into the water, the two girls swimming out together to the middle of the pond. Everett pretended to be busy with something at his feet though his gaze followed the girls in the water, Shanti practising the butterfly while her sister treaded water nearby. A few minutes later, when they came up to shore, Everett watched Shanti as she stood, water streaming off her dark hair and down her front. He saw the sharpness of her hipbones and her small breasts pressed flat by her bathing suit.

One evening, at dinner, the Molls joined the rest of the group at the long centre table and Everett found himself beside Shanti. She kept her elbows close to her sides, eating delicately, barely touching the carrots and rice. She liked meat, preferably mutton, her mother explained. The Doctor said that meat was a rarity here. What was eaten was taken from the land, and the only animals to be had were the bull in the pen that was waiting for a mate, and the goat that provided the group with a small amount of milk. "Can't eat our provider of milk," he said. "And sheep we do not have. Though we have thought of purchasing a cow from the Blaines up the road. This would be good for both us and the bull. And we have the boy who brings us chickens twice a week. And sometimes rabbits." He looked at Lizzy.

Everett imitated Shanti's method of holding her knife with the right hand and the fork with the left. It was awkward, and he managed to mangle a carrot and work it up towards his mouth.

"What kind of fancy knife work is that?" his father asked, grinning.

Everett, his face heating, ducked his head.

"Leave the boy alone," his mother said. She was wearing a short red dress and a string of pearls. Her hair was swept up to reveal her long white neck. She had taken to dressing up for the evening meal, as if each occasion were a banquet. She usually put fresh-cut wildflowers in sealer jars and she always lit the stubby candles that she had found in one of the cabinets in the Hall.

Everett wanted Shanti to recognize his mother for her beauty and sophistication. It might, he thought, make her notice him and want to be his friend. He leaned towards her and said that his mother had just finished reading a book by a Russian author that was eight hundred pages long. Shanti seemed unimpressed. She raised her chin; her small dark mouth worked at a tiny piece of carrot. She turned to her father and said, "Geoffrey, when should we put on the play?"

"Wonderful. You have something to show us?" the Doctor asked.

"Yes. Yes, we do. The play we might suggest is a hodge-podge," Shanti's father said. "A tragical-comical-historical-pastoral." He lifted his eyebrows at Lewis.

Everett sensed that his father did not like Mr. Moll. They seemed to be angry at each other. Once, in the evening by the fireplace, Everett had heard them argue about whether Shakespeare had actually written any of his plays. Mr. Moll was emphatic that he did not, and Lewis thought this was naive.

"My daughter Lizzy is an author," his mother said. "She writes plays as well. And poetry. And some fancy-pants prose."

"Don't," Lizzy said.

Shanti tittered and made a face as if she had tasted something bad.

"I have seen some of her writing," Harris said, "and it is quite mature." He rarely spoke, and so now to hear this announcement was quite a surprise. Everett was aware of Lizzy and how she stared defiantly at her mother, though she seemed pleased by Harris's claim.

Shanti said that she had written the play with her father. It had demanded so much work, she said, looking at Lizzy. Her nose was like a small button. Everett wanted to touch it.

The Doctor thought it would be marvellous to see a play that evening. "Do you need help with actors?"

"Oh, not at all," said Mr. Moll. "It's just a simple four-hander."

Lewis had called the play dire. The actors were like spent swimmers who clung together and choked their art. Though these had been their father's words, Lizzy echoed them now. Everett asked Lizzy what *dire* was and she said, "Desperately bad." They were in bed. Fish and William were sleeping. Lizzy was lying under a pool of light, writing in her notebook.

He said, "Dee Dee was good."

Lizzy allowed that Dee Dee had played a good flirt, but that that was easy for a fourteen-year-old girl who was flirtatious in real life. "That's not acting," she said.

In the play, Shanti had been a boy, Dee Dee a girl, and Shanti had wooed Dee Dee, who came from the other side of the tracks. Dee Dee's parents, played by her parents, had forbidden any sort of relationship because Shanti wasn't a Christian. There was much arguing and tears, and in the end Shanti had become a Christian and the two lovers had gone out together. Everett had found Shanti quite believable as a boy, but he felt confused by his emotions as he watched because he was hearing Shanti's voice and watching Shanti's gait, and he was conscious of Shanti's body beneath the flannel shirt and dark wool pants. She was angular and thin, with a narrow chest.

"It's not believable," said Lizzy, "that someone would convert to Christianity in order to get laid."

"They didn't have sex," Everett said. "They just went out."

"You know what I mean," Lizzy said. "Besides, the writing was terrible. Clunky and wooden."

Everett lay on his back and imagined a block of wood with words on it. He thought about Shanti with a moustache, pretending to have a penis. What a surprise then to find no penis when he undressed her. And so he put her in a skirt and then undressed her. At the edge of his sleep, she became a boy with a penis larger than Everett's; they compared, and Everett came up short.

The next day, down by the pond, Fish nearly drowned. It was late afternoon, and Lizzy and Shanti were arguing about comedy and tragedy. Lizzy said that the best stories were a mixture of both and that comedy only sharpened a tragedy. Everett was lying on a large flat rock close to the pond, eyes closed, listening. He admired his sister's way with words and her ability to argue. At one point, she looked at Shanti and said, "You think that sneering is the way to win an argument. That's stupid. I'm willing to hear a good point, but you haven't come up with one."

Shanti said that the play the night before had been a good example of comedy. There was nothing tragic. All had ended well.

For a long while Lizzy did not answer. Then she said that

the play was a black-and-white tale. "Not a bad one," she said generously. "But still, its goal was to teach."

"Of course," Shanti said. "What else?"

They were on their stomachs, side by side. Lizzy was wearing a bright blue bikini and Shanti wore her black one-piece. Everett saw their bums and their backs and the angle of their necks as they lifted their heads to speak. The string of Lizzy's top was untied. Lately, she had seemed to him impatient with the younger boys, who were at that moment down by the water's edge, building a dam out of stones.

A voice entered Everett's head, soft and low. "I want to see the Lookout. Would you take me up there?"

Dee Dee was standing beside him. He saw her feet and ankles, and looking up he had an elongated image of her: thick legs, crotch, round stomach, barely formed breasts, the bottom of her chin. She walked off to the edge of the bush and looked back at him and he rose and followed her. The sun hit his shoulders, Shanti's voice poked away at the hot air, and he heard Fish squeal with delight at something.

The Lookout was about a mile into the bush. A narrow trail led up to the top of a large rock that overlooked the camp to the north. To the south, far off, you could see the roofs of the larger buildings in town. Sometimes the children went up to the Lookout to watch birds and chase squirrels, or in the evening their father led them there to study the constellations. Dee Dee had heard of it, but had not yet been there.

For a while, Dee Dee walked ahead of him on the path. As Everett followed he was aware of her shape and how unlike her sister she was. And then, as if she knew Everett's thoughts, she said that her sister was boring. "She thinks she's always right."

"Maybe she is right," Everett said.

"You just like her," Dee Dee said.

"I don't," Everett said.

Dee Dee stopped and turned to face Everett. She grinned. "Really? Then why are you always watching her?" She had her hands at her sides. She was carrying licorice strings in a paper bag. Her small mouth and the round slope of her bare shoulders. She was barefoot and wore shorts over her black bathing suit. He shrugged and pushed past her and led the rest of the way, walking quickly, forcing Dee Dee to run.

"Hey," she called out, but he ignored her. The path narrowed and the branches of the bushes scraped his arms. Mosquitoes flew up and came to rest on his neck and back. He slapped at them and kept going.

When he reached the Lookout, he turned and saw Dee Dee coming up the trail. When she finally caught up to him she was breathing heavily and her voice was panicky. "You pig," she said. Her arms were scratched and the left side of her face was bloody from where a branch must have caught her below the eye.

He reached out and touched the scrape on her cheek, showing her the blood. She licked her fingers and rubbed at her face, then sat down and rested her chin on her knees. Everett sat beside her. He said that he had hated the Retreat from day one. He hated the mosquitoes in his ears at night, and the lousy food, and the long days of nothing. He said that she was lucky because she would be climbing into her bus soon and leaving.

"Yeah?" Dee Dee said. "To go where? To another nowhere place." She said that she couldn't wait till she was eighteen and then she would leave home. She turned to study Everett and said, "Shanti couldn't care less about you. She laughs at you. Says you smell like shit. She has a boyfriend back home. He's twenty-six. An actor. That's why we're travelling. To get Shanti away from Bryson."

Everett's chest felt hollow. He didn't speak.

"Anyway, she's terribly dull," Dee Dee said. "Not to mention frigid."

Everett lifted his gaze and studied Dee Dee's mouth. She was chewing her licorice and still talking.

"She won't put out. Not even for Bryson. She's *saving* herself." She grinned, lifted an end of the licorice, and reached it out towards Everett's mouth. "Here," she said.

He took it. Dee Dee's mouth approached. Curious, he watched her gobble up the red line of licorice and then she was there, at his mouth, and she was kissing him. Her small mouth had suddenly opened and was offering him her tongue. The sun was bright behind her. She pulled away and stood and hoisted him up so that he was facing her. She slipped her shorts down and her bathing suit sideways and took his hand and put it at her crotch. "Put your finger inside me."

He was helpless, so she guided him. They stood face to face. Dee Dee watched his eyes but did not kiss him again. She pushed against his hand and closed her eyes. Her eyelids trembled. The muscles moved on her face, and then, without warning, she said, "Okay," and she took his hand away and readjusted her clothing. He tried to kiss her, not because he desired her, but out of obligation. She turned her face away and stepped backwards, tilting her head as if to consider what she saw.

"Nice," she said. "You're very nice."

Walking back down towards the pond and the other children, Everett heard Dee Dee's footsteps behind him and her quick short gulps of air. The human body was a veil with holes and he had put his finger into one of Dee Dee's holes. He hadn't hurt her. She was still behind him, talking now and then, chewing on the last of the licorice, complaining about the bugs and the heat. On her face was the scratch, another hole of sorts. He was ashamed. He wanted to turn and tell Dee Dee that he was sorry, but it wouldn't be clear what exactly he was sorry for. She had asked him to help. She had taken his finger and put it inside her and he had not felt anything erotic. It had all just evolved as an experiment of sorts, as if they were conducting research. So, this is it, he had thought at one point, and then realized that it wasn't, not really, because he himself didn't have an erection, nor did he feel the possibility of one. Dee Dee's lightheartedness was so different from his own distressing view of the event. He might have been a carrot, or a cucumber. She hadn't needed him, really, though she had called him very nice. But this, too, seemed wrong.

Coming down into the clearing that would soon offer a view of the pond, Everett heard shouting and then the sound of a voice calling, "Fish. Fish. Fish." A game, he thought at first, and then, because the voice was piercing and panicky, he imagined that Fish had been hurt, or had committed some innocent crime. Crime ran in the family. And then, entering the field of grass, he saw Lizzy near the water's edge. She was on her knees, pummelling a shape beneath her and then calling out. Standing off to the side was Shanti. William was running across the rocks and through the trees towards the camp.

A shimmer of heat, like a false wave seen on the highway in summer, had settled over the scene. Everett walked into and through that gauzy lake. Fish was on his back. Lizzy had her mouth on his. And then she pushed his chest, and blew into his mouth again. Everett found himself beside Lizzy, looking down at Fish's dead body. He was dead because Everett had finger-fucked Dee Dee. And now Dee Dee was over there, holding her skinny sister's hand. Dee Dee's fat, pale face. The crotch of her shorts, slightly twisted, her chubby thighs. Everett shivered. "Fish," he whispered. "Breathe, Fish." And his little brother opened his eyes and from his mouth flowed water, a soup of snot and brine and the dark pond itself. Fish coughed and spat and sucked for air and spat some more and then he sat up and said Lizzy's name and she took him and he pushed himself against her chest.

There was a time when Mrs. Byrd had been happier, light-hearted and carefree, but when Fish was born, she descended into darkness and she gave Fish over to Lizzy, who was too young to say, No, this is not mine. And she went away, sometimes for long periods, and when she finally returned she could not remember the children's birthdays or where the salt shaker was kept. And yet briefly the gloom would lift for a while, and during this momentary drift from sadness, the mother held and cared for her baby, and Lizzy was for a time set free.

There had been, in the first two years, a woman called Minny who came in to care for Fish during the days when Lizzy was at school. Minny was large and old and she wore sensible tan shoes and she suffered from pitting edema. She was constantly pressing a fat thumb against the dough of her flesh and showing the children how the imprint remained. She was from some foreign place where greasy soup was made in large vats. Fish did not like her, he wanted Lizzy, or his mother, but Mrs. Byrd had disappeared. She had been, in their father's words, vacuumed up by the black dogs, and she came out of her bedroom only intermittently to view the state of the kitchen, or to stick her pale face into the den where the children had gathered to watch TV after school. Her wan pretty head, her grey eyes, her hair gone limp because she no longer bathed properly. Everett often curled up beside his mother and read while she slept. And when she woke, he silently combed her hair.

Their father's work was a short walk from the house. He came home for lunch and attempted to get Mrs. Byrd to eat. She sat with him at the kitchen table and studied the food on her plate, and then pushed it away. He tucked her up in bed before he left again, telling her to sleep, and that when she woke the world would certainly be a brighter place.

And then, one evening, when Lizzy was caring for Fish, offering him sliced pear at the kitchen table, her mother returned from a night out. She'd gone with a friend to a talk given by a doctor of philosophy and religion. Lizzy heard her enter the house, and she knew, by the tenor of her mother's voice and the way she sashayed into the kitchen, that something large had taken place. Her mother lived for big things, and when she found them, she became giddy and breathless. Mrs. Byrd stooped to kiss Fish's head, and then Lizzy's cheek, and she said that the Doctor had been absolutely amazing.

"Amazing," she said again.

Lizzy could smell her mother, a mix of cigarette smoke and perfume and the outside air.

"That man. He talked about, about" — and here her hands moved around as if seeking to gather a spirit from the air — "he talked about being mortal and about how I belong to myself and I am nobody else's." She paused and grimaced slightly, perhaps for Lizzy, who couldn't help looking skeptical, and her mother said, "I'm okay. I am." She pinched Fish's cheek and squealed, "Who's your mummy?" Fish squinted and chewed thoughtfully, as if an answer was required. But she was already gone, into the next room where Lizzy could hear her talking and talking to her father and she thought about how long it had been since her mother had been like this.

That night, from her own bed, Lizzy heard her parents whispering and then it was quiet, and then her mother's voice called out. At first Lizzy thought that her mother might be asking for her to come help with something and she started to get up, and as she put her feet to the floor, her mother let out a sharp yelp and then a series of cries and Lizzy crawled back into bed and pushed the heel of her hand against the hard bone of her crotch.

And then again, in the middle of the night, her mother's cries startled her, pulling her up from a dream in which she was using Fish as a top, spinning him round and round, and he was squealing with delight, and when she woke she heard the squeals next door and realized that her mother and father were having sex once again. In the morning, her father made scrambled eggs for everyone and sang "Summertime," and when he came to the line about the mama being good-looking, he swung about and grinned and pointed the spatula at Lizzy, who shook her head and turned away.

The day Fish almost drowned, her mother had come running down the path to the pond, calling Fish's name, but by the time she got there, Fish was already looking about, cradled by Lizzy. Her mother was wild, violent. She clamped

Lizzy's wrists and cried out, "What happened?" Lizzy began to explain but her mother scooped Fish up and held him to her chest. William, slower than his mother, had arrived in her wake and was standing off to the side, surprised that Fish was alive. Lizzy was faced with her mother's bewilderment, her rage, as she stooped and hissed at her, "What were you *thinking*?" And then she turned and walked up the trail, and Lizzy saw her mother's back and Fish's small wet head, his chin resting on her shoulder.

That evening, after supper, her father took William and Everett into town for ice cream. Lizzy went to her parents' cabin. She found her mother and Fish lying on the bed and Fish was sleeping, his head resting against his mother's underarm. Her other arm, with a cast, lay across her stomach, making her look vulnerable, off balance. Lizzy stood in the doorway and said, "Is he all right?"

Her mother turned slightly, as if to determine the distance between herself and her daughter. She said, "Close the screen door. The mosquitoes."

"It was awful, Mum. He wouldn't breathe. And I did everything I'd been taught, the clearing of the pathway, the pumping of the chest, but it all seemed so hopeless. I didn't think it would work."

"William said he was dead. He came running up into the Hall and said that Fish had drowned. So, until the moment I got there, I believed that Fish *was* dead. Imagine that, Lizzy. Imagine how I must have felt." She sat up, shifting Fish away from her. "What were you doing, Lizzy? What was going on out there?"

Lizzy said that she had been talking to Shanti. They had been arguing about the play, about comedy and tragedy. She said the word *tragedy* and she stopped, knowing that there was no reasonable excuse that her mother would accept. "Maybe once, you could try to imagine *my* feelings. I didn't *try* to drown him."

"No, but today, by the water, he was yours. You took him there. He's four years old, and he nearly drowned. On your watch."

A lamp glowed by the bedside table. In its light, she saw her mother's elongated neck, sharp nose, the shadow of breast and nipple. "*My* watch? You take him next time, then. He's *your* child, not mine. Instead of talking to that stupid Doctor, *you* can take care of Fish. And what about Dad? I can see what's happening." She was crying, and she only knew this because she felt the tears on her face. She wiped at them with her hand and abruptly turned and left. Her mother called after her several times, but Lizzy kept going, out into the dim light of the clearing towards her own cabin.

The next morning, at breakfast, her mother sat at the far end of the table, close to the Doctor, with Fish at her side. Her mother cut up Fish's eggs with a fork and leaned into him, showing him the utmost care. Lizzy ate quickly and then walked out, meeting her father at the doorway as he was entering. He said good morning to her, and though she responded, she did so grudgingly, feeling resentment at his ignorance.

Later, as she sat unhappily on the porch of her cabin, she noticed Raymond's pickup parked near the Hall. She watched for him, and when he didn't appear she walked up towards the kitchen and just as she was about to go in, the screen door swung open and he was there. He stopped and then his mouth lifted slightly on one side and he said, "Lizzy."

His voice, and the way he said her name so lightly, opened something in her and she said that Fish had nearly drowned the day before, down by the pond, and that everyone was blaming her and maybe it was true that it was her fault. She stopped, looked at Raymond, and said, "Why are you smiling like that?"

"*Is* he dead?" Raymond asked.

"No."

"So, you saved him. Good for you. If *I* were drowning I'd want you close by."

As Raymond walked past her towards the pickup, she followed him and said, "Where you going?"

"The golf course. Work."

"I had fun. Up at your place."

He nodded. "It was good." Then he said that Nelson sometimes said the wrong thing. He could be an asshole.

"Oh," she said. "I didn't think so." She leaned towards him and then took a step back. "We could maybe see each other again. With or without Fish. He doesn't *have* to come along. You know?"

Raymond had propped himself against the pickup. One leg bent, boot planted against the door. He studied Lizzy and said that she probably had parents who didn't want her being seen with someone like him.

"Are you dangerous?" she said, and made a fist and pushed it against his stomach, not hard, but enough to feel the coil of his body, his solid mass. She laughed, as if to hide her own surprise at this sudden boldness.

He said that he wasn't, actually. Dangerous. He reached up a hand as if he wanted to touch her shoulder, her arm, or maybe her hip. Then his hand fell and he nodded and climbed into his pickup, waving to her as he backed up. She stood motionless, thinking about how close he'd been to touching her.

All that afternoon, she took care of Fish. Her father had taken her mother to the hospital in the late morning to have a smaller cast put on. Lizzy had seen them leave, her mother talking and laughing in the front seat, as if Lizzy's words of the night before, and the meaning behind those words, had not affected her. There was a brief thunderstorm in the afternoon, during which Fish napped on Lizzy's bed, his arms thrown back over his head, his brow wet with sweat. William and Everett had found an old Monopoly game and were playing in the Hall. Everett had seemed happy and for this she was grateful.

The Molls had left that day, early, before anyone else was awake, and later in the morning, Everett had told Lizzy, when they were alone on the sand by the pond, about his experience with Dee Dee. He said that he was to blame for the family leaving. Lizzy had not been surprised at Everett's honesty, though she had been amazed at how clear he was in telling his story, how matter-of-fact, as if what had happened to him was not at all sexual. She thought then that he might not have understood what Dee Dee had wanted. She told him that the

Molls had left because they had not liked the Retreat. It had had nothing to do with him and Dee Dee. The morning was cool, the sky grey. Lizzy smoked and she and Everett talked as they huddled under a blanket. She had loved her brother magnificently at that moment.

Now, watching Fish sleep on the bed beside her, she heard the family car pull up, and she heard the doors slam, and then the sound of her parents walking past her cabin. They did not appear at dinner and when Fish asked for his mother, Lizzy walked him up to their parents' cabin. She walked in without knocking. Her mother was lying on the bed, a wet towel across her forehead and eyes. Her father was sitting in a chair, leaning towards the lamp on the side table. He did not see or hear Lizzy above the sound of his own raised voice. "You're living a pipe dream, Norma," he said. "Maybe I'll just hit him in the lip."

Fish called out, "In the lip, hit him in the lip," and he ran to his father and jumped onto his lap. "Who? Who?" he asked. Lewis placed a large finger against his son's mouth. He looked over at Lizzy and said, "Next time, knock, all right?"

Lizzy was still standing in the doorway. She rolled her eyes and said, "Jesus Christ. Who am I? The nanny?"

Her mother groaned. With the cloth still covering her eyes, she told Lewis that she had misbehaved the day before. She'd been so frightened by the possibility that Fish might have died, that she'd blamed Lizzy. She said that she'd thrown her fear onto Lizzy. She called for Fish. "Come," she said.

Lizzy glanced at her father, who was studying her mother with what seemed utter weakness. The argument they had

been having, the one in which he was going to hit a man, probably the Doctor, in the lip, seemed to have been forgotten.
Lizzy realized that her parents, even when in conflict, were a
team. And she was only their daughter. She felt acute sadness,
a deep pity for herself. She left Fish with her parents and went
back to her cabin and changed into jeans and a flannel shirt.
William was sitting on the floor, studying his collection of
glass jars, into which he had placed bugs and worms and pieces
of grass and leaves. He had, in the last while, become a collector like Emma Poole, who he sometimes followed about. Lizzy
had seen him talking to Emma, asking her questions, showing
her his own collection of bugs. Everett was lying on his bunk,
watching Lizzy. He wore shorts and his bare legs were long
and bony and his feet, reflected in the mirror of the bureau,
appeared oversized. He had inherited his father's feet. They
were scooped slightly, shaped like spades.

"Where you going?" Everett asked. "Can I come?"

Lizzy pulled her hair into a ponytail and shook her head.
"I'm tired, Ev. Anyway, I'm going to visit a friend." She had
not known of her own intentions until she said the words.
And then, after saying them, it became clear that this was
what she wanted; to ride the bicycle up to the golf course and
meet Raymond. She asked Everett if he was going to be okay.

"Yes," he said. "I guess."

She said that he should go play chess with Harris or
someone. She said she wouldn't be long.

As she rode up towards the golf course she saw cattails in the ditch, and small birds that swept along beside her, and she felt the warmth of the evening sun against her neck. Lizzy thought of her mother on the bed with the wet cloth across her forehead, her arm thrown backwards as if she were falling, and the weak defence that she had offered. Her mother only cared when something threatened to brush too close to her life and alter her happiness: Fish drowning, her husband accusing her of some betrayal, Lizzy opposing her.

The golf course wasn't far from the Retreat, and she realized that she had never considered whether Raymond would be finished work, or whether she'd be interrupting him. He wasn't expecting her and he hadn't exactly invited her, and this filled her with a feeling of excitement. Maybe he would tell her to turn around and go home. A few days earlier, she'd borrowed the Retreat's pickup and driven to town because her father wanted her to be more independent, and Everett had come along and they'd bought food at the Safeway. Later, they'd driven down to the wharf by Canadian Tire and sat on the benches close to the houseboats. A group of men had approached them. The men were drunk and one, older than the others, had asked for beer or money, or anything of value. He'd said the word *value* and Lizzy had looked up into his dark and slightly ravaged face and she'd thought of Raymond and wondered if Raymond knew this man. And then the thought had flown away.

She had been writing lately. Her letters to Cyril had become letters to herself, and when she mentioned this fact to

Harris several days ago, he had encouraged her. He offered suggestions, he told her that the material world had much to offer, and that it was dangerous to be too ephemeral or romantic. She had thought at first that he was talking about falling in love with an actual person, and then she'd understood that Harris was referring to language and words. He'd said, "Name things. If a shoelace is blue, say that it's a blue shoelace. Or, play with some variation of it. And, of course, lie. You have to lie to make everything clearer." She'd wondered about this and decided she didn't have to lie. She'd written something about her mother, about the bone-coloured dress her mother liked to wear, and the buttons that were like tiny bones themselves, and about the shape of her mother's bones within the dress. And the bone of her mother's wrist cracking as she fell down the stairs. "How nice to imagine the snap of my mother's ulna."

The clubhouse was lit up and inside there were two men drinking at a small round table. Looking through the large plate-glass windows, Lizzy thought she saw Raymond, but it turned out to be another, a younger boy, who was wiping the tables. She stood alongside her bicycle, near to Raymond's pickup, and she wondered if she had made a mistake. She was about to climb on her bike and return home when Raymond appeared. He did not seem particularly happy and so, as he approached, she said, "I shouldn't have come."

He looked behind him, and up at the sky, and then back at her and he said, "Did someone tell you that?"

She said, "No, but it's strange, me standing here waiting for you. I mean, we didn't plan this."

Without asking, he took her bike and laid it in the back of his pickup and he got in. Tentatively, as if still expecting to be scolded, she climbed in and shut the door, which creaked and then clicked.

"Another day, another dollar," Raymond said. He turned and said that this was a surprise. A good one though. Then he told her that he used to caddy for an older woman who wore pink skirts and now she had married a Texan and was living in the States. He said that it was funny because he knew nothing about golf. He had been a mule, that was all. He said that his brother Marcel claimed that the woman had probably liked young boys. "You know."

The cab of the pickup, as they sat there, not moving, felt like a small room, and Lizzy felt safe as she listened to Raymond's voice inside that room. She asked where Marcel was.

"He lives in Montreal. He calls me sometimes and lectures me on life. He's a lawyer, so he figures that's his job." He said that Marcel didn't like white people. Lizzy looked at Raymond, as if to see if this were a joke. She couldn't tell.

The two men who'd been drinking in the clubhouse walked out onto the parking lot, their golf shoes clicking on the pavement. Raymond waited till they had left and then pulled a joint from his front pocket. "You smoke?" The match flared and revealed his right eye.

She shook her head.

"Never, or just not now?" he asked.

"I never have," she said, and she felt embarrassed.

He held it out to her and told her to try. It was nothing, he said, just a little buzz in the brain. For floating.

She took the joint, raising it to her mouth, and then pulled and exhaled, coughing.

"Hold it as long as you can," he said, and motioned her to go again. She did, and closed her eyes this time to concentrate, aware of expectations and the need to discover some small key that would unlock her longing. And then, as if to throw off some awkwardness, or perhaps to fill in the blank spaces she thought might exist, she began to talk. She told Raymond that she had come up to see him here because she didn't know where else to go. She'd been angry at her mother and she didn't want to stay back with her family and so here she was. She said that her mother never talked to her. She always talked at her, through someone else. This had always been the case.

She paused. Said, "Oh, boy. Fuck my mother."

"Okay," he said, and he laughed and told her that he was joking. He took tweezers from his front shirt pocket and used them to hold the last bit of joint. He said that the night before he'd gotten stoned with Nelson, and everything had been very funny. He could get Lizzy a little bag, neatly packaged, fresh. "I have a great supplier. A seventy-five-year-old man who lives in town. White. Big citizen. Used to own some fancy shop. Now he sells great shit to kids. Weird." He pulled in smoke from the little bit of joint that was left and offered a last drag, but she waved his hand away, thinking that this was not what she had imagined. The weed was doing nothing good for her. She felt a little dizzy, but that might be her own sense of panic. Raymond had slid down in his seat so that his head was resting against the top of the seat. He had lifted his right leg and rested his boot on the dash and she realized that he was far away. She felt disappointment. She said that she should go. She had to go. She opened her door and waited for him to stop her but he was just looking at her. Then he said that she probably wasn't as far along as him and he could fire up another, to help her. Or, he said, they could walk out on the golf course. He liked doing that at night, when everybody was gone, and the animals came out. He said that animals were beautiful. He dropped his leg, opened the door, and said, "Let's go." And he walked out down the fairway, with Lizzy tentatively trailing behind him. It was fully dark now and the bushes were black and the grass at her feet was black; she could only see the sky above her, which opened up onto far too many stars, which swam and fell.

"What kind of animals?" She ran slightly to catch up to Raymond.

He lay down on the short grass of a green and told her to join him. "Don't worry," he said.

She laughed and said, "I'm not worried." And saying this, she began to calm down.

They lay side by side and gazed up at the sky. Lizzy could hear Raymond breathing, and though she wanted to turn her head to look at him, she didn't. He began to talk. He said that he had hardly known his father and that his mother had died when he was six. Ever since, his grandma had raised him. He loved his grandma. She was there, and sometimes he thought she might always be there, though he knew that that was impossible. He said that last year a cousin had told him his father was living in Winnipeg, and so he'd taken the bus to the city and looked for him. "That was the easiest part. Took me half an hour. Asked a few people where Tom Seymour was and they led me right to a bar off of Main Street." He said that he had lived with his father for a while then, but it was awful. His father stole from him, and he wasn't interested in talking, and he had a girlfriend called Clara, who thought Raymond was going to take his father back home to Kenora. "So, she didn't like me much. I lasted a few weeks and then went back to my grandma."

She said, "When your brother went to live with that family? Was he in some kind of trouble?"

Raymond didn't respond at first and Lizzy thought maybe she'd said something wrong. Then he said, "It wasn't a big deal. It was decided he would live somewhere else. The government has its plans." He paused. Then asked if she played basketball. She said that she didn't, she wasn't any good at sports.

He said that he was a good point guard and if they were on the same team and she were just a little free, if she had even just one hand free, he would get the ball to her. "Pinpoint passing," he said. "That's what my coach always told me."

The sound of Raymond's voice lifting and then fading made Lizzy shiver. She'd been hearing Raymond, aware that even as he spoke he seemed ill at ease to be speaking. And so, attempting to find some balance in the conversation, she talked about her mother. She said that these days her mother seemed unhappy and that this made her father unhappy. "They're all twisted together." Then she said that she had had too much opportunity to watch adults these days, and she had discovered that most adults wanted what they couldn't or didn't have, and they would hurt people to get it. She said that when she was older and married, or if and when she had a lover, she would not be weak. She said, "Wouldn't it be right, if someone is being betrayed, that they stand up for themselves?"

Raymond took her hand. She opened her palm and received his hand, and then closed her fingers around his. She was trembling.

He asked if she was cold and she said no, that sometimes her body shivered when it was happy. She said that she would like to run away like he had.

He said that he hadn't run. His uncle had given him the cabin to use every spring and summer. He said that running away meant leaving everything you knew and understood, and finding a place that was completely unknown, where you could be a different person. "You don't want that."

Lizzy thought how clear and true this sounded and she was surprised that he would have the knowledge to say these words. She was about to say something, when he kissed her. He was suddenly up on one elbow and leaning into her and his mouth was on hers and then he was finished and lay back beside her, looking up at the sky.

He was quiet for a while and Lizzy thought he might have fallen asleep, but then he turned and he took her head in his hands and this time his tongue was in her mouth, and she considered pulling away but she didn't, and his hands were around her neck and up and down her arms and he was making noises and she breathed deeply so that his smell would stay with her the rest of the night. They kissed for a long time and Raymond touched her breasts through her shirt and she let him.

Then she said that that was enough for tonight, that she felt like a cup that was spilling over and she didn't want to waste anything. They walked back to the truck without touching. Lizzy was slightly ahead of Raymond, aware of the silence between them, but knowing too that the silence might be all right. He smoked a cigarette while he drove her back to the Retreat, and he offered her a drag now and then, which she took willingly, thankful to keep herself busy. She was still shivering a little, and thought it might be the wetness from the grass against her clothes.

Just before she got out of his pickup, and before he lifted her bicycle from the back, she said that there was going to be a dance at the Retreat on the weekend. He should come, she said. And Nelson too. And anyone else he wanted to invite. He should come for supper as well.

He said that he had been at one dance there last summer, so he knew about them. Besides, the Doctor liked it when he showed up for dinner or at the dance. "He likes to hang out with an Indian or two." He smiled and said that he might come.

She thought he might want to kiss her good night, but this did not happen, and it did not trouble her. He simply got into his pickup, waved goodbye, and was gone.

In bed, later, she lay staring up into the darkness and she touched her throat where Raymond's hands had been. He had calluses on his fingers and his hands were large, and they had encircled her throat and she had felt his strength. She willed herself to dream of him, to fall into the shadows and find him there. But she did not. She dreamed instead of following a man whose face she never saw, who led her down a twisting path that was thick and matted with branches. They arrived finally at a clearing where there was shade and sunlight and she knew, waking from this dream, that there had been danger in that place.

On Saturday evening after dinner, the furniture in the Hall was pushed back and fairy lights were strung at the edges of the walls and across the ceiling. The room still smelled of fried sausage from the dinner, but someone, Mrs. Byrd perhaps, had lit candles and placed them in low glass jars on the sills of the windows, and the waxy scent of the candles eventually overwhelmed the smell of the food. Ian, a young man who had arrived with his girlfriend Jill just the week before, had a collection of records. Jill and Ian ventured out onto the floor first, moving to "Love Train." Then Mrs. Byrd joined them, sliding across the floor all alone to "Some Kind of Wonderful." She was wearing a white skirt with pleats and an orange top, loose and thin. She had wrapped a colourful scarf around her new cast, and she danced with her eyes closed, arms slightly raised. She was barefoot. Lizzy watched her mother and felt both mortified and envious. She wondered if her father would show up.

Fish wandered out onto the floor and Lizzy followed him. This brought out the rest of the adults and children, save for Big Billy, who sat in a corner eating chocolate cake. William, in a rare moment of abandonment, danced and skipped about the room. At some point, to the sound of "Free Ride," Emma had her arms around Franz's neck and Mrs. Byrd was dancing with the Doctor, one of her hands pushed against his chest, the other around his waist. She was looking up into his face, and she was talking, her white teeth flashing.

Margaret came in, holding a plate with raw carrots and broccoli and a parsley dip. She put the food on the table and walked over to Lizzy's mother, tapped her on the shoulder, and stole her husband back. Mrs. Byrd let go easily, still moving her feet to the music, and it seemed to Lizzy her mother wasn't worried that she appeared to be openly flirting with the Doctor. Lizzy made a decision to go look for her father. She found him in his cabin, a book in his lap, but he didn't appear to be reading. The music drifted faintly across the clearing. She went to him and took his hand and pulled him up and said, "Come, Daddy, we're dancing." He said that he was not particularly interested, and she said, "You should be," and she hooked her hand under his arm and led him out his cabin door. She saw Raymond's pickup at the edge of the clearing, and her heart moved.

When she entered the Hall he was sitting with Nelson, a large woman older than him, and a young girl. The four of them were on chairs near the back wall. She waved at them and Raymond waved back. Then she walked her father out onto the dance floor. "Relax," she said and she put her arms lightly around his neck, and they danced to Marvin Gaye. He said that some Woody Herman would be nice, and just then her mother passed by and said, "Hi, Lewis," and Lizzy handed her father to her.

She had noticed Raymond watching her dance, so she went to him now and said, "Here you are."

"I am," he said. He introduced the young girl, said her name was Lee, and that she was his niece. "And this is her mother, Reenie, my sister." He motioned at the larger woman who wore around her neck a crucifix that seemed to have been hammered from scrap metal. She said hi to Lizzy and then laughed and turned her head. Lizzy thought she might be nervous. Lizzy said she had a brother, Everett, who was maybe close to Lee's age. He was fourteen. She pointed out at the dance floor, where Everett and William were dancing near to their parents. Lizzy reached for Raymond's hand and said, "Come." He followed her, and when they reached the centre of the room, she moved around him as he shuffled his feet. She said that she was glad he was here.

"I'm not a good dancer," he said. "You'd be better off with a dead tree."

Nelson had found a beer and was standing at the edge of the room. Reenie and Lee were dancing and giggling, holding their hands over their mouths. The room was hot and Lizzy smelled her own sweat and the pale sweetness of the perfume she'd put on earlier in anticipation of Raymond coming. She had never touched him in public, and now, as a slower song played, she took his hands and put them around her waist and she laid her head against his chest. She did not talk, because then she would have had to lift her head in order to make herself heard, and she would then have lost the sound of his heart in her ear. Her mother was standing to one side with her hand on her hip, watching. When the song was finished, Lizzy took Raymond's hand as they walked to the chairs where Reenie and Lee were again sitting. She offered to introduce

Lee to Everett, but Lee shook her head no. Reenie chuckled. Her large hands were folded in her lap.

Against the far wall, Lizzy saw Harris, drinking from a flask. He noticed Lizzy and raised the flask and smiled. Lizzy waved back. She told Raymond that she was going to dance again, in fact she would be dancing all night, and if he wanted to see her, he would have to come find her on the dance floor. Okay? And she turned, not completely willingly, and she scooped up Fish and walked out onto the dance floor. His eyes were bright. He was wearing shorts and she felt his firm, cool legs and this made her think of Raymond's hand on her breasts several nights earlier. The force of his mouth on hers. She turned and saw Raymond leaning towards Nelson, whispering something. He was looking right at her. She smiled.

Late into the night they danced. Nelson finally made it out onto the floor with Reenie and Lee. At some point, he was sitting at one of the tables, talking to Everett and moving his hands in the air as if making a point about something. During the slower songs, Lizzy danced with William, and then Raymond again, the movement of his back muscles against her hand, and then with Ian, who kept reaching out to brush her arm or her shoulder. He said that she was good-looking; he'd never really taken note. "That boy. Your main man?" he asked. He moved closer and tried to take her in his arms, but she slid away and went over to where Everett was sitting with Nelson and pulled her brother out onto the floor, letting her wrists rest on his shoulders. Everett told her that Nelson was nice and that he liked chess, just like he did. "That right?" Lizzy said. "I'm happy for you." Later, the Doctor asked her to dance with him; they moved slowly, an arm's-length apart. The Doctor's shirt was unbuttoned halfway and his bony chest was visible. He dipped towards her like a large white bird and then leaned back and moved his hips, as if offering his crotch for assessment. Lizzy wanted to laugh, but she stopped herself, because she knew she would have to explain her laughter to him. Once, looking back over her shoulder at Raymond, she saw her mother talking to him, reaching out a hand as if to drag him out onto the dance floor. He was seated and she was standing, bending over, and Lizzy imagined Raymond might see down her mother's top and this made her suddenly angry. He saw Lizzy watching and he shook his head. Her mother straightened and backed away.

She found Lizzy not long after that. Trapped her near the tub of beer and placed a hand on her shoulder and said, "Is that the boy?"

"What are you talking about, Mother?" Lizzy asked.

Her mother said that he was handsome, wasn't he? She said that she was glad to know that her daughter had good taste. "And don't let people tell you differently," she said, and she slipped away, seemingly pleased with herself.

And then, at the end of the song, Raymond came to find her. He told her Nelson and Lee wanted to go. "Already?" she said. She took his hands and tried to lead him onto the dance floor, but he pulled away. At that moment she saw herself as desperate and so she said, "Okay." Then he said that he would come by the next day, about noon. Maybe they'd drive to town. Or around. He lifted his hand in a slight wave and turned away. Lizzy circled the room, suddenly lonely,

and looked for someone. She found Fish and they went over
to a chair and sat, Fish on her lap.

On the far side of the room, her parents were dancing. Her
mother had her face against her father's chest. He was talking
into her ear, talking and talking, and then she smiled and
pushed away from him. She found Lizzy and came to her
and bent over, touching her mouth to Lizzy's temple. "Can
you put the boys to bed? Now that your boyfriend is gone."
Her orange blouse, the tops of her breasts; Lizzy saw what
Raymond would have seen. And then, without waiting for a
response, she went to Lewis, took his hand, and they left.
Lizzy watched them go, feeling sad and jealous in some odd
way, and confused by how easily her mother could call
Raymond a boyfriend.

William had already gone up to the cabin. Ian and Jill
were slow dancing to some French-sounding song with an
accordion in the background. Harris had sipped his way into
a dreamlike state and was tapping at the arm of his wheelchair with his right hand. Emma had disappeared long ago
with Franz.

After the last song, Lizzy passed Fish off to Everett and
asked him to take him back and put him to bed. She went to
Harris and told him she would bring him to his cabin. He said
that she should not feel sorry for him. They went out of the
Hall and up the path. In the moonlight she saw the back of
Harris's head, his slight shoulders, his hands gathered in his lap.

He said that he had to empty his bottle. Could they pass
by the bathroom.

She pushed him up towards the outhouse, thinking how proper he was, calling it a bathroom when it wasn't that at all. It was a shack with two holes. A shithouse. The door was open and there was the smell, which always depressed Lizzy, and she breathed through her mouth.

Harris set the brakes on his wheelchair and pushed himself upwards. He picked up his bottle and clutched it.

"Here," Lizzy said, and she held his arm as he hobbled forward.

"I'm fine," he said, and closed the door behind him.

She walked down the path and waited. A mosquito landed on her neck and she slapped at it. A long while later, the door opened and Harris stumbled and almost fell forward into the darkness. "Jesus Christ," he said.

Back in the chair, he sighed and said, "Kill me already." It was like the cry of a small bird.

At his cabin, Lizzy parked the wheelchair under the awning and helped Harris up the stairs.

"Come in," he said. "Please."

She continued inside, holding his arm. He lit a lamp and sat on a chair, breathing heavily. He motioned at the desk in the corner. "There's a bottle of Scotch in the drawer, and two glasses. Have a drink with me. I've been drinking all evening but it would be nice to have company."

"I don't think so," Lizzy said. "I gotta get back to my brothers."

Harris waved a hand. "They'll be fine. Everett's a big boy." Then he said, "He's a different one, Everett."

"What are you talking about?" She went to get the bottle.

"He might not know it yet, but I can see it. There is a marked circle in which we all exist, and Everett is at the edge of the circle, on the verge of leaping out."

"He's just Ev," Lizzy said. "Doesn't talk much, but knows everything that's going on."

Harris shrugged but didn't pursue the topic. He took the Scotch from Lizzy's hand, squeaked open the cork, and poured two glasses. "Here." He handed her a glass and then he drank from his own.

Lizzy looked at her glass and then drank. The liquor burned her tongue and passed down her throat and she coughed.

"Good for you," he said. "Sit." He motioned at a second chair by the desk, and she sat cross-legged, aware of the room now in the dim flickering light. There were the two beds, both made. There was a bookshelf and a desk and a table with Emma's butterfly paraphernalia. Against the far wall stood a wardrobe, and beside that was an easel and brushes, and beside that another desk that held a typewriter and nothing else.

"You're wondering where my wife is," Harris said.

Lizzy didn't answer.

"It's fine. Everything's fine. We have this arrangement that must be obvious to everyone else. Though she always makes it back here, so that she can help me. Tonight, I fear, she forgot me. Didn't she?" He looked at his glass, which was empty, and he poured himself more. "Highland Scotch," he said. "Not as musky as the Lowland." He drank. "Quite the

saviour." Then he smiled and said that it was unfortunate
that a girl her age should have to witness the idiotic failings
of adults. "I love my wife," he said. "And I need her." He gestured at his legs. "With these useless legs, what else would
I do? Hire a girl like you? You're rather a good dancer, by
the way."

Lizzy wondered if he was going to cry, and she wondered
what she would do then. She thought she should be frightened, but she wasn't. He leaned forward and watched her cir-
cumspectly. His nose was suddenly large. His glasses had
slipped slightly. He drank again and then said, "I hear you're
reading the novels I gave you, first to last. Your mother told
me, she was proud of the fact, though I'm sure there are better
things to be read." He paused, studied her, and then said that
he wasn't going to ask what she thought, because it wouldn't
make any difference, he wasn't going to change anything.
"These days I'm like a dull moth banging at an unlit lantern."
He drank and then said that he seemed to have lost his muse
at about the same time he lost the use of his legs. "I was
loved," he said. "And I loved back, ferociously, and now I
appear to be flapping uselessly in the wind. Funny."

Lizzy didn't respond. She thought she should leave, but she
was curious too. This frail man, with his sticks for legs, and
his clumsy hands, was so different from the man who fumed
and ranted in *All Leer's Women*, the novel Harris had handed to
her one day. It was the story of a real estate salesman, Richard
Leer, who talks his way into the underwear of every woman
he meets, young or old. Maybe Harris would try to seduce
her, though she could easily outrun him. The possibility

intrigued her. She wanted him to be pathetic. She wanted to say no to him.

He was moving his crooked fingers, as if attempting to pick some slippery idea up off the floor. He said that once upon a time there was a man who took his wife on a long trip to southern Europe, and then across the Mediterranean to Egypt and on to Tanzania. This was not long ago. Three years, maybe two. The man's wife was unhappy; she suffered melancholy, she was dissatisfied, she wanted to hold something in her hands that she had not yet held. He said that this was not unusual, especially as one grew older and discovered the darkness at the edges of the path. He said that the man thought that he could cure his wife of her unhappiness, and travelling might be that cure. One afternoon, in Egypt, in a place called Aswan, the two of them sat on a small balcony and watched a crowd of men with horses gather in the courtyard below. There was much yelling and shouting, and then a stallion was brought out and it was made to mount one of the mares. When the stallion was finished, one of the men jumped on the mare's back and another man took off a shoe and hit the mare on the rear end and the mare took off madly down the road and then returned. A celebration ensued and then the process was repeated with another mare. The man and woman watched this for a while and then the crowd of men and the horses disappeared and it seemed as if the scene had never actually happened, that the horses and the men and the shouting had all been imagined, though there was horse dung on the cobblestones below.

Harris stopped as he poured himself more Scotch. Held up the glass and dipped towards it as if he were a bumblebee hovering over a newly opened flower. Lizzy saw the shadow of his mouth through the bottom of the glass; the candle flame mirrored there as well. Harris recalled that the daylight disappeared quickly. It fell away as if a curtain had been suddenly drawn. The woman was cold and so the couple went into their room and lit a candle and drank some wine and ate some pita and shared the boiled eggs that they had purchased in the market. The woman went to bed early and the man stayed sitting in the chair and he watched her sleep beneath the mosquito net and then, finally, because he too was cold, he climbed in beside her and she woke and said that she had dreamed of the horses.

Harris paused. Lizzy wondered if he was about to fall asleep, but he was simply resting. He said, "The next day they flew to Tanzania, and that is where we meet Franz." The flame from the candle on the desk wavered, and then renewed itself. Harris shifted and looked at his empty glass and then at Lizzy and he said that he would drink a little more. He said that the story he was telling was long and it didn't have an ending yet. As he poured more Scotch, he said that his wife had been jealous of his success. "It was as if I had been anointed in some way, or perhaps it was simply chance that threw success my way, and suddenly the world was at my feet and Emma did not recognize the man she had married. Or she did not like what I had become. Or she wanted what I had. I do not know." He said that she had wanted children, and when that proved to be impossible, she became interested in insects. In bugs. Then he said, "Look at your mother. Four children, like four novels with endings yet to be written. Wonderful. Emma would have liked that."

And this idea appeared to rejuvenate him and he sat up and said that in Tanzania the man and the woman fought. They fought as soon as they woke and they fought through breakfast and on into the day. The arguments were about African politics or the efficacy of malaria pills, or whether or not the fish had been cooked enough, or about money. Pointless disagreements, he said. But beneath the arguments was a deep sadness, as if they both knew that the man's increasing inability to walk was a symptom of everything wrong in the marriage. "Suddenly, she had the advantage," he said. "And she was merciless."

He said that they flew over to Zanzibar and hired a car to take them up to Chwaka where they stayed at a run-down villa that had, in its prime, been an estate of a German family. It belonged to the government now and it was in disrepair. Rats had made homes in the mattresses, the windows were broken, the few chairs left were wobbly and unsafe. There was little to eat and they made do with fish that was delivered by a local villager.

Harris said that it was impossible to predict how a decision, like his and Emma's choice to spend a week in Chwaka, could change one's whole life, but this was what happened, and it was only in hindsight that the evidence could be sifted through and understood. Or sometimes not understood. He said that on a weekend afternoon, while sitting out on the beach, he and Emma met a German man who was staying in a house up the coast. The man invited them for dinner. Emma accepted with great alacrity and this surprised Harris because usually she was hermetic and antisocial. He couldn't walk to the house, and so the German man, who was Franz, picked them up by jeep and drove them to his villa, which was beautiful and well kept, with the requisite cook and gardener and liquor cabinet and a fine view of the ocean. In a large room just off a wide hallway, Franz had a solarium in which there were plants and mounted animals. The animals weren't all large, in fact the majority were lizards and birds and all of them were placed strategically in trees and on rocks, so the effect was surreal. Harris said that it was like walking into a photograph. Franz was very proud of his stuffed animals, and of course, Emma was intrigued. After all, she collected butterflies.

Harris paused, drank, and then said that it was a fascinating thing to observe the disintegration of a marriage. This last gasp. He said that love should not be taken for granted. "It is so often a doomed enterprise, and typically perceived by the outsider to be doomed before the players are even slightly cognizant of the carnage. Franz knew immediately. And, delicately, as if he were a man who might wish later to claim innocence, he seduced my wife."

Here, Harris stopped talking. He closed his eyes for a long time, and then he opened them and said that he knew that the point of view was awry in this story, but would Lizzy bear with him? Please? In any case, it wasn't necessary that she follow exactly, and wasn't it more interesting to have to work at the threads of the narrative? He said that there were moments when he was overcome with anger and shame and he saw his wife as a whore. But he said that there was also curiosity and a certain macabre objectivity. "As all of this was happening," he said, "I imagined writing a story about a cripple whose wife takes on a lover and the three of them, the two men and one woman, live together and in fact quite easily fit into the quotidian of eating meals together and travelling, but never really talking about what is actually happening. My own life was producing the fodder for my next novel." He said that he was a puppeteer. That was what he did for a living. He wondered though if he had been deceiving himself all along, and that in real life, his life, the life of Emma and Franz, and even in Lizzy's life, they weren't all puppets being manipulated by some higher puppeteer, some malevolent and disinterested God who smiled benignly at his puppets' foibles. "Perhaps there is nothing more than this. A kind of luck or fate. Or not even that, because that is being too generous. Luck implies the possibility of blessing, hope, redemption. I have given up on all of those." He chuckled. Not happily. And then he said that it was unfortunate that she, at her young age, should have to listen to the indiscriminate musings of a disappointed cripple. "I do not wish to steal hope from you."

And then he was quiet and Lizzy waited, but he did not say anything more, though he had promised more. She had listened to his voice lift and fall and she had wondered if the story he was telling was true or if it had been made up for her benefit, as if he might be trying to tell her something about her parents, or even about herself. Harris had been watching her dance all evening, and he had seen her with Raymond, and though he had said nothing, and she had asked nothing of him, she did wonder if he was trying to protect her in some way. In the light of the flame, Lizzy saw that his eyes had closed and that his glass was slipping from his hand. She took the glass and put it on the table, and then she stood and looked at Harris, and knowing that she couldn't leave him in his chair, she shook him awake and said, "Harris, you should go to bed." She stepped backwards and then turned and left the cabin.

There was a quarter moon just above the treeline. It offered a pale light that allowed Lizzy to find her way to the out-house. She sat and wondered how it was that older people could complicate what should be simple and clear. What res-onated with her was Harris's use of the word *puppet*. It had been like a slap and she had wanted to protest, but she hadn't.

Coming out of the outhouse she came down the path and met the Doctor, who was standing and observing the sky. He turned to her and said that a sky like this one — and here he lifted a hand towards the stars above them — made immortal-ity seem possible. He asked Lizzy if she believed in everlast-ing life.

She shrugged and stepped sideways. The moon was behind the Doctor's head and it lit up the path and the trees. She said, "I should get back to my cabin."

The Doctor appeared to not hear her. He said that he had seen her come out of Harris and Emma's cabin. "You were with Harris," he said. Then he said that Harris lacked both conviction and faith and that he was suffering from a failure of ego. "This happens to men sometimes. We're swimming along, taking our good fortune for granted, and suddenly we begin to sink." The *s* of the final word whistled from his mouth.

Lizzy was aware of the Doctor's youthful face and she was suddenly conscious of his vanity and of the night sounds and the late hour. She said, "My mother loves my father. She's been sick and he knows what she needs."

The Doctor nodded, as if her statement made perfect sense. "Of course he does." He paused and then said that he had seen Lizzy with the Indian boy. He said that he was worried about her. It appeared that her parents didn't worry, or didn't take any responsibility for her choices, and so he was offering some advice. He said that she should be careful. She was a stunning young girl and she could do better than this Raymond Seymour. Did she know that?

"What are you talking about?" Lizzy said. "You don't even know him."

"But I do," the Doctor said, and he motioned that she could pass. She hesitated and then moved past him. He said good night and she said good night in return, and then she walked quickly up the path to her cabin.

She stepped inside and heard the sound of her brothers breathing. As she undressed in the dark, a voice whispered, "Where'd you go?" It was Everett. He was sitting up, and she could see his shape in the dim light.

Lizzy sat on the edge of her bed. "The Doctor was out there," she said. "He was looking at the stars."

She lay down. It was quiet for a long time and then Everett said, "You sleeping?"

"No, you're not letting me."

"I'm not tired." Then he said, "Mum danced with Dad."

"I know, I saw them."

"That's good."

"Hmmm."

"Raymond's brother Nelson's nice. He has a gun and he shoots rats down at the dump. He's gonna take me. He drew me a map so I'd know how to get to his cabin."

"You aren't going to visit Nelson."

Everett was quiet, then he said, "You like Raymond?"

"No. But I like his truck."

"Mum isn't very happy, is she?"

"Don't worry about her."

It was quiet then for a long time and Lizzy was almost asleep when Everett said, "I don't want to be old."

"Go to sleep," Lizzy said. And she heard nothing more as she fell sideways and then downwards, and a light flickered briefly across her vision, and then it went out.

In the clearing, by the Hall, William was swinging Fish. Lizzy had asked him to take care of Fish and he'd been doing that since mid-morning, when Lizzy had begun to prepare. She'd showered and shaved her legs and she'd tried on various skirts and shorts and tops. Everett had been in the cabin, lying on his bed and helping her, and as she slipped the clothes on and off, he looked away and then offered his judgment when she was ready. He had good taste, and they'd settled on a fringed white skirt that dropped to mid-thigh, and a black plain T-shirt that wasn't too tight. He said that if it were him, he'd wear their mother's red dress, the sleeveless one with the zipper up the back. She said that that was for evening wear, in the city, and this sure as hell wasn't the city, and besides, they might end up at the dump, shooting rats. She put on flip-flops, looked down, and said that she hated her feet. "I wish I had Mum's feet."

She smoothed her skirt and studied her brown legs. It was just before lunch. She went outside and sat on the steps, and waited.

Her father walked by, appraised her, and said, "Hey, beautiful, goin' fishing?"

"Raymond's picking me up."

Her father squinted at the sky, as if ascertaining some possible revelation, and then said, "The boy with the chickens?"

"He's not a boy."

"I'm afraid that's true." He looked at her and said that she should take a jacket, it looked like rain. "Remember who you are," he said, and he walked down towards the kitchen. Lizzy watched him and thought about how fragile he seemed. His neck appeared to be too thin and his back was slightly bent.

She watched the rest of the group enter the Hall. William and Fish, her mother, dressed in pink shorts that were too small on her, Ian and Jill, who looked as if they'd just climbed out of bed, and then Emma, pushing her husband's wheelchair, as if they were a normal couple. Harris saw her and waved and Lizzy lifted a hand in response. Emma looked back over her shoulder at Lizzy and then leaned down to whisper in Harris's ear. Lizzy felt self-conscious, unsure if Harris would even recall their late-night conversation. He had been quite drunk.

She sat on the stairs through lunch, aware of her hunger, but not wanting to embarrass herself by joining the group. She went into the cabin and looked at her face in the small mirror hanging beside her bed. She glanced at her breasts. She took off her T-shirt and unclasped the bra and removed it. Put the T-shirt back on. Looked in the mirror again and deemed it okay. She went back outside. Watched a trail of ants pass across the bottom step and disappear under the stairs. She wondered if Raymond, when he reached up under her T-shirt and discovered her bare skin, would think she was too easy. The door of the Hall opened and out came William and Fish, who both squatted in the dirt and poked away at the earth with newly found sticks. Lizzy knew that if Fish saw her, he would come running and climb on her lap and push his dirty hands against her clean skirt, so she stood and walked up the driveway towards the main road, thinking that she'd flag Raymond down on his way into the Retreat. When she reached the main road, she paused and looked east and then west. A car passed, a purple Cutlass like the one her father used to drive in Calgary. The driver honked and Lizzy waved. She stood on the shoulder. Within half an hour three vehicles had passed, two of them logging trucks that left in their wake a backdraft that lifted her skirt and dusted her hair and face. She moved off the shoulder and down into the ditch, where she sat on a rock. A baby frog leaped by.

By now the wind had picked up and she heard a vehicle coming up the path from the Retreat. She wondered for a moment if she had missed Raymond, but then the utility truck came into view, a white rusted half-ton with no front panels. The truck pulled over onto the shoulder and her father leaned over and called out of the passenger window and asked if she wanted to go to town. He was picking up some lumber and if she was tired of waiting, she could join him.

Lizzy stood and went to the truck and got in. Her father put it into first and pulled out onto the road. He steered with his left hand and his right rested on his thigh, and over the sound of the engine he shouted that he'd thrown out his back dancing last night, you know. He winked at Lizzy and said, "Your mother loves to dance. In fact there was a time when I thought she'd run away to Las Vegas to be one of those dancers that kicks in the air, you know what I mean, and so now when she gets the chance, it's good. Really good. You know?"

Lizzy offered a grimace, then turned away.

At the lumberyard, while her father paid for his order, Lizzy stood on the asphalt parking lot and leaned against the pickup and watched a young man operate a forklift. He knew she was watching him; he drove with greater abandon and when he climbed down off the forklift to adjust a load he looked at Lizzy and nodded. She looked away. When she looked again, he was walking towards her. He said that his name was Chuck. "How much wood would a woodchuck chuck if a woodchuck could chuck wood?" he said, and laughed. "My dad used to say that to me. How 'bout you?"

"My dad never said that," Lizzy said.

"I mean your name."

Lizzy studied him, and then she said, "Lizzy."

"Thin Lizzy," Chuck said. "My favourite band. You waiting for someone?"

"Hmm-mm."

Chuck looked around. He took off his cap and pulled up his T-shirt so that his stomach showed and he wiped at his face. He had a line of hair running just below his belly button. His belt buckle was wide and it said "Chuck." He lowered his shirt and asked if she liked fishing.

"Not really," she said.

"Probably never been," he said.

"Maybe not."

"Then how can you know whether you like it or not?"

"I guess I'm guessing."

Chuck snapped his fingers. "Come fishing with me. I'll take you on Saturday morning. We'll leave early, you can catch all the walleye you like, and then I'll bring you home. I'll supply the beer, you can keep the fish. I'll even fillet it for you."

"I'm busy Saturday."

"How 'bout Sunday?"

"I got church."

"That's a lie. You married?"

"Whaddya talkin' about?"

He squinted. Then said, "You gotta man? You know, like a ball and chain?"

"Yeah. Raymond Seymour." She said it so quickly, so matter-of-factly, that she surprised herself and, it appeared, Chuck as well.

"Seymour? You his squaw?" Chuck laughed and said, "Jesus."

Lizzy wanted to take back what she'd revealed. She had not expected that this boy with his bullet-shaped head would know Raymond, and even if he had, she would not have expected this response. She touched at her mouth, and then pulled back on a few strands of hair that hung loose by her cheek, and she said, "You know him?"

"Sure. Went to high school with him. For a while. Until he left. These days he lives with his brother who works at the dump." One eye closed and opened. "No, no, no, Lizzy. You can do better than that. I'll take you out on the lake."

Her father came out of the store and walked over and looked at Chuck and then at Lizzy and got into the pickup. "I guess I gotta go," Lizzy said, and she moved past Chuck. She could smell him, a mix of freshly cut spruce and sweat, and she liked it because it was a sign of something, perhaps of work and brawn and stomach muscles and the hair on his body. She could imagine pushing her nose against the dampness of his underarms. Her father started the engine and pulled into the loading yard and said, as if he had been asked, "Stay away from that one, nothing between his ears but sawdust."

They went for a Coke at the hot-dog stand, the same place Raymond had taken Fish and Lizzy, and she looked around as if expecting to see him again. But there were only two old men smoking, and a young mother screaming at her toddler.

Her father sat down across from her and said, "So, little Lizzy, tell me where your head's at."

"I don't know."

"You like it here?"

"Not really."

"I didn't think so. But then, we can't always get what we want. Look at me."

She didn't want to talk about him and about his disappointment. This grand idea of the Retreat and her mother's vision of salvation, the Doctor as a guide to a higher plane, hope for the family. And then the emptiness, the lazy people, the paltry meals. The night before it had been little heaps of corn scraped off wilted cobs and then cooked in chicken broth and served up as stew. Slices of dry white bread that had been picked out of the Dumpster.

Lizzy put her mouth over her straw and sucked her Coke slowly. Her legs were sticky with heat and sweat and she uncrossed and then crossed them again. A flip-flop dangled from her toes. She felt sluggish and restless and recalled Chuck's midriff. A shimmy between her legs. She shifted. Her father was talking but there were no important words. Something about the Doctor and then he said, "Everett," and then, "How about you?"

"How about what?"

"These talks, these speeches he's making, dragging kids into his dingy den and doing God knows what, and doing this all in the name of community. You been in there?"

"Yeah. Once."

"Really? Where've I been? Where's your mother been? Why would you go into the Doctor's den? He's got nothing, absolutely nothing to offer you."

"How do you know, Dad? You've never really talked to him."

"Don't have to talk, you just have to listen for thirty seconds and you know. Man doesn't have any idea what a wrench is, or what a hammer's for. What does a man need to survive? The words to talk about some old and tired idea or the hands to replace a generator that will run the electricity to heat your stove or bake your bread? You can't eat words."

"Maybe the Doctor's ideas are useful."

"That's bullshit. He wants to make everybody into a copy of himself. I told him that he wasn't ever to ask one of our children into his office again unless I was invited as well. I was furious, I'll tell you, when I heard that Everett had been in there."

"Mum knew."

"She couldn't have. She wouldn't abide such twaddle." Then he said that that night, when she'd walked into the cabin, he'd been talking off the top of his head. "Shouldn't have said what I did. And then Fish hearing my nonsense. And you." He paused. "I love your mother. And she loves me."

Once, mid-afternoon, Lizzy had seen the Doctor come out of her parents' cabin, hopping cheerfully down the stairs, as if it were his pleasure to make house calls. Lizzy had turned and walked away, not wanting to meet him; she had felt shame and imagined that by talking to the Doctor she would be conceding that she and her mother thought alike. She looked at her father now. His wide jaw, the manner he had of pushing it out as if determination alone could drive away all trouble. He was very handsome. Sometimes, when she watched him too carefully, she got sad. Her father lifted both hands as if he were a juggler and said that William concerned him. So resolute, creeping after Emma. "He just sits and watches. I can't tell what he's thinking. Can you?"

Lizzy shook her head. Felt a sharp ache for William, who didn't seem to know what he wanted.

Her father stood and said that he liked the land here. "All this water, the lakes you can get lost in. Beautiful, deep, black lakes that go on forever."

"You're never *on* the lakes, Dad," Lizzy said.

"Oh, I will some day. Soon." He started walking towards the pickup and said, "Maybe we should move here permanently."

Lizzy didn't answer. She knew it wasn't true, like much of what her father said. Let him talk.

They passed down the Main Street and then up the 71 and past the mill. Three boys on bicycles wove into the traffic and then stopped to throw rocks at the highway sign. Lizzy waved and they waved back, and then one of them gave her the finger.

At the turnoff to the Retreat there was a police car and beside it was a young cop. Lewis slowed and turned onto the small road. Down near the clearing Lizzy saw Raymond's pickup. She saw another police car and a group of people gathered in the clearing by the dining hall. And then her mother was running up the path towards the pickup and she was crying and calling out, and she was saying Fish's name, and as she drew nearer, she said what Lizzy had already feared was true. Fish was gone.

In the Hall there was a map and the map had been drawn into grids, and when a grid had been searched, it was coloured in by a chubby police officer, who also took notes in a little brown book and asked questions of the searchers, many of whom were volunteers who had arrived from town.

Mrs. Byrd, pale and helpless-looking, was sitting on the stairs of her cabin, waiting. Lizzy saw her and then she saw Raymond at the edge of the clearing and she went to him. He took her hand, saying that all would be fine. He said it so confidently, with utter clarity, that Lizzy had for a brief moment been overwhelmed with relief. But this had passed. One of the police officers was a red-haired man named Vernon, who when he wasn't directing the search, was watching Lizzy and asking her questions about where she was from and why did she live in this place and was she a hippie or any such thing. "What are you talking about?" Lizzy said, and she turned away. The third policeman was Constable Hart. He was an older man, with a squat neck, and he was the one in charge, asking to interview everyone from the camp. When Hart questioned Lizzy, he asked about her relationship to Fish, when she had last seen Fish, and if Fish had been alone. He was sitting so near to the edge of his chair that Lizzy kept picturing him falling. He asked about Raymond. What she knew about him. What time he had come to the Retreat that day. He seemed less interested in finding Fish than in finding someone to blame for her brother's disappearance. Lizzy didn't like him.

"I was with my father in town," she said. "When I left, I don't remember seeing Fish. Anyway, it's not anybody's fault. Fish likes to explore, to wander. He's curious."

Lizzy's chest felt scooped out. She swallowed and tried to rid herself of the hollow feeling, but it wouldn't go away and she knew it was because Fish might be dead. When she told Hart this, in the corner of the Hall, he looked at her and said, "Why would you say that?" He said that many people survived the bush. Even a child could survive. He had to be found quickly though. The thing to be worried about was the insects. They could make a person go mad. Then he asked if Raymond Seymour was her friend.

Lizzy nodded.

"Boyfriend?"

She shook her head. She asked what that had to do with her missing brother.

Hart didn't answer. He nodded and wrote something down. He asked what Raymond was doing here at the Retreat.

Lizzy looked about. Over by the map the fat man was marking something down on the map. The Doctor was leaning close to him and they were talking. Everyone else was out searching. She turned back to Hart and said, "He comes here a lot. He brings us food. What are you saying?"

"Not saying anything." He patted Lizzy's knee with his left hand. "Don't worry," he said. "We'll find your brother."

Raymond refused to be interviewed by Hart. He said that he would talk to anybody else, but not Hart. He told the officer named Vernon this and Vernon went over to Hart. They conferred for a time in the corner. When Vernon came back he said, "Fine, let's talk."

Lizzy had been in the kitchen with William, and when she came out she saw Vernon and Raymond talking. Later, outside, she went to Raymond and said that she wanted to search with him. They were supposed to go in pairs and would he go with her. He ran his hand over his head and looked around and he said that sure he would go with her, no problem.

They carried flares and flashlights and radios and water and whistles. The grids were small and had been marked off with yellow tape and Lizzy could hear other searchers in the bush calling out. There were shouts of hello and there were shouts of Fish's name. The only one not searching was Harris, who stayed in the Hall, drinking coffee, shaking his head, waiting for news.

They scoured the bush. This had been the instruction. If you see a clump of shrubs or a fallen log, approach it, lift it up, look inside, underneath. Fish might have fallen, he might have lain down and be sleeping, he might have broken something. Don't leave anything unturned.

Raymond walked carefully, his gaze swinging from side to side, and Lizzy walked behind him and called out Fish's name again and again, and Raymond never told her to stop. She was aware of Raymond's boots, and of his back and the blue-checked shirt he wore, of his long hair. If only he had come earlier to meet her, and if she had not gone to town with her father, Fish would not be lost. This was all so illogical that she thought it might be true. She said, "You were late." He turned and studied her and then turned back and continued on through the bush. She said, "I waited and waited."

He said, without turning back to her, that he had come. Maybe not when she'd planned for him to come, but he'd come. And she wasn't there. Then he said that he was sorry that she hadn't been there. He stopped walking and she stood beside him. A swamp lay before them. Mosquitoes lifted and swarmed them. Lizzy panicked and windmilled her arms, but Raymond seemed not to notice the insects. He looked at the swamp, and past the edges of the swamp, and Lizzy felt help-less and she began to cry. Raymond said that Fish would be absolutely safe. "This happens all the time. Marcel, Nelson, me, when we were young we all got lost in the bush sometime. And look at us. We survived. He'll come back smarter."

"Really?" Lizzy said, and then she went, "Oh," and her voice broke.

As darkness fell, the search was called off for the day, and the group gathered in the Hall. Her father stood and spoke. He thanked everyone for helping. He said that with so many people out in the bush they were bound to find Fish. "Fish is okay," he said. "He's curious about things. He'll see this as an adventure. It'll be something to talk about. We'll call it 'The Day Fish Got Lost.'" He paused. Her mother was crying quietly, Everett at her side. Her father looked at them and at his other children. Then he turned to Constable Hart and he said that trying to figure out who was responsible wouldn't help get Fish back. No one would be made a scapegoat. Despair and finger pointing weren't helpful at this point. His shoulders were bowed and he appeared tired and angry. He took in a breath and exhaled slowly and he said that a bonfire would be built in the clearing. This would be a beacon for Fish. The fire would need tending through the night; two people working in two-hour shifts until dawn. Then he asked for volunteers and Lizzy said that she and Raymond would go first. She turned to Raymond, who nodded.

They sat beside each other on stools by the fire. The sparks lifted into the dark and then faded and went out. Above them the sky was clear and if you moved away from the fire and looked upwards, you could see the stars, bright and plentiful. Lizzy wondered what Fish was thinking, or if he would be capable of thinking, or if he was just terrified.

"He'll be scared," Raymond said. "But he'll sleep too."

Lizzy saw the outline of Raymond's face in the firelight, the slant of his shoulders. He was different from the city boys. His hands were rough, his fingernails dirty. And his slight limp, his small ears, the mole on his neck, and his mouth with the scar on the upper lip. She knew what he tasted like. She wondered if he'd thought about their time together at the golf course; if he had kissed and touched her because he wanted to, or out of some sense of obligation, because she had come to find him. His elbows rested on his knees. He was drinking coffee from a tin cup. He smoked and studied the fire, occasionally looking up when a sound came from the bush.

"What are you thinking?" she asked.

When he finally answered, after a long silence, he said, "What you're really asking is am I thinking about you. Right? Well, I was. About how kind you are with your brothers. And how lucky they are. And I was thinking about how young you are. And then I wondered, What is Raymond Seymour doing?"

"I'm seventeen," she said, with clarity and force. She felt insulted by his comment, and she said that she wasn't a vulnerable child.

"That's not what I said. And I know you're not a child. You certainly don't kiss like one. Ha." He pushed his elbow against her shoulder and looked at her face. She saw that he covered up his discomfort by being physical.

The fire crackled, a log popped. He said that Hart scared him. Not just a little bit, but a lot. "I wouldn't talk to him, you know. That's why you saw me talking to the other cop."

She said, "When my dad was talking about a scapegoat, it sounded like someone was being blamed."

"Don't know that word."

"Like Fish disappearing. Whose fault is it? Who's to blame?"

Raymond made a clicking sound with his mouth and spread his hands towards the fire. "Hart's an asshole, okay? I know."

She asked Raymond why Vernon had been talking to him. "He looked so serious."

"He wanted to know how much time I'd spent with Fish. When. Where. Stupid questions. What he was really asking was if I liked little boys."

"Fuck. What a jerk," Lizzy said. "Can I?" she asked, and without waiting for an answer she put her arms around Raymond's neck and laid her head against his shoulder. His wool jacket was rough against her skin, but she didn't move. They sat for a long time in silence. Lizzy thought, what if something did happen to Fish, Raymond would be blamed. She said, "Don't worry about Vernon. I know what's true and what isn't."

A door banged and in a few moments her father appeared. He squatted by the fire alongside her. "Your mother's going mad. So are we all." He looked up at the sky, checked his watch, and said Lizzy should go to bed. He thanked Raymond for his help and said that he could go home. "I'll keep watch until Ian and Jill get here. I finally got your mother to lie down and rest. Go." He waved them off.

Lizzy walked Raymond up the path to his pickup. Their shoulders touched and she placed a hand on his waist. "Little me," she said. In the dark, she thought she saw him smile. Raymond got in and rolled down the window and looked out at her as he started the engine. Lizzy asked if he would come back, in the morning. He hesitated and then said that he didn't know if people wanted him here.

"I do," Lizzy said. "I want you here." She stepped away from the pickup and lifted a hand into the air and then let it fall down by her side. And then he was gone.

She found her father in the Hall, drinking coffee. He said, "What he should do is burrow under some leaves and bushes and pull his T-shirt over his head so the bugs can't get him." He reached out and pulled Lizzy close. "Jesus, Lizzy," he said. "Jesus Christ."

In the warmth of her father's body, she felt sleep approaching. She nodded and jumped and her father told her to go to the cabin to sleep, or lie down on the old couch by the fireplace. She sat straight and said she was fine.

Her father said that Raymond came from a completely different place.

"Yeah?" Lizzy said. "What if I like that place?"

"You don't know it, Lizzy. You don't know *him*. You get told over and over that you're this and you're that and you start to think maybe you are this or that. Just be careful is all I'm saying."

Her father stood, pulled her up, and guided her to the couch. She fell asleep instantly. When she woke the sky was growing lighter and she was alone. She went outside and found her father standing by a tree, tying the chainsaw to a rope that hung from a tree branch.

"This is it," he said. "This is the answer. Fish loves the sound of the chainsaw. Fire it up and run it and when he hears it he'll come home." And he took the cord in his right hand and he made solid the chainsaw with his left and he pulled the cord. The saw sputtered and cut out. Another pull and the motor cracked and started and the racket lifted into the air and echoed around the clearing.

Others emerged from their cabins. William and Everett and Franz, and then Emma appeared, looked about, and then went back inside her cabin. The Doctor and his wife came out, Margaret wearing her housecoat and slippers. The chainsaw clattered through breakfast, a background buzz that alarmed William, who had not eaten anything since Fish had disappeared, and on that morning only nibbled at a piece of toast. The Doctor thought it impossible that Fish would be able to follow the sound of the saw. The sound would seem to be coming from all directions. Fish would be running in circles.

"Nonsense," Lewis said. "He'll come."

He was lying in a hole. Not a deep hole like in the hot-house where a man lived with long arms, but a hole shaped like a plate with space for his bum and his back. In the hole at the hothouse there was a man who kept flies and the flies always banged against Fish's bare bum. "Hi, flies," he would say. And the eye of one fly was bright and black, dark like the hole. The fly lifted and dropped and banged against his leg and then his bum. Then there was another fly, and another, a whole family like his with brothers and a sister, big and little, and a mother and a father. A baby fly landed on his finger. "Where is your mother?" Fish asked.

The first time he read words, his mother was very happy. She called the family around and he read for them and every-body clapped and said, "Wow, listen to Fish read. A four-year-old! What a genius!" But at night, in the cabin when he was tired, his sister Lizzy read to him. He put his ear against her chest, against the soft cloth of her shirt, and her voice was inside her and outside her and he saw the words at the edges of her hands that held the book, and his ear was against her chest, like the Doctor's ear against his mother's chest that afternoon in the nail place, where Lewis kept his hammers and saws. The Doctor tipping forward. His mother's fingers in the sunlight. Knuckles and wrists. Knuckles and wrists. The sunlight. The wind behind him. The Doctor listening to his mother's chest. She had her eyes closed and was whispering and then the Doctor licked her, one lick, two licks, and his mother pulled the Doctor's ears and said, "Oh." And Fish asked if she was sick.

His mother's eyes, like the sky in the morning. She had said his name, Fish, like a dog's sharp bark, and she pushed the Doctor away and picked her shirt up off the floor. It was next to the chainsaw. Her chest went away and she buttoned her shirt and kneeled and held him and he smelled the gasoline in the shed and felt the heat of her cheek and she said that she was fine. "Okay? The Doctor says I'm all better."

The Doctor going down the dark path into the woods. Gone. His mother holding his hand. They walked up the path. She said that Doctor Amos wasn't always a doctor-doctor, but today he was and now she was better. Did he understand? Her knuckles in his hand. Her wrist there. She broke it. The step on their cabin broke and she fell and snap went her wrist and she went to the hospital and came home with a cast, heavy and white. The fucking wood was rotten. Dad said that. He had built new steps, with the nails from the nail place. Dad fixed things. That was his job. Maybe Dad could fix Mother's chest. And later, in the evening, Lizzy reading to him, her voice inside her chest, and he asked if Dad could fix Mother's chest. Lizzy's voice went up and down. He was inside a tunnel. She asked what he was talking about. He saw the bottom of her chin. He was going to marry his sister. The skin on the backs of her legs was soft.

And under her arms. He liked to smell her arms and her neck. She snuck him candies from the kitchen. Ate the peas off his plate. Before bedtime she whispered that the dish ran away with the spoon and then took him in her arms and ran with him. He slept with her and in the morning her breath smelled hot. Again, Lizzy had asked what he was talking about, and he didn't answer.

The sound of the wind. And then nothing. The bottom of the plate was wet and cold. He stood and he looked down at the hole. He bent and scooped more leaves into the hole. And then he settled back in. He slept. And woke. He stood and peed off to the side of the hole. The hole was his safe place. Nothing could get him if he stayed in the hole. He closed his eyes and then opened them. The leaves were moving. The sky was moving. He thought about his father. He would be worried. And his mother would be worried. And Lizzy. He liked Lizzy best. Then Lewis. And William. He liked him too. Though he never let Fish play with him because he was too young. So, Fish followed his father. They built things. Bunk beds for Everett and William. A pump with a black pipe that came from the pond and under the kitchen and up into the sink where Doctor Amos's wife washed her hair and other women with white legs sticking out from under their dresses cleaned potatoes for supper. And an outdoor shower with a rain catcher where he showered with Lizzy and Lizzy spilled warm water from the hose onto his hair and onto her hair and then she put soap on her body and told him to clean himself and he did.

Just before he was lost, he'd been sitting on the cabin stairs and a frog had hopped under the cabin. He'd followed it, sticking his head into the darkness, then he'd come back out into the light. He climbed the stairs where his mother fell and snapped her wrist. *Snap.* And then Doctor Amos had come and taken her to the hospital and Doctor Amos had hair on his face and hair in his ears and in his nose and Doctor Amos kneeled and looked him in the eyes. The Doctor's lips were pink but not special, no different than his mother's lips or Dad's. Lizzy had big lips. Sometimes Lizzy said "Fish" really softly and put her lips on his cheeks and mouth and ears. Lizzy had soft lips. He sat down on the stairs and looked for William or Everett or his mother, but there was only the light and a butterfly in the clearing. He stood and went to the kitchen and looked in the fridge. Margaret was there. She was making her nails pink. She asked him what he was doing and he said he was going on a trip and she said, "You betcha. Have fun."

He took a carrot. A piece of chocolate. Closed the fridge door and went outside and up the path. There was a loud wind and it moved trees and on the path the shadows of the leaves were dancing. He tried not to step on the leaves. It was hard. The path went sideways, but always it came back, and then he was on a big rock that went up and the path was gone, but the path would be over there, and so he went up the rock and found blueberries, lots of them. His mother loved blueberries. She was. always walking up into the rocks and trees to look for patches. This was a big patch.

He took out the chocolate and sucked on it. Then he ate the carrot. He climbed over the big rock and looked for the path. It was gone. He sat down. He looked up at the sky and he looked at the trees and he heard the wind and he heard voices in the wind. Then he began to walk. He went up and down hills and through bushes and sometimes he stopped and listened and then he kept walking. At some point he sat down and began to cry, and when he was finished crying, he dug his hole.

The wind was in the trees and something was calling *Fish . . . Fish . . . Fish*. He stood and ran through the trees towards the place where Lizzy was calling him. Then he fell and hurt his knee. His pants were torn and there was blood, but Lizzy was still calling so he got up again and ran. He found Lizzy. She was in the tree. She was a big blackbird calling *Fish . . . Fish . . . Fish*. He sat down. He was thirsty. He lay back against the rock and watched the bird. The sky was grey now and the bird was blacker and the wind still blew through the trees. Then Lizzy was in the shower and pouring warm water on his legs. He opened his eyes. It was dark and his pants were wet and warm. He had wet himself, which is what William sometimes did in the morning. He took off his pants and his underwear. Put them in a pile. The sky was dark. The forest was dark. There was no more wind and Lizzy was gone. He cried. He cried for a long time and then he stopped. He opened his eyes and saw an animal beside him. The animal was very still. It was curled up and it didn't move and when he talked to the animal it just sat there and when he poked it the animal became his pants and underwear. He stood and walked out into the darkness. He walked until he fell and where he fell was very soft so he lay there. There were bugs and the bugs were biting his bum and legs and neck and arms. He touched his forehead to his knees and waited for Lizzy to find him.

In the morning there were flies. One fly had crawled to the edge of his mouth. He made it go away and then he got up and walked. He was missing one shoe and his pants and he tried to find them, but they were lost. After a while he stopped walking and he lay down under a big tree where the ground was bare and soft and he fell asleep. When he woke he felt happy. The sun was warm, the birds were singing. He stood and walked. He found a trail and the trail went up and down. The leaves and trees were making shadows again, but there was no wind. He didn't like the wind. Then he heard the sound of a bee. He sat up. The bee was above him, and all around him. He listened. Then he got up and followed the sound of the bee. He went round and round. He saw again that he had no clothes and he worried his father would be unhappy and his mother would tell him to go find his shirt and pants and underwear. He walked and walked and the sun was on his back and a shadow was in front of him and he stepped on the foot of the shadow and when he looked down he saw his feet and the scratches on his legs and his bare stomach and he heard the saw and a sound like someone talking. The voice was saying *Come, come,* and so he did.

Lizzy waited for Raymond to return, but by mid-morning, when everybody had already been searching for a number of hours, she gave up waiting and headed into the bush with Everett. They walked side by side. The distant sound of the chainsaw was a persistent whine, like a mosquito buzzing in your ear. She thought about the words Fish had recently learned: *clutch* and *sapling*. There was the clutch on Raymond's pickup and here was the sapling scratching Lizzy's arm. She saw him on his back looking up at the sky, which was black with many bright holes and out of the holes came insects that landed on his ears and cheeks and arms and chest, and the insects were eating him. He opened his mouth to call out but there was no noise, only the sound of his breath going in and out, in and out.

The sound of a whistle nearby. A voice called out. It was Franz. Lizzy and Everett made their way towards him. Emma was with him and Franz was holding a runner. It was Fish's, orange with black stripes. It was all he had found. There was nothing else.

Lizzy took the shoe and held it and looked about and then pressed her fingers against the inside sole. The shoe was damp, perhaps from dew. The lace was untied. She fell against Franz and hit at his arms and chest and screamed at him. She said that the runner was useless, useless. Everett stood to the side and watched his sister flail. Franz held Lizzy and Emma went over to Everett and put her arm around him.

Together the four of them walked back to the clearing. There was no one there. The chainsaw spun and cried out. Franz sat Lizzy down and Emma brought her tea and someone wrapped her in a blanket. She huddled and shook.

Later, after everyone had gone out to search again, she willed Raymond to arrive. She willed and willed but it did not work. She eventually went and sat on her stairs and she gave up all willing. She said, "Fish is dead." The chainsaw sputtered and quit. It must have been out of gas. It hung from its branch, finally quiet, spinning uselessly.

And then the trees opened up to the path that led up past the outhouse towards the Lookout. Down the path came a little naked boy wearing one shoe. He was Fish. He was walking and his face was dirty and he went to his parents' cabin and sat down on the bottom step. And then Lizzy was running towards him, calling, and he looked up, and he saw her. He stood and smiled.

One evening, Lewis gathered up his children and drove them into town for dinner. William had wanted them to take the pickup so they could sit in the box. Lewis drove slowly, checking the rear-view mirror, watching Fish on Lizzy's lap, and calling out the window at William to sit down or he was going to fall out of the truck and crack his head on the pavement. The children were excited to be eating restaurant food, to be away from the Retreat, and Everett had already written down on a piece of paper what he wanted to eat: flatiron steak, root beer, french fries, and chocolate ice cream. Lewis had looked at the list and said, "What if they don't have flatiron steak? What if it's filet mignon?" He saw his children in the mirror and heard their voices lift and then fly away, and he thought how fragile everything was.

For a brief period, after Fish had been lost and then returned, and in that week before Norma left, they had been able to talk more easily, with an open honesty and with no inclination towards sex or disagreement. Norma had spoken about the foolishness of having taken all of them out to this place, what had she been thinking, and she talked about Fish almost dying, and how after Fish had come back, she had seen herself as a terrible person. She was not a good mother. She had been much more interested in freedom than in the welfare of her children. She said she had been mad, a completely different person. She went up on an elbow, the moon fell through the window onto her bare shoulder. She was wearing a white undershirt with narrow straps and Lewis saw the sheen of her skin. Her cast had been removed earlier that day and her arm was thin and vulnerable-looking. He did not move. He waited. She said that the Doctor had offered sex, but she did not accept. "I was like a virgin. Touch me here and here and here, but no penetration. Am I scaring you, Lewis?" And then, not waiting for an answer, she said that she had wanted to keep the Doctor holy. "The idea of him. This I wanted."

"So you didn't kiss," Lewis said. His voice was low, and he repeated the statement, as if repetition might make it fact.

"Why do you keep asking that? Do you want it to be true?"

Then she lifted her thin shoulders and turned to him and said that yes, they had kissed and he had touched her and he had seen her naked, though only briefly. "Oh, Lewis. In the tool shed. Imagine. The smell of gasoline, the Johnson motor at our feet, washers, oil, grease, and I'm removing my bra. It was like I was thirteen again and showing my breasts to Mickey Ketler."

"Why are you telling me this?"

"There's something more to tell you. We were interrupted by Fish."

Lewis began to shake his head. "Norma. Norma. What the hell did you do?"

"I told him everything was okay. I'm pretty sure he didn't really see anything."

Lewis closed his eyes.

"It wasn't me. Don't you see?" She reached across to touch his face. Her hand went flat against his chest and rested there.

"And now? Are you *you* now?"

She was quiet for a long time and he imagined that she might have fallen asleep and then she said that she didn't know. Everything felt out of control. He needn't worry, she was finished with the Doctor. They had traded kisses, that's all.

And then on another night, she said that she couldn't breathe. "Remember in Calgary, after Fish was born, and I wanted to bludgeon someone or something? And you took me away from the children because you saw danger? I'm not saying this time is as grave or dangerous, but I'm feeling wild, Lewis. The day Fish got lost? I was supposed to be watching him, and I went to the Hall to get something. I can't remember any more what I wanted, but I got delayed. There was this furious discussion taking place, about some ancient philosopher, and I got involved for a time, not long, at least it didn't feel very long, but when I came back, he wasn't there. I can't forgive myself." She said that she had gone to the children's cabin just before and found Fish asleep. "Everything is so uncomplicated when a child is sleeping, don't you think? I found myself wishing he would stay sleeping."

She said that she'd been thinking that she would leave for a while. She would visit her sister in Chicago. Saul Bellow also lived in Chicago. Did he know that? She had been reading Bellow. She carried *Herzog* around as if it were a gift to her, as if Mr. Bellow had sat down to write a novel for Norma Byrd. It had become her Bible, and one night, reading by flashlight,

she offered the image of Herzog pressing his daughter's little
bones. Her face had softened, and Lewis wondered how it was
that the woman he had married could feel more love for a
child who was not real than for her own flesh and blood. She
said that she would marry Saul Bellow if he asked. "Would
you let me do that, Lewis?" Her mouth had twisted into a
smile. She was teasing both of them with an impossible desire.

The night before she intended to leave, he sat at the edge
of the bed in his jeans, and he said that he didn't know what
to do. He said that too much was being asked. He wanted her
to stay; he asked what it would take to make her stay with the
family. He got up and kneeled before her and held her hands.

"Don't beg, Lewis," she said. "That's not you." She touched
the back of his neck and drew her hand down his spine. "This
is not about you," she said. "You shouldn't take responsibility.
I feel ashamed. I don't want to face these people any more. It's
possible you'll all be better off without me here. I'm not asking
for your pity or your blame, Lewis. Can you understand?"

"I'm trying to," he said, and he pushed his face against her
and said no more.

She wanted to have sex that night. She wanted him inside
her. Would that be okay? Not waiting for his response, she
came to his side of the bed and sat beside him so that their
thighs touched. She was wearing light blue panties and an old
T-shirt of Lizzy's. They lay on the floor, on a blanket. Norma
lay on her back and put her legs over Lewis's shoulders because
this was her most pleasurable position, and when she came
she made the smallest of sounds, like the muted bleating of a
lamb, and Lewis, as he came, pushed his face against Norma's

neck, where the collar of the T-shirt lay, and he smelled there the residue of his daughter. His anguish surprised him and Norma's tears surprised him, and later, as he lay awake listening to Norma breathe, he was sorry that he gave in so easily to what was being asked of him.

The following morning, early, Lewis drove Norma to the bus station. Before they left the Retreat, he asked her if she was sure she didn't want to say goodbye to the children. She stood in a light rain by the car and shook her head. She said that if she did that, she wouldn't be able to leave. It would break her heart. "Tell them," she said, "I love them terribly."

"Are we supposed to stick it out here for the next month without you?"

"Oh, Lewis. I'm not leaving for good. I *will* be back."

At the bus depot, saying goodbye, she had clung to him and at that moment he had experienced a loosening in himself and it had felt right to hate her.

That day he'd broken the news to Lizzy. He took her into his cabin and sat her down and told her that her mother had gone away for a bit. "She's beleaguered," he said. A light rain still fell, and though it had been mid-morning, it felt like dusk in the cabin, on the verge of darkness. Lewis was standing by the small table in the corner of the cabin, and as he talked he looked straight at Lizzy. "She's gone to Chicago to stay with her sister for a while. Fish getting lost, that pushed her over the edge. She needs some time."

"She couldn't even say goodbye?"

"Don't be angry, Lizzy. I know it's hard, but don't be angry."

"Oh, no, why would I be *angry*? It's always been all about

her anyway. But how are you going to explain to Fish that his mother is gone. Or to Everett and William. Don't expect *me* to do that."

"Of course not, I'm not asking you to do anything. I'm just telling you first because you're older and self-possessed and strong. Okay? She doesn't want to hurt you. She just needs some time, a safe place to push the pieces around in her head."

"But *this* was the place," Lizzy said. "Right here. That's why we came *here*. What'll we do now?"

"We have some time left here. We'll wait here for her to come back. She will be back. She's gone before and always come back."

Lewis had been suddenly very tired, exhausted by his optimism. He thought of Fish. And William, who, ever since Fish got lost, was suffering terrible nightmares, waking up at night sucking for air and calling out, so that Lizzy had to come get Lewis to talk to him until he went back to sleep.

He went outside and walked through the rain and found the boys in their cabin. He sat with them and explained that their mother had gone to Chicago to visit their aunt Anna and she would be back soon. William wanted to know how soon, and Lewis said that he couldn't be sure, perhaps a week or so. Everett had listened to this explanation, and then asked why they hadn't all gone, and why his mother hadn't said goodbye. It was a challenge, and Lewis ignored it. He said that their mother would come back refreshed, with a new view of the world. "This is a good thing," he said.

The restaurant Lewis had chosen was attached to a hotel and there was an elevator that Fish had to ride up and down in before they ate. Lizzy and William went with him while Lewis and Everett sat and studied the menus. There was round steak with mushrooms and a salad. Everett lifted his head and said that that was fine. His eyes were dark and hollow from lack of sleep.

"We're kings tonight," Lewis said. He ordered a beer. Everett asked for a Coke. Lewis said that when he was a child he'd been taken to a restaurant in Vancouver, down by the harbour, and he'd ordered fish and hated it. "The head was still on the fish, imagine that, and it lay on my plate and I thought it was still alive. It was staring up at me. My father ate the eyes."

"I know, Dad. You've told that story before."

"Have I? Well. That's why steak is safe. No chance of the steer landing hooves and all on your plate. I considered, for a time, when I was fourteen, being vegetarian. That lasted all of two weeks. My mother refused to feed me." He studied Everett. "You miss her."

Everett shook his head and said he was fine.

"That's all right."

Fish flew in, his brother and sister in his wake. He climbed onto the bench seat beside Everett, put his fists on the table, and said, "Chocolate milk." Lizzy put William between her and Lewis. She was pensive, untalkative, and when Lewis tried to draw her out, she ignored him. They ordered and when the food arrived they all ate quickly and greedily, as if they had come on a long voyage with little food. When he was finished eating, Lewis put his cutlery down, ordered coffee, and said that the ease with which the food had appeared and then been devoured was a delight. "A real delight," he said again, and he tilted his head. "This is very nice, sitting here with my children." He put his hand on William's head and said that sometimes he failed to keep an eye on things and so he lost track, and he had every intention of keeping his eye on his children from now on.

"Mum?" Fish asked.

"Oh, sweetie. You know she went away for a little while. Like a mother bird that's gone out to look for worms to feed her babies. She'll come back."

"With worms?"

"Of course."

Fish grinned and looked at Lizzy, who wrinkled her nose at him.

"You're full of shit." This was Everett. He was holding his fork. On his plate there was a pile of mushrooms that he'd scraped away from the steak. A smear of ketchup beside the mushrooms.

"Ev," Lizzy said.

"Fullashit," Fish said. He blew bubbles into his chocolate milk.

"Your words," Lewis said. William was beside him, a stoic little boy, already thick at the neck and waist. He had his father's hands, his father's mouth. The boy got lost in the melee of the family. He was a listener; he observed and reflected. He would never act impetuously like his mother, he was too careful. Lewis looked down at him. "You okay?"

William nodded. He'd eaten a hamburger and taken out the pickles and lettuce and they lay on his plate. He had a tiny bald spot on the side of his head.

"What's this?" Lewis asked and touched it.

William pulled away and put his hand over the spot.

"Size of a dime," Lewis said.

Fish had unearthed *shit* and was using it to make compound words: *fullashit, cuppashit, forkashit*. Lizzy reached out and put her hand over his mouth.

Everett was angry.

"Ev," Lewis said. He let the first letter of the name stretch out and then closed it down with a quick drop into the *v*, as if he had arrived at a dead end. The boy usually liked that.

This time he didn't. He said, "You're a liar, Dad. You always do that, make things up to make us all feel better."

"Whoa," Lewis said. "Not everyone's fourteen or older here."

"Fish? William?" Everett's voice was quick and bitter. "They know Mum's gone. They know she doesn't love us. Fuck the Doctor and his stupid ideas."

"Fuckthedoctor," Fish said. He stretched for his straw and closed his lips around it.

For a moment Lewis was without words. He took a breath. Finally he said that their mother had not betrayed him or the children. "She loves you. Absolutely. No question. She just isn't happy with herself. She went away and at some point she will miss you all so much that she will come back. Very soon, I think."

"Jesus, Dad." This was Lizzy, shaking her head in disgust.

Lewis ignored her. Then he said that it was a warm night and they would walk down to the wharf and look out at the lake.

And so they wandered outside, Everett following sullenly behind the group, and they walked down to the wharf and sat on benches while Lewis commented on the last remnants of the blood-red sunset.

"Look at that," he said, and they all looked.

S everal days later, in the evening, Lizzy walked out to the main road, stood on the shoulder, faced the oncoming traffic, and held out her thumb. The first car that came along picked her up. The driver was a woman who was camping at Rushing River and had come into Kenora for supplies. When Lizzy got into the car she tried to make her voice sound confident and assured, though she did not feel confident. When she saw the sign for Bare Point she asked the woman to stop. She thanked her and walked up the gravel road, past the houses on the reserve, and into the tunnel of trees that led towards the turnoff to Raymond's cabin. It was nine-thirty in the evening and the sun was setting; she had an hour of light left. She would get to the cabin before dark and then later Raymond could drive her back. She missed him. She had seen him only once since Fish had wandered off. He'd come back the next day, and arrived to discover everyone in the Hall, gathered around the little boy. He had stood on the outside of the group and to Lizzy it seemed that he had been unwilling to share the joy, or that in some way he did not understand it. He had seemed weary and uninterested, and had disappeared before she could talk to him.

The road she walked on was narrow, and with each step dust rose and then settled onto her runners. Clouds of mosquitoes floated above her and occasionally some would find and circle her, and then rise again. She could hear birds in the bushes and other sounds that might have been made by larger animals. She did not think of fear, because if she allowed that, then anything might be possible in this place that was unknown to her. She heard a vehicle approaching, and as it came up behind her, she stepped down into the ditch to let it pass. It halted and from the driver's window a man in a straw cowboy hat studied her and then asked if she wanted a ride. The man's face was in the shadows and she could not see his eyes. She shook her head. She said she liked walking. The man, as if understanding her unease, removed his hat and she could see he was elderly. He said that his name was Joe and he lived on the reserve and he was going up to Bare Point. She could take a ride, or she could walk, it was her choice. She stepped up onto the road and came around to the passenger's side and got in.

The man didn't say anything more, in fact he didn't really look at her. Lizzy glanced at him and she saw that a finger was missing on his right hand and that his face had deep lines. She told him that she was thankful for the ride, and she hadn't realized the road would just keep on going. The old man nodded at this as if what she had said had been well thought out and then offered for him to ruminate upon. He said, "Roads," and he nodded again. They rounded a curve and he slowed and stopped before the lane that led up to Raymond's cabin. She got out and closed the door and it was only when he was gone that she wondered how he would know her destination. She climbed the grade towards the cabin, thinking that she had just had a dream in which an old man named Joe appeared and had given her what she wanted but not asked for. Raymond's pickup was parked in front of the cabin. There was a car there as well and a dog lying beside the car. Lizzy said, "Hey, girl," and walked around the dog and hesitated at the door, and then knocked. When it opened, Nelson was standing there, blocking the light from the oil lamp and his face was hidden. He said her name and then stepped back and she saw into the room where Raymond was sitting with two men. The two men were drinking beer and Raymond, when he saw her, raised his head in recognition but said nothing. One of the men, who had been speaking, stopped and looked at her.

"Hi," Lizzy said. "I walked up." She shrugged.

Nelson pulled her in and gave her a warm beer and introduced her to the men, Lionel and Gary. He sat down and lit a cigarette. No one spoke, and then finally Nelson said, "It's okay, you don't have to worry about her."

She sat at the edge of the room, her bare knees touching, feeling that she was too dressed up in her short skirt and tank top, and also feeling that she was not trusted. She said, "I'm sorry, I can go." Raymond said that she should stay. He would drive her back in a bit.

Then the man named Lionel turned away from her and said that they were a bunch of shit, you know, because they still weren't getting anywhere and all they wanted was to identify with the white man. "With his money," he said. "Always knocking their ass off for money. For money. For money. This is why we need to organize. If we are going to get killed here, I want to know that I've asked for everything. I want to die right. I'm not just going to ask for a piece of bread and then get shot without even getting that much."

The other man nodded and then looked straight at Raymond and said that big things were going to happen up at Anicinabe Park. "We want you to join us. Both of you," he said, turning to Nelson.

Nelson, his feet resting on a chair in front of him, drank and didn't respond. Lionel said that Judge Nottingham had to fucking go. That would be one demand. "And we won't get any demands met until a lot of white people out there sit up and say, 'Well fuck, look at that blanket-ass Indian. He's starting to figure out where his head's at and he's starting to know what the fuck's going on.'"

Raymond grinned and looked over at Lizzy. There was a wine bottle hanging from a rope above the table and there was a candle in the bottle. A moth banged against the bottle. Outside, the dog barked briefly and then stopped.

Gary stood. He looked at Raymond and walked outside, followed by Lionel. Raymond went out as well and Lizzy could hear Gary's voice and then Lionel's, but she didn't hear Raymond say a word. Nelson was still sitting. He said, "You watch. Ray'll get sucked right into that shit." Nelson put his bottle on the table. He said, "And your brother?"

At first it wasn't clear to Lizzy what Nelson was asking and she began to say, "What," and then Nelson laughed and said

that he'd been lost when he was seven. "Ran around in the
bush for three days, crying like a little shit. My brother Marcel
found me and hit me across the head and called me stupid.
Learned my lesson."

The dog barked again, wildly this time, and then an engine
started and idled, and finally there was the sound of their car
driving off.

When Raymond came back, he motioned for Lizzy to
come outside. She followed him and they got into the pickup
and Raymond rolled down the window. The two of them sat
looking out over the hood of the pickup into the darkness.
Raymond reached out a hand and put it on her neck and
pulled her close and she didn't resist. Her head rested on his
shoulder. Beyond the windshield, framed in the light of the
doorway, she saw Nelson looking out at the pickup, and then
he disappeared from view. As if this were a signal of some
kind, Raymond leaned forward and turned the key with his
left hand and in doing so she felt the movement of his body
against her chest.

She thought about her father, who was sleeping alone. She
thought about her mother's red dress, which Lizzy had in her
own bag back in the cabin. She'd taken it on a whim one night
a while ago. She had imagined that Raymond would like the
dress, like the shape of her long legs falling below the hem.
She felt an urgency pressing down on her, which was perhaps
what her mother had felt before she left; the sensation that
danger or something necessary and calamitous lay just around
the next corner and that action had to be taken. It was like
walking into a clearing and understanding that of all the

numerous directions to take, only one could be chosen. She told Raymond this. She offered him the vision of the open space and the choices encountered while crossing that space.

Raymond said, "Maybe there's only one path and that's all. No choice. Ever think of that?"

"I don't want to think. I want to feel and then act. Or maybe act and then feel. Thinking makes everything far too complicated. Like now, I'm thinking too much. Next time I won't talk so much." She laughed weakly and said, "You think there'll be a next time?"

Over the following week she saw him almost every night. He picked her up, or she met him out on the highway, standing in the ditch until she saw the one headlight of his pickup approaching, and she felt as if she were moving into the outer dark, a new and exacting place where others might have gone before but no signposts had been left to guide her. They stopped one night in town for condoms. They had discussed who would go in and buy them, and grudgingly she agreed to because he said that everyone knew him in town and it would be too obvious. So she stood at the counter and an older man took her money and looked at her and then away and then studied her again with what seemed a slight smirk. She was wearing her mother's red dress. She'd changed into it out near the road, slipping off her jeans and T-shirt and putting it on while she waited for Raymond. The brief act of being nearly naked in the ditch at the side of the road had left her giddy. The dress was tight and the man behind the counter was looking at her breasts. Beyond the store window, in the darkness of the outside, she saw Raymond sitting in the cab of the pickup. He lit a cigarette; the brief flare of the match and then the glow. She bought a chocolate bar and a small tin of baby formula as well in order to appear wholesomely purposeful, or domestic, as if she'd stepped out of her own home and was running an errand. She blushed, took her change, and left the store.

They went up to the dump. Nelson worked there and Raymond had the key to the padlock that held the gate. It was north of town, up past narrow roads and clear-cut paths that the hydro workers had made, and down a rutted drive to a chain-link fence, seven feet high. Raymond got out of the pickup and unlocked the padlock, removed the chain, and swung the gate open. His outline, the thin shape of him, moved in and out of the beam from the headlight. There was a song on the radio by Pink Floyd, and the sound of it made Lizzy's heart ache, and she knew that whatever she might want, she could get.

The road into the dump was rough and the pickup jolted and threw her about. Raymond stopped at the edge of the pit, which dropped down below them. The one light probed the darkness and fell onto the trees on the far side. Raymond killed the engine. He said, "Wanna hear something funny?" And then not waiting for her answer he said that his last year in high school his science teacher, Mr. Schneider, had hit him. One time he had forgotten his textbook and Schneider came at him with a ruler and hit him across the side of the head. "He said I would make an excellent garbage collector. That's what he said, and then he looked at the class and asked if he wasn't right and some kids laughed, but nobody said anything. I thought of standing up and walking out, or maybe grabbing his ears and banging his head against the desk, because I'm bigger than Schneider and could've done that, but I didn't and later I wondered why not, what stopped me." He shrugged and said it was funny, because Schneider was right. Here he was, sitting by the garbage dump.

"So," Lizzy said. "That doesn't make him right. You should've clocked him."

"Yeah, should've. And then I'd've been charged."

"Was he charged for hitting you?"

Raymond laughed and looked over at her. "Come on," he said, and he took her hand.

They walked down the path to where the Caterpillar was crouched. Raymond climbed onto the tread and then reached out his hand and said, "Here." Her dress was too tight. She was wearing runners, so her feet were okay, but she couldn't stretch her legs in any way. Finally, she hitched the dress up over her hips and stepped up onto the tread. She was wearing white underwear and she told Raymond not to look. The cab was small, with little room for two, so Lizzy sat on a side console while Raymond fired up the Cat. There was no steering wheel, just a number of sticks that Raymond moved back and forth. As they crawled down into the pit, the Cat's spotlight fell onto the space before them to reveal the garbage and the movement of rats.

"My brother and I sometimes come up here to shoot raccoons," Raymond yelled. "It's easy at night. Sitting ducks, eh?"

He taught her to operate the Cat. Let her sit between the sticks and showed her how to advance, reverse, and turn. She rolled the Cat up out of the pit and stopped just before the pickup, which appeared toylike in front of them. Later, back in the pickup, the dim light of the dashboard reflecting his face, she saw his teeth appear and then disappear, and she was struck by the brief image of something animal-like and feral in him. She pressed a hand against his mouth.

He said that they should go into town for a drink. Then they could go up to the cabin, later. Nelson had gone to Winnipeg, so they would be alone.

"You don't drink," she said.

"True. But that can change. For tonight."

Lizzy said fine, if he wanted. She leaned back and said that she liked it when he liked her. That he wanted to be seen in public with her. "Who do you want to show me to?" she asked. Then she said that it went both ways. She wanted to show him off too. With her index finger she touched his forehead and said, "I love this," and then she touched his chin and his jaw and she said, "And this, and this." He stopped at a bar on Main Street. Parked down by the wharf and they walked up past a patio full of people and then around to the front door. They sat in a corner booth, looking out at the crowd. Lizzy ordered a beer and Raymond a whisky neat. Lizzy looked at him when he ordered and she raised her eyebrows.

There was a band playing country music and Lizzy asked Raymond to dance.

He shook his head.

Lizzy grinned. She tugged at Raymond's left hand. "Come on."

"When I'm drunk," he said.

"You're embarrassed."

They sat and watched the crowd, and the people dancing, and Lizzy took Raymond's hand and played with his fingers until he laced them into hers. She said her mother used to play this game with her, when she was younger, where she would fold her hands together and ask Lizzy to close her eyes and count her fingers to see if she could find all ten. Sometimes she got nine, sometimes eleven, rarely ten. "I couldn't do it." She paused and said, "She went away. She's done this before. We wake up and she's gone. She doesn't leave a note, doesn't come and say goodbye. It's like she doesn't have children. I'm okay, but I feel sorry for my brothers, they're too young to understand."

Raymond watched her, and then he said, "You still have a dad."

Lizzy smiled, and then began to laugh. She said, "Stupid me." Then she said, "I like you."

A girl in a tam walked past their booth, looked at Raymond, and stopped.

"Hi, Raymond," she said.

Raymond lifted his head and said her name, "Alice."

Alice looked at Lizzy and then back at Raymond. She smiled and in the smile Lizzy sensed a possible threat.

"How've you been?" Alice asked. She was wearing tight jeans that went wide below the knee and she wore a vest over a plaid shirt. She looked like a cowgirl. Her mouth and eyes were small.

"Okay," Raymond said.

Alice nodded. She didn't say anything more, but she made no move to leave. Finally, she said that it had been a long time.

"I guess so," Raymond said.

Then Alice stuck out her hand at Lizzy and said, "My name's Alice. Alice Hart."

Her grasp was poor and slightly off-centre and Lizzy thought then that this might be a girl that Raymond had known quite well. She said her own name and took her hand back.

"You're not from here," Alice said.

"The Retreat," Lizzy said. "That's where."

Alice nodded and then her eyes brightened and she said, "Uncle Earl told me about you. Your family. It was your little brother who got lost, right?" She seemed happy to have situated Lizzy in this way. She said that her uncle Earl had been the policeman in charge of the search. She didn't look at Raymond as she said this, but she turned at some point and faced him and said that she was getting married. Maybe next month.

"Really," Raymond said. "That's fine."

"'Course it's fine. Aren't you going to congratulate me?"

"I guess that depends," Raymond said.

"On what?"

"On who you're marrying."

"Vernon." The corners of her small mouth lifted. "He's here, you know," and she looked over her shoulder, then turned back to Lizzy. "Ray and I knew each other in high school. Didn't we, Ray? Very good friends." She waited, as if there were more to add. Then she told Lizzy that Vernon was a constable on the police force. Just like her uncle. "But then you know that. Vernon helped look for your brother, right?"

Lizzy nodded and said that she remembered him.

Alice went pensive and leaned towards Raymond and asked him if he had a joint. Even half a joint. Or some crumbs. "You got some?" she asked.

He said he didn't. He said she should ask policeman Vernon. He probably had lots of prime confiscated shit.

Alice's mouth drew into a neat pucker. "You don't have to make fun." And she turned and walked away, disappearing through the crowd on the dance floor.

Lizzy watched Raymond. "She calls you Ray," she said.

"True." He drank the remainder of whisky and when the waitress passed by he asked for another. He studied Lizzy.

Lizzy smiled briefly.

Raymond's shot glass arrived. He drank it in one go, grimaced, and set the glass down.

"She was your girlfriend?" Lizzy asked.

Raymond seemed to ponder this question, as if he wasn't sure of the answer. Then he said, "For a while. Last fall."

Lizzy touched Raymond's fingers. "Your hands. They're shaking."

He stood and reached into his jeans' pocket and took out some cash and laid it on the table. He walked out and Lizzy followed him down the hill to the pickup, stumbling slightly in her shoes, unable to keep up.

"Hey," she called.

Raymond didn't answer. He got in the pickup and sat there. Even after Lizzy had climbed in he made no move to start the engine. Just sat and looked out the windshield at the harbour in front of them. The float planes, the slips of the dock, the barrels of fuel.

"What's going on?" Lizzy said. "Was it Alice?"

He started the engine and drove up the hill, past the bar, and down Second Street. They crossed over the intersection near the baseball diamond. Up past the prison and down onto the flat stretch towards Raymond's turnoff. Lizzy said that she didn't know what had happened back there in the bar, but she didn't care about Alice. Not one bit. Anyway, Alice was getting married and she didn't seem that smart and what frightened her, she said, was that Raymond might not know the difference between her and Alice. "You know? What do you see when you look at me? A white girl? Because if that's all you see, then there's a problem."

"That's not all." He said that Alice had been his girlfriend in high school. "Her father wasn't happy with this, but I didn't give a shit. Alice was this girl who had pointed her finger at Raymond Seymour. I wasn't very bright back then." He poked around in his shirt pocket for his cigarettes. "Wanna?" he asked Lizzy. She took one and waited. He struck a match and held out a shaky hand. She held his hand as she bent to the light.

"Hart told me to stay away from Alice," he said. "I tried, but she kept coming back. And I wasn't interested in sending her away. And then one night Hart found us. Put us in his police car and dropped Lizzy off at home. I was in the back of the car. I got into the car, see, and once I was in, I couldn't get out." He opened his window and ashed the cigarette. He didn't speak for a long time and Lizzy thought that this might be the end of his story. She wanted to ask questions, but she didn't. She saw that this was a sad and private story and she felt her own sorrow, which she experienced as pity.

Raymond said, "So Hart takes me out to my boat, and he puts me in my boat. He gets in and I get in. Just like that. Maybe I'm thinking we're just going for a ride and he's going to talk to me. Huh."

And he was silent again. And again, Lizzy waited. Only this time Raymond didn't continue. He tossed the cigarette. The truck was crawling now. The tunnel of trees, the corners around which there was the promise of something, and then nothing except another tunnel and more trees and one more corner.

"He put me on an island," Raymond said. "And he left, and for nine days I waited on that island until finally a barge passed by. I remember thinking that I couldn't let myself go crazy. By the end, I was walking in circles and talking to myself, to my brothers, my grandma. I knew I couldn't last much longer on a small island where there was no food or shelter. I *was* going crazy. The thing is, I climbed from the boat and put myself on the island and I let Hart take off. That was the worst thing. I didn't fight back."

"You didn't *let* him put you there."

"No?"

"You reported this," she said.

"Oh, yeah. Sure did. I walked into the police station and made my report and then they arrested Constable Earl Hart and had a big trial and he's still in prison. Even as we speak. You don't get it. There're two kinds of laws, one for your people, one for mine."

"But you could have told someone. Nelson. Your grandma. The counsellor at school."

"Nelson wasn't there. I did tell him, but way later."

"This isn't right, Raymond. Does Alice know?"

"Sure she knows." He said that his rescue had been written up in the local paper. She had to know.

"And nothing? She did nothing?"

"You met her," he said.

"Oh, Raymond." She put her hand on his shoulder. "Poor boy," she said. And she slid across the seat and put her arms around him as he drove. "Do you want to cry?"

He said no, he didn't. He sat, stolid and resolute.

Instead she began to cry. Not loudly, but her eyes filled and she said that she loved him. Did he know that? She did. She loved him. She didn't say anything more until they reached his cabin.

In the darkness, Lizzy found two small candles and lit them. Then she went to Raymond and kissed him and when she pulled away she said that she wanted to stay here, in this room, where the candles were, and the windows. She took off her shoes and looked down at herself and saw the dress she was wearing as excessive. It was as if she were playing at some-thing, as if everything in her own life was frivolous. Raymond went into the bedroom and returned with a woollen blanket. He placed it on the floor and then took off his boots. They were cowboy boots, well worn, and his socks had holes. He took off the socks and threw them in the corner.

"Music would be nice," Lizzy said.

Raymond looked around, as if something that could produce music would magically appear. Then he said, "Okay," and he went outside in his bare feet. Lizzy heard him open the door to the pickup and then the radio was on and music fil-tered through the door. The tinny voice of a radio announcer and then the Doobie Brothers singing "China Grove."

Lizzy slid out of her dress and removed her underwear and bra. She blew out one of the candles and the shadows in the room extended. She stretched out on the blanket. The floor was hard, the blanket was itchy. Her breasts were too small. She sat up and took the dress and spread it out underneath her and lay down again. The dress was cool and soft on her bum and on her back. She sat up again. Her breasts were fuller this way. She pressed her legs together and positioned them sideways, so that her feet were tucked behind her bum, rather like a princess. This did not feel right and so she lay down and lifted one leg so that it was bent slightly at the knee. When Raymond came back inside he had the long view of her, from her toes to her head.

He moved his eyes down her body and back up again. "You're naked," he said. "I go out to find some music and when I come back, you're naked. How does that work?"

"Lucky, I guess."

"Music okay?" he asked. He hadn't moved from the doorway. Then he said that she could still choose. She could get dressed and he'd take her back to the Retreat. "I don't want trouble."

"You see me as trouble?"

He shifted his weight and said, "It's me. I'm the trouble."

She shook her head. "No. No, you're not. Come."

"You sure?"

"Yeah, I'm sure."

"You want the light?" He motioned at the candle. And then, without waiting for her answer, he leaned towards the table and blew and it was immediately dark.

At night, she woke and heard rain. There was music playing; the sound came from far away, intermittent and faint through the noise of the downpour. Raymond was sleeping beside her. She reached out and shook him and said his name and then she stood and felt her way to the table. She found the matches, lit one, and held it to a candle. It caught, then flared. Raymond was on his back beside the blanket, one arm thrown back. Lizzy went over to the doorway and the light flickered behind her. She briefly saw her own shadow, wavering and elongated. He had held her head in his hands and asked several times if she was okay. She had said yes, yes, and then her own hands were everywhere and a gust of wind entered and a door swung wildly, back and forth, and she had pulled him hard against her chest. She felt all of this more accurately now than when they had made love. She pushed the door open, reached out, and felt the rain, then ran through the mud to the pickup and turned off the radio, taking the key from the ignition and picking up the plastic bag that held her jeans and T-shirt. When she got back inside, Raymond was awake.

"I have to get home," Lizzy said. She'd found her under-wear and bra and she was slipping her jeans on. She pulled her T-shirt over her head.

Raymond got up and walked over to the open doorway and stood there and peed into the rain. Then he got dressed and asked if she wanted something to drink before they left. Tea or coffee? He could start the stove. She said no, that people might be looking for her and they should go.

They drove down the slippery road and the pickup tried to slide into the ditch. Raymond swore and steered wildly. The headlight caught the falling rain and it seemed to Lizzy that the world was swollen and angry, that she was hovering some-where between heaven and earth, that what had happened up at the cabin was an act of little consequence, a mere scrap in the history of the world.

"Are you all right?" she asked. "You're not disappointed?"

"Not at all," he said. "Never." He took her hand.

By the time they reached the driveway that led to the Retreat, the rain had stopped. Lizzy asked Raymond to let her off at the highway, it would be quieter that way. He pulled onto the shoulder, turned to her, and said, "Hey," and he drew her close and kissed her on the mouth.

"Oh," she said. "You."

Then she climbed from the pickup and turned at the last moment to watch his tail lights disappear. Walking down the path in the black night she lifted a hand to her face and found Raymond there at the tips of her fingers, a pleasant and burnished scent, not unlike the warm smell of Fish when he had come up from the pond and lain down and dried himself in the sun.

When he could not sleep, Lewis sat in a chair by the window that looked out over the clearing and plucked at his cobwebbed brain, knowing that any brilliant and important thoughts in the night could, in the light of day, be reduced to neurotic nonsense. He neither drank nor smoked and so to keep his hands busy he knit. Norma had never liked him to knit, she thought it effeminate, or perhaps it went against her image of what she wanted him to be, but now that she was gone he was free to knit during the day or in the evening, on the porch, in the Hall, or now at night, as he sat insomniac by the window. He knit by feel, he had no need to bend his eyes to his task. He was making caps for his children, skullcaps that would sit like beanies on their heads. He had given Everett his already; the boy had taken it, studied it with some doubt, tried it on, taken it off, and said thanks. Lewis had not seen him wear it.

A week after Norma left, a letter had arrived. She talked about Chicago and the heat and about going to a baseball game with her sister. She said, "Don't tell the boys, Lewis, they'll be terribly jealous." She said that the weight she'd felt at the Retreat was gone now. Everything was lighter, even the air was lighter. "Maybe I'm a city girl," she wrote. She said that she missed the children and that Lewis should be sure to give them her love. "Especially William," she said. "I've been thinking too much about his reticence, the shell he puts himself into. He reminds me of me." Then she told Lewis that she loved him. She said nothing about when she was coming back.

He had told the children that their mother had written, and that she missed them. Fish had looked up and asked, "When is it a week?" and Everett said, "It's already been, stupid." Fish looked confused. "Don't call him names," Lewis said. He gathered Fish in his arms and tickled him and said, "Come, my sweet little chickens," which was a line from a story Norma liked to tell. Fish, gasping, said, "Again," and so Lewis told his boys the story one more time.

He had thought of calling her. One evening he'd stood by the phone in the Hall and dialled the number, let it ring once, then hung up. He knew Norma, and he knew that his calling would appear desperate, make her feel pursued, and this might drive her further from the family. He decided instead to write a casual letter, but when he was finished, he reread it and saw that it seemed indifferent, as though the family did not need her, as though they were doing much better now that she was gone, and so he tore it up.

Lizzy had shown no interest in the letter when he told her about it. Lately, she had become more aloof and Lewis knew that she was spending time with Raymond again. Over the last while, almost every night, he had observed her step out of her cabin door and walk up the path that led to the main road. She always returned around one or two, and he'd see her tiptoeing up the steps and through the door of her cabin and then, inevitably, a candle would be lit and he'd see her shape moving back and forth. Once, briefly, he had seen her undress, lifting her arms above her head as she removed her T-shirt. He had looked away, affording her her privacy, and when he had turned back moments later, the cabin was dark. He had talked to her about Raymond, but it had not gone well. He had felt helpless and overwhelmed. In his concern he had been too harsh. She had refused his advice and talked about her mother, about how selfish she was, and said that she had her own life to live now, and that life included Raymond. He was good and kind, Lizzy said. There were no bad intentions, and even if there were, it wasn't any of Lewis's business.

Norma, if she'd been around, would have asked her if she was having sex with the boy and, if so, was she using protection. Norma was good at that. She was not a prude. Norma had had no problem baring her breasts for the Doctor and then talking about it. She'd always leaned towards a brazen lightheartedness, referring to her pussy and Lewis's cock as if they were domestic pets. Lewis disliked this. Sex was serious and could be ruined by too much talk.

Lewis preferred the secrecy of his own thoughts. Some time ago, he had become more conscious of Emma Poole, and there were times, at night, when he would imagine having sex with her. Her demanding voice, her requirements, her needs, all of this made him excited and anxious. He felt both lust and irritation. He was taken aback one night, as he imagined Emma's thin arms falling backwards onto the moss of the forest, that he saw Norma instead, and a deep loneliness invaded him. He had leaned against the window jamb and breathed greedily, trying to regain a sense of the world outside of himself.

Emma Poole did not in fact seem to like Lewis. She had, during a discussion about politics once, called him passive-aggressive, said that his hands were always clenched, his mind limp. And she looked down at his crotch as if the association was obvious. A half-knit cap lay in his lap. Usually, she just ignored him, and it was this that depressed Lewis. He was often ignored. Lately, however, he had been talking to Margaret down by the garden. It had begun one day when Fish wanted to dig in the dirt of the garden with his toy loader and Margaret had been picking beans while her boy Billy flattened a tin can with a large stone. Margaret had whispered that her son had an eating problem, he was fat, and she had said this so matter-of-factly, and yet so filled with worry, that Lewis had suddenly seen her in a new way. She was no longer the complicit partner of the Doctor, allowing him to forage for other women and cheering him on, but she had become instead a mother who sat up at night, worrying about her child. He had lifted his head and said, "No, I don't think he is," and she said, "You sound like Amos. Like most men. Always in denial." She said that she had been reading medical journals, and there were clear signs that her boy leaned that way. "When he was born, for the first two years, he wouldn't let go of the breast, he was insatiable. He doesn't know his limits. It's like his body is missing the regulator that kicks in to tell him he's had enough." She was on her knees now, tending her plump tomatoes. Lewis saw her round face, the scarf covering her hair, her wide shoulders. She was a tall, large woman. Standing, she rose above everyone else at the Retreat. Norma had joked once that in bed she must smother the Doctor. Lewis studied her now and wondered what she looked like naked. For a big woman, her breasts appeared dramatically small. He imagined one in his hand. Fish came to him and pulled at one of his shirt sleeves. He had to pee.

"Do it in the garden," Margaret said. "The ammonia will do the earth good."

Lewis nodded at him to go and he did, aiming at the rocks that rimmed the patch, rocks that Lewis had laid out on a hot afternoon, just after the family's arrival. He had been looking for a job to do, had hated the desultory nature of the camp, the indolence, the lassitude, and so he had created a bit of a rock garden, to no one else's pleasure it seemed, not even Margaret, who had studied the job when he'd finished and said, "Oh, rocks."

Over the last while, Lewis's habit had been to slip down to the garden and talk to Margaret, or to meet her in the Hall where they shared tea, or sometimes Lewis sat in the kitchen and watched her bake while they chatted. She was more complicated than he'd imagined. One afternoon, when the Retreat was quiet, Lewis had found her on the front step of her cabin, patching a pair of jeans. He had sat on the stair just below her, and she began to talk about her husband and the Retreat. She said that what Amos believed in was freedom at work and at love and at play. Freedom was ultimate. She said she still wasn't sure what that meant but she believed that there was some truth to Amos's notion of freedom. She said that she was not caught in the spiral of sexual desire like her husband, and so in some ways she was freer than he was. She said that the year before, a young man named Kyle had come to the Retreat and Kyle had fallen in love with her. She smiled briefly. Her eyes closed and opened again and she looked at Lewis. "Kyle told me and I told Amos and Amos said it was fine. I could sleep with him; it might liberate the boy." She said that Kyle had spent his days in the field, meditating. He rarely ate, he didn't bathe, and he was constantly going on about his visions. "Personally, I think he was suffering sunstroke," she said. In any case, she had had no interest in sleeping with Kyle. She loved her husband. She said that the problem with sex was that people saw it as a form of salvation. It wasn't. She said, "Take my husband and your wife."

Lewis just looked at her.

"Let's face it, we both knew," she said.

"They didn't actually have sex." Lewis's response was so quick, so emphatic, that it seemed untrue. He felt that he'd been wrong about something, and he wondered now if Margaret had not minded her husband seducing Norma. He said that Norma had told him that the affair, if you could call it that, had been intellectual and spiritual.

Margaret smiled and said that in the last while her husband had changed. He now entertained notions of being like Christ. "He believes he exists above the fray." Then she said that though Norma was a beautiful woman, she hadn't ever felt threatened by her. "People feel sorry for me," she said. "Don't. I know where I am."

Lewis gazed out across the clearing and realized that Margaret was as arrogant as her husband. The Doctor had never acknowledged Norma's departure, and to Lewis it felt as though he didn't care. This lack had at first pleased him, but then it had angered him to think that Norma should be seen as so disposable. These days he couldn't stand the sight of the Doctor.

When Margaret had talked about Norma and of her husband, he had felt affection for her. How practical she had seemed; her efficiency and honesty, even her air of superiority, spoke of someone complex enough to understand things in a certain way. He had wondered, very briefly, if she found him attractive, or if, like Emma Poole, she thought he had a limp mind.

And now, at night by the window, waiting for Lizzy to return, he imagined lying down beside Margaret. She was willing and calm and her long legs held him. He stood, looking out at the wet dark clearing, and masturbated, saying Norma's name.

☙

At breakfast the next morning he sat beside William and noticed that the spot on his head had grown to the size of a quarter. Not wanting to frighten the boy, he said he was going into town and perhaps he wanted to join him. Just him, no one else. William was eager; he climbed into the car and let his hand catch the wind as they drove. Lewis talked to him, said that the spot on the side of his head was a curious thing, wasn't it, and maybe a doctor should look at it, just to make sure. He'd felt in the last while that he and the children were standing at the edge of a cliff and that he didn't have enough arms to hold them back, and that the worrisome thing wasn't so much that they might fall as that he would somehow cause their falling. William was stubborn and said that there wasn't anything wrong. He said he'd shave his head completely so no one would notice.

"Does it hurt?" Lewis asked, running his hand over his son's head.

William said it didn't.

Lewis said they would drop by the hospital for just a quick visit. It wouldn't take long.

The doctor on duty inspected William and said that the boy was stressed or malnourished or both. He asked if something bad had happened lately in his life. He asked William if anything was bothering him. The doctor was facing the boy, their knees almost touching, while Lewis sat in the background. William shook his head. He was thinking, his dark eyes not moving from the doctor's gaze. The doctor asked if he was getting enough to eat up there, and as he said "up there" his voice dropped, as if the father and son had descended from a sinister place. The doctor turned to Lewis and said that his son should get plenty of sleep. He should be encouraged to talk. He should eat more green vegetables. There was science and then there was voodooism, he said, and science made more sense. He wrote out a prescription for an ointment and handed the paper to Lewis.

They drove to the drugstore where Lewis had the prescription filled and then they went to an outdoor market and Lewis bought broccoli and fresh peas and corn and carrots. He climbed back in the car and William pointed with his nose out the window.

Lewis leaned down and looked through the passenger window to see Raymond passing by, singing or talking to himself. Lewis watched him for a bit and then told William to sit tight, he'd be right back. He got out of the car and called Raymond's name. Raymond looked sideways and paused. He nodded. Then continued to walk on. Lewis fell in beside him and said, "You have a moment?"

Raymond stopped and turned.

His dark eyes found Lewis, then fell away.

"You and Lizzy," Lewis said.

Raymond nodded.

"She's been spending time with you," Lewis said. "Do you love her?"

Immediately he knew that this was wrong. The boy couldn't know if he loved her. He had a hard enough time loving himself. So Lewis backtracked and he apologized. He said that that wasn't the point, except he was concerned for Lizzy, that she would get hurt, and he didn't want that, no father wanted that. He said that he knew Raymond had a grandmother on the reserve, Lizzy had told him, and he thought that his grandmother must be concerned about Raymond as well. Wasn't she? And when he was older and had children he would learn all about this part of being a father, not much fun, really, and so Lewis wasn't saying he couldn't see Lizzy. But.

He stopped talking.

Raymond looked down at his feet and then back up at Lewis.

"I won't hurt her," he said. "I have no plan to do anything like that. She knows it."

Lewis nodded. He raised his chin as if to add something, but then he stopped and said, "Okay, good," and he reached out a hand to shake, as if they had, the two of them, struck a deal. Raymond looked at Lewis's hand and then took it and they shook briefly and let go at the same time. Lewis turned towards the car and he saw that William was watching, pressed against the side window, no expression on his face.

One morning, when Raymond drove past Anicinabe Park on his way to work at the golf course, he saw police cruisers and barricades at the gate entrance, and he recalled the time up in the cabin with Gary and Lionel. The occupation of the park had been part of their plan, and now it was happening. A few days later, in the afternoon, he parked his pickup a ways back from the gate entrance and he stood watching in the sunshine. There were four police cruisers parked alongside the road and a number of constables patrolled the barricade. Inside the gate stood two men wearing bandanas and carrying rifles; bandoliers criss-crossed their chests.

That night he told Nelson that he was going to join the protest. He didn't want to just watch from a distance. He'd heard that the best way to get into the park was by boat, from Bare Point. He would go that night and he said Nelson could join him if he liked.

Nelson laughed. "Don't be stupid, Raymond. You're walking into a mess. Lizzy not exciting enough?"

"This isn't about her."

"You haven't even fucked her yet. Have you?"

"Piss off. You think everything's about sex. It isn't."

"I'm a pacifist. I don't believe in guns." He lifted a hand, showed Raymond his thick fist, and said, "Though I could beat the shit out of you."

Raymond turned and walked away. He heard Nelson call out that he was joking, but Raymond didn't turn back. He drove down to the highway and sat the pickup on the shoulder and turned off the engine and killed the lights. The windows were down and the night sounds drifted across the highway. When they were young, before Nelson was taken away, they used to walk out into the bush to an abandoned shed where they would build fires on the large bare rocks and let loose. One time, in the oppressive heat of a summer day, they ran naked through the bush, laughing and chasing each other. At some point Nelson tackled Raymond and sat on him. Raymond struggled to free himself, but Nelson had held him down. "Gotta boner," Nelson said, and he punched Raymond in the chest, hard enough for Raymond to bruise up later. Another time, he'd fallen from the roof of the shed and landed on his back, all the air knocked out of him. As he gasped and thrashed, believing he was dying, Nelson kneeled beside him. "You're okay. Suck in the air, that's all. You won't die." And he'd been right.

And then Nelson had been taken away and the sadness was absolute and complete and there were days when Raymond would go out to the abandoned shed and he'd imagine Nelson arriving. He had not known, at that time, that Nelson would be gone for ten years, or that when he returned he would be unrecognizable.

Raymond drove his truck to Bare Point, unmoored his boat, and headed out onto the lake. He approached the park landing in the dark, cutting the engine and drifting towards the shore. A man holding a rifle stepped out of the darkness and called out to him. Raymond said who he was and why he was there, and he was taken to see Gary, who was sitting by a fire, rifle at his feet.

Gary said that he remembered that night with his brother Nelson. And he remembered the white girl.

"I'm alone," Raymond said. "I want to help."

Gary looked him up and down, told him to sit. He said that the police were trying to starve them out of the park. "They arrested four of our people today as they were leaving the park." He asked Raymond if he had a vehicle.

Raymond said that he had a pickup, he had a gun, and he had a boat.

Gary nodded, lighting a cigarette. Then he moved away from Raymond and talked to the other men.

That night Raymond lay under a picnic table, close to one of the fires the men had gathered around to talk. He slept off and on, the conversations drifting around him. Sometimes the only sound in the night was the wood cracking in the fire. He wished Nelson had come with him. They'd be talking right now, just the two of them, telling jokes, pretending to know things that they didn't. It felt good having him around, and sometimes up at the cabin, when Nelson wasn't aware, Raymond would watch him closely, as he would a stranger; this person who had seen a different world, who knew things, and who never spoke of the past or what had happened. He didn't seem to hold it against Raymond that he was the one who got to stay.

Just before dawn, Raymond woke and went to stand by the fire. After a while, Gary came to him and said he had a job he wanted him to do. He handed him a bundle of money held together with a rubber band, and he put a grocery list into his pocket. He said that everyone had something to do and this would be Raymond's something. He didn't ask if Raymond wanted this job, he simply instructed him. He said that Raymond shouldn't buy all the supplies at one place, as that might cause suspicion. He said that food was the priority. Some food had been brought in two days earlier by bus from Winnipeg, but then the police had laid barbed wire across the entrance to the park and no more outsiders were allowed in. He would have to bring in the food by boat. Adults were now limited to one meal a day. The children were fed twice a day, morning and evening.

Raymond wondered where the children were. He'd seen only one, an infant at a young woman's breast. He pushed the money into his pocket, looking up at the man beside him. Then he went down to his boat and pushed it off of the shore and climbed in. By the time he'd reached Devil's Gap, the sounds of the men had faded and all he heard were the waves lapping at his boat. The campfires on the shore flickered and then disappeared.

The journal had been deep in the back of the top drawer of the dresser in his parents' cabin, wrapped in a silk scarf, a small notebook with a black leather cover, dated on the inside. Everett had found it one evening when he was looking for matches to light the lamps, and he read it clandestinely and with guilt.

The writing was intimate and bold. His mother wrote that she had put on the red dress for the man and danced and imagined she was someone else. She sat on the man's lap and they kissed. Another time she sat on a chair and smoked while the man was at her feet and he touched her while she blew smoke in his ear.

Everett looked for his own name and he found it near the middle of the journal, where she said that she worried about him, about his lack of friends, and wondered if she was maybe too entangled with him. She said, "Everett looks at me oddly sometimes and I tell his father to do things with him, play hockey, or box or wrestle, but Everett's not interested. He lies on the bed and watches me get ready for work and asks about the nurses and the doctors and we gossip and laugh. I love him." She wrote that Fish made her feel sadness. It wasn't

Fish's fault, but he was one too many. She had three too many, maybe all of them were too many, because if she didn't have any of them, she would be free to run. She said Lizzy was not a worry, but Everett was.

He liked that he was a worry. He thought that if he had known he was a worry, he would have worried her even more so that she would have been obligated to stay. She had loved him. This was a revelation, something that he might have sensed but never truly understood; these words written down, the sentiments both amazed and depressed him. He did not understand how she could choose to leave if she loved him. He remembered his mother hugging him a few days before she left, as if she had known already that she was leaving. She had held him and he had been keenly aware of her body and her smell and the sound of her voice.

He wondered who "the man" had been and how it was that his mother would let a stranger touch her. She had blown smoke in the man's ear. His mother adored her cigarettes. She would light one and hold it aloft, and then open her mouth and draw and squint, and sometimes she laughed her big laugh. Everett liked to be across from her then because he could look deep into her mouth and experience a shiver of intimacy. The man was not the Doctor, whose hands were fine and hairy and whose fingers were narrow. It might have been the surgeon from the hospital where his mother worked in Calgary. A Doctor Thu. A man she had talked about often. Or someone Everett had never met. At this moment his mother was with people he would never meet. .

Or she was dead. His mother *was* dead. Though his father said she had written, Everett had never seen the letter and he imagined now that he might have been lying. To make him feel better. Harris said that she would come back. They had been sitting at the edge of the pond. Some mothers were like that, Harris said. They flew away with one kind of message clutched in their claws and returned with a different message. Not better, just different. But they always returned. Harris looked at Everett. "How old are you?" he asked.

According to his father, Harris was ineffectual, crippled physically and emotionally, and he was a cuckold. Everett remembered this when the man asked his age. There was little comfort in Harris's words. And with Everett's response, Harris nodded. He ducked his small chin and asked if he should read to Everett. In the last while, he had been reading *Gulliver's Travels* to anyone who wanted to listen. Usually in the late after-noon, by the pond, when everyone was tired and stretched out on the sand, Harris would read and laugh and then cast his gaze about, seeming to expect others to laugh as well, and sometimes they did, but not as enthusiastically as Harris.

Everett said that he was going for a bike ride, and he picked up his towel and walked back to the camp. He wanted to go up to the cabin to visit Raymond's brother Nelson again. He had already been at the cabin, Nelson had invited him, and when he got there they had played chess and then they'd driven to the dump where Nelson taught him how to shoot a gun. Later, they had shared a beer, and Nelson had asked if Everett wanted to smoke a joint. He didn't. Nelson smoked

and talked and at one point he said that these were the con-
fessions of a resolute sinner. He had not stopped talking, and
Everett felt like they were equals, that Nelson saw him as
someone worth sharing things with.

And so he set out now, down the highway and then onto
the long road towards Bare Point, thick bush on either side
and in the bush his mother's body. She'd been picked up by a
hitchhiker and been strangled and dumped in the bush. A bird
called and it was his mother's voice. He pedalled faster, panicked now, breathless, up the narrow road to Raymond and
Nelson's cabin, where he found Nelson before a small fire
near the swing, roasting wieners. Nelson showed no surprise
when Everett appeared. He said he was alone, Raymond was
out on the lake with his boat. "Hungry?" Nelson said.

Everett laid his bike on the ground and stood beside
Nelson and watched him eat and then took a wiener himself
and roasted it and ate it plain, chewing slowly. He said that
he'd been bored at the Retreat and he hoped Nelson didn't
mind him coming to visit. He said that his mother had left,
and ever since then the Retreat seemed different. His father
was different. He was always alone and it made Everett sad,
and so he tried to stay away from him. Lizzy had changed too.
"She's quiet and keeps to herself," he said. "And she thinks
about your brother a lot." He said that the only one who
hadn't changed was his smallest brother, Fish, at least as far as
he could notice.

Nelson went inside and came back with a bottle of whisky
and two glasses and poured the whisky into the glasses and
handed one to Everett, who drank, a little fearful but curious

about something he'd never tasted before. He shuddered, hating it, but he drank again. The whisky sat in his throat and chest and then all sad thoughts gradually floated away and disappeared.

They sat by the fire on lawn chairs patched with bicycle tubes and Nelson told Everett how he had shot a skunk the night before, down by the well, shot him right through the head and buried the little thing out in the bush so the rotten smell wouldn't drift up to the cabin. "Got him before he could spray." He said that he used to shoot birds in Lesser, down by the river, him and Lawrence Neufeld. "We'd lie and wait and the idea was to take off the head without damaging the body. I was good. Larry called me a fucking potshot, which I was, and we'd laugh and shoot some more. Larry's in Bible school somewhere. B.C., I think. For a time in my life, six months maybe, I was going to be a preacher. I got baptized. Had a girlfriend, Dorothy Stoez, who wanted to be a preacher's wife. You know? In grade seven, Mr. Arndt took us to see a dead body, a young boy maybe nineteen or twenty who had fallen from a radio tower. Three hundred feet and all he had was a slight bruise on his forehead. We traipsed by the coffin and went up on tiptoes and looked in and then we went back to class. I don't know what the point was, though I remember the assignment. Write a poem. About anything. So I wrote about Grandma Seymour. She's still alive. Has a house on the reserve and lives with Reenie and company. She'll live forever. Goddamn invincible. The poem was about her dying. Huh. Funny, that."

He paused, lit a cigarette. He said that when he came back here, to Kenora, he saw that his grandmother hadn't changed at all. She was still his grandma, though not the same with him. Like he'd gone away and been someone else for ten years and then he'd reappeared but she didn't know him any more. You know?

He said that at Everett's age he had been a pretty good viola player, was in the community orchestra out in Steinbach and played in church Sunday mornings and all the women swooned, especially Mrs. Pauls, who always wore something different with her dangly earrings and high heels. "I loved imagining what she'd wear next. Then, I went to a music competition in Winnipeg and I was smoked. Little fish arrives in big pond. I didn't play much after that."

Everett could feel the warmth of the whisky in his head and chest. Nelson's voice was soft, his eyes were dark. His life seemed so much larger than his own, and everything seemed to come easily to him.

Nelson leaned forward and said in a confidential tone, "In school, I took German for five years. Mr. Goertzen beating me about the ears, trying to augment my vocabulary as I struggled with insane passages. *Ich.* Weird. Me speaking German. *Na, Sie sieht immer noch ein bisschen blass aus.* 'My, she's still looking a little pale.'" He paused, then said, "Looking pale. *I* was very pale. So pale, I didn't know who I was. This is what I learned."

He sat back. "By the way, your sister left a dress here some time ago. Red."

Everett said that that might be his mother's dress.

Nelson motioned inside. "Go ahead. You'll probably want to take it back when you leave."

Everett stood and stumbled slightly. Nelson chuckled. Everett moved into the house and found the dress in a plastic bag beside the mattress. He picked it up and smelled it. Cigarette smoke and a hint of Lizzy, but mostly his mother. He breathed in deeply, then put the dress back in the bag and carried it outside. Nelson was standing, urinating in the bush. He looked over his shoulder and called out, "Find it then?"

He zipped up and turned, saying that he'd come across it the day before. "It's a beauty." He said that he used to go shopping with his stepsister Emily, for her clothes. "Girls are lucky, don't you think, all that choice." He said that he once tried on one of Emily's dresses, just for fun.

A cool wind came up the hill. "Wanna go in?" Nelson asked, and not waiting for an answer he walked into the cabin and sat and poured himself another shot. He did the same for Everett and said, "Drink up."

Everett looked at the whisky in his glass and then took a sip. Bull passed by and rubbed against his legs. Everett reached down and scratched her head. "Where'd the cat come from? Is it yours?"

"I found her wandering around the dump, scavenging for food, and I thought that's no life for a lady and I brought her home." He sat back and smiled at Everett, who smiled back. A hazy glow. Wind in the trees.

"When you have to go, I'll drive you," Nelson said. "I have Reenie's car. Throw the bike in the trunk. Easy. Very easy. Like speaking German. *Ich.* Go ahead, say it. *Ich.*"

"*Ich*," Everett said.

"Attaboy."

"My father likes to mix up languages," Everett said. "Throws in a bunch of French words and makes my mother laugh."

"Sure it does." Nelson studied Everett and then said, "She'll come back."

"You think so?"

"I'm certain."

Everett smiled. "Am I drunk?" he said. "I think I am." Something had been set loose inside of him.

"First time?"

Everett nodded.

"Oh, boy."

"*Ich*," Everett said. He laughed.

Nelson said, "Go. Why don't you try on the dress."

Everett looked at the bag in his hand, at Nelson, then back at the bag. He took out the dress and held it up. "This?"

"Yeah. Put it on. It'll be fun."

"I'd look stupid in my mother's dress."

"Why don't you just try and see."

Everett stood, stumbled, and moved to the bedroom. In the dim light of the room he laid the dress on the floor. He stooped to untie his runners and fell over onto the mattress. He could feel the beating of his heart. Then Nelson called out. Everett lifted himself and said, "Almost done." Seated on the mattress, he removed his shoes and socks. Pulling his T-shirt over his head, he lost his balance and fell backwards again, then managed to remove it. He stood and unbuckled his jeans and dropped them. Kicked them away and stood in his underwear. He thought for a long time about his underwear. He had the beginning of an erection and he looked down at himself. He took off his underwear and picked up the dress and undid the zipper. He pulled the dress on, as he had watched his mother do so many times. It slid easily over his shoulders and hips, the arms went in, and there he was, clothed. His hard-on was real now. He reached behind his waist for the zipper and then called out that he needed help.

"Come here," Nelson said.

Everett backed out of the bedroom and stood waiting. His erection embarrassed him and he didn't want Nelson to notice. The light was weak. Nelson came up behind him and took the tongue of the zipper and pulled it upwards. A soft insectlike sound. Nelson's hand against his back.

"There," Nelson said. "Let me see."

Everett swivelled, his hands in front of his crotch.

"Well. That's good. Very nice. Whaddya think?" He motioned at the chair and said, "Sit."

Everett sat. Crossed his legs so that his right foot extended towards Nelson who reached out and touched a toenail and said, "Next time you can bring up some nail polish and we'll paint your toes. Red. Or something groovy and bright." He laughed.

Everett was shaking. He wasn't cold, but he was shaking, and it came from deep inside.

"Hey, don't worry," Nelson said. "We're just fooling around. Nothing to worry about. It doesn't mean we're perverts or anything, if that's what you're thinking."

Everett was conscious of Nelson's mouth and of his hands flitting through the air. Nelson said that a friend of his, a good man, had once said that the happiest man was the one surprised at nothing.

A draft of air came in through the open door and passed over Everett's neck. He looked down at his bare legs and saw the hem of the dress. He heard the wave of Nelson's voice, and he saw the way Nelson was watching him, and he was surprised. He didn't want to be surprised but he was, by the erection he'd had, by Nelson's easy manner, by the hollowness inside him that felt like when he was hungry, and yet it wasn't exactly hunger. He was surprised by all these things and so he knew that he couldn't be happy. Perhaps Nelson had tricked him, or he had tricked himself. He stood and reached for the zipper. "Please," he said, and he turned and asked Nelson to unzip him. He wanted to change and go back home.

They drove down towards the main road, sliding through dusk. On Everett's lap was the plastic bag holding the dress. They drove in a silence that confused Everett. He wondered if he had done something wrong, if Nelson still liked him. At the Retreat, Everett climbed from the car and Nelson took the bike out of the trunk. He leaned it towards Everett and said that they never had their game of chess. "You come back any time and we'll play," he said.

Everett stood and watched Nelson disappear, then he looked up at the sky, which was clear and full of stars, and it felt as if he was standing at the bottom of a deep well.

News of the native protest at Anicinabe Park arrived at the Retreat via radio and newspaper. Early on, the protestors had threatened to blow up both the hydro dam and the pulp-and-paper mill. The town might also go up in flames. One of the leaders of the occupation asked, "What are a few houses when every Friday and Saturday night blood can be seen running down the sidewalks because of vigilante actions against native people?" At breakfast one morning, the Doctor unfolded the newspaper and read aloud from an interview given by Gary Cameron, the leader of the occupation. Cameron said that one of their goals was to take back the park that had been sold out from under them years earlier, another was to draw attention to their people, who suffered at the hands of the government, the courts, and the police. He said that natives were tired of being beaten up and handcuffed and thrown into jail and paraded up and down the main street of Kenora in police cars. Houses on the reserves were death traps. There were no social services. He had a list. The people were tired and fed up and now they were taking action.

The Doctor laid the paper down. Lizzy noticed that he had voiced no opinion about the protest, for or against, though when it came to social justice, she knew that he favoured the underdog and liked to quote from Christ's beatitudes.

That evening, she rode the bicycle up to the cabin where she found Nelson sitting on the swing, Bull in his lap. She approached him and straddled her bike and asked if Raymond was home. He wasn't. Lizzy looked at the open doorway and then asked when Raymond was coming back.

Nelson said that he didn't know. "He's a political protestor now, up at the park. Sometimes he comes back for the night, sometimes he doesn't." He shrugged. Lizzy looked at Nelson and shifted her weight onto one leg, her hip pushed out. She was wearing jean shorts and flip-flops and a T-shirt and aware of how Nelson leaned forward as if to inspect her. He said that Raymond might be back at any moment. Or he might be back in a week. He said that his brother was naive. He had discovered justice and protests and guns.

"Raymond's too smart to do anything stupid," Lizzy said.

Nelson laughed. He said that Raymond was in danger of being fired at the golf course, so he was doing the job. "I now punch his time clock." He smiled, looked Lizzy up and down. "I'm becoming Raymond," he said.

"I guess that would make you my boyfriend then," she said flatly. "Anyway, I just came for a dress," she said. "I left it here."

"Look around, absolutely." Nelson waved a hand.

She went into the bedroom and came back into the main room where Nelson, inside now, was sitting on a chair, waiting. She sat on a stool at a distance from him and said that the dress was gone.

"Your brother probably took it. He's come up to visit me a couple of times," he said.

"What are you saying?"

"Everett. Funny guy. Reminds me of me at that age. You know?" Nelson appeared slow and sleepy, as if he had been working at getting drunk.

"He came up here? How?"

"Like you. Bicycle. One time he carried the chess set with him. At the dance he said he liked chess and so I invited him up here to play and drew a map. Very eager boy. Awkward. Making sense of things. Not messed up."

"He would have gotten lost, map or not."

"He didn't. People surprise us sometimes, don't they? You think I'm messed up?"

Lizzy shook her head. "I didn't say you were messed up."

"Okay. But, the question. What's the answer?"

"I don't think so. You're maybe a little sad. That's one thing."

"That's right. Sad. Raymond says I should talk to someone." He smiled briefly and then said that when Raymond came back he would tell him she had come by. He said, "You can visit any time. I'm not dangerous, you know."

"Really? Why aren't you up there at the occupation?"

"Me? I don't believe in that shit. You watch, after all the threats and the talk, they'll give up their guns and go back to their shacks. Thirty years from now, nothing will have changed." He stood, leaned towards Lizzy, and said, "Raymond's got this big vision and don't be thinking that you fit anywhere inside that vision. You know?"

"I don't think that's true."

"No? Has he told you you're special?"

Lizzy was quiet. She remembered Raymond holding her in this room, the two of them on the woollen blanket and him asking if she was okay. She wavered now and felt Raymond's absence and Nelson's cruelty. She said, "He told you something?"

"Naw, he didn't tell me anything. I don't even know Raymond, really. I'm just the prodigal brother. So, I can see things you can't, and I'm telling you not to get too excited. Maybe he just wanted a white girl."

Lizzy stared at him for a moment, then turned and went to her bicycle and got on. When she looked back, Nelson was standing in the doorway. She called out, "Everett won't be coming up here again. You stay away from him." Nelson was gazing out into the distance, not at her, but at something beyond her, and he didn't acknowledge her words, though she saw his head move, as if he were ducking a blow.

That night, in the quiet of their cabin, when everyone else was sleeping, Lizzy told Everett that he was not allowed to visit Nelson again. She said, "I talked to Nelson and told him. What were you *thinking?*" Lizzy's voice rose in whispers. "You don't know anything about Nelson. He's got nothing. He's a talker. He makes things up. He can be mean."

Everett hesitated, then said, "He hasn't been mean to me. He talks to me and makes me feel good."

"I love you. I worry. And I don't like to be worried because then my chest hurts. You know?" Then she said, "What did you do with Mum's dress?"

There was a pause, and Everett said, "Why?" Then he said, "I put it back in Dad's cabin."

It was quiet for a long time and finally Lizzy said, "Go to sleep."

Silence. The soft pat of Fish opening and closing his mouth. Then, "Lizzy?"

"Hmmm."

"Do you think I'm strange?"

"Don't be stupid."

"Am I bad?"

"You're only fourteen, Ev. No, of course not."

"But you think Nelson's bad."

"I didn't say that. I said he was *mean*. He can be cruel."

"He said he knew a man in Winnipeg who operated an elevator, one of those old ones where you can see through the grating. He said he would take me there sometime."

"Yeah? That's wonderful, Ev."

"He lived with that man for a bit. He learned how to box."

"Maybe he's just a little bit full of shit."

"*I* don't think so. You worry too much."

"I've got lots to worry about."

"You're not my mother."

Lizzy made a very soft humming sound, and then she was quiet. Everett heard her breathing and he knew she was sleeping. He lay there a long time, looking up into the darkness.

Outside, an animal moved alongside the cabin. A skunk, perhaps, or a bear. His father had seen a black bear the day before, out at the edge of the clearing, and he'd warned the children. The berries were gone, the nights were getting colder, the bear was looking for garbage. Everett fell asleep, holding the twinned thoughts of capture and escape.

The following morning, Lizzy found Franz and told him she wanted to go up to Anicinabe Park with him. "When you go," she said. "If you're still going." He'd gone the day before and come back to announce that there was a huge police presence and anyone who tried to get into the park was being searched. He told Lizzy that he was going after breakfast and he would be pleased to have her join him. Lizzy wore a yellow sundress with thin straps over her bare shoulders and Franz said that she looked very handsome. She said nothing and turned away and rested her arm on the rolled-down car window. This was how Franz talked to her. Once, when she had come into the kitchen for a late-night snack, she found Franz eating bread and butter at the table, just sitting alone in the dark, a knife in his hand. He had asked, after some small talk, if she had a boyfriend. It was the kind of question that a man liked to ask, as if he was playing a game in which there was a stone fence, she on one side and he on the other, and he was asking if he could climb over the fence and join her. She also understood that some men liked to look at maps and that they dreamed of visiting foreign countries, countries that were out of bounds, and that the possibility of invitation to those countries was exhilarating to them.

That night, in the kitchen, she had quickly made a sandwich and left, aware of the glint of the light off of Franz's knife. Now, sitting next to him, she was conscious of her own curiosity about him. Then Franz spoke, and the silence dissipated, and with it her mood. He said that the occupation was a good thing, the government was fascist, and he was all for the Indians blowing up a few buildings to make a point. "They're oppressed," he said. "And they want a voice. Who wouldn't want a voice?" He said that this sort of oppression would never happen in Europe.

The entrance to the park gate was blocked by six police cars. Two officers held rifles. One of them approached the car. Lizzy recognized Vernon. He leaned in to talk to Franz and he saw Lizzy. "Miss Byrd. Sightseeing?" he asked. He shifted his rifle. Held it higher as if to make certain Lizzy caught a glimpse of it. "Because if you are, this is not the place to be. We've got a bunch of Indians with guns and Molotov cocktails who want to take down the town. I'd suggest you go back to your commune." He said *commune* slowly, as if it were a strange and unwholesome word.

"Franz is from Germany and he wants to take some photos."

"I know he's from Germany," Vernon said. "I remember your little brother. How *is* Fish?"

"He's taken care of," Lizzy said. She stared out past the windshield towards the gate and beyond as if she might catch a glimpse of Raymond.

Vernon said, "It's not wise coming up here. It makes it look like you're sympathetic to the Indians. Yesterday, three communists from Winnipeg tried to get through here with a semiautomatic rifle. All the wackos are coming out of the closet. You don't want to be counted as one."

Lizzy didn't answer. Franz held up his camera and said that he was interested in recording history. "You, for example," he said. "Could I take a photo of you?" Vernon looked amused at first, as if unsure about the request, and then he smiled and said, "I don't see the problem."

He posed beside his police cruiser, one arm resting on the roof of the vehicle, a leg slightly bent, his rifle slung over the shoulder.

Lizzy stood behind Franz, who asked Vernon to hold his rifle in both hands. "Is it loaded?" Franz asked, and when Vernon grinned and said, "Of course," Franz snapped two quick photographs.

Vernon took one step forward and said, "Enough," and waved them away. He halted before Lizzy and, nodding back at the park, said, "Your Seymour friend in there?"

Lizzy shrugged. "No idea."

"Be careful," he said. And he walked away.

The following day, Lizzy saw the newspaper on the table in the Hall and picked it up. There was a photograph of a group of protestors, about twelve in all, raising their fists and rifles in the air and, according to the caption, singing the American Indian Movement anthem. Lizzy studied the photo and thought she recognized one of the men who had been up at Raymond and Nelson's place.

She put the paper aside and lifted Fish and walked to the pond. William followed them, dragging a stick. Lizzy sat on the grass while the boys looked for frogs in the reeds at the edge of the water. At night, she had woken frightened and breathless from a dream in which Raymond had been standing with his back to her. She had circled him, trying to catch a glimpse of his face, but there were shadows and he appeared not to see her. When they had made love he hovered close to her and sniffed her all over. There had been no words, just the sound of him breathing as he moved over her. Perhaps Nelson was right and Raymond's vision did not include her. She took a cigarette from her bag and lit it. Fish came up out of the reeds and said, "You're smoking."

"You're right," Lizzy said, and pointed affectionately at his nose.

His eyebrows went up. His mouth puckered. He turned away and surveyed the pond. Then he sat down between Lizzy's legs and pushed himself against her chest. Lizzy lifted her head as she exhaled. She imagined Raymond admiring her neck. Fish was hot against her. "Go swim," she said.

He didn't move. He was humming and touching the down on her arms.

She put out her cigarette. Everett had arrived earlier, wheeling Harris to the edge of the pond, and now Harris had swivelled his chair so that he was facing her and she caught him sneaking looks at her legs and breasts. "Go," Lizzy said, and she gave Fish a push. He stumbled upwards and walked over to Everett and sat on the sand beside him. "Ev," he said.

Harris called out that he wanted to move away from the edge of the pond. Lizzy stood and went to him.

"Sorry," he said. Since the night of the dance, they had not really talked again. It was as if after sharing an intimacy there was nothing left to say between them and they were strangers again. They had seemed to avoid each other. A door had opened and then been slammed shut, and in some way she felt bad.

"Don't be sorry," she said. "You have no reason to be sorry. You need someone to help you and so I'm helping you. Where's Emma this morning?"

"She went out early to paint. She likes the morning light."

Lizzy snapped back the brakes and spun the wheelchair so that Harris's feet dragged through the sand. She wondered if it hurt him, but he didn't say anything.

"This okay?" She had placed Harris so he was facing the sun. She set the brakes. He observed the sky.

She told Fish she was going back to the cabin to read. Did he want to go see Dad or did he want to stay?

"Stay," he said.

"Don't go in the water without Ev." She turned to Everett. "That all right?"

"Fine."

The skin on her back and shoulders was breaking out again. Tiny bumps, a form of acne that she couldn't get rid of. Her mother had once asked if she wanted to go on the pill, but Lizzy had refused. She pulled on her shorts over her bathing suit, and she picked up her shirt, and walked up the path through the clearing and past the outhouse and the garden where the Doctor's wife was tending her vegetables. Her father was standing beside her, hands in his pockets, talking. He didn't see Lizzy, and she didn't call out or wave. She passed the Hall, imagining that she heard her mother's sharp, bright laugh. Instead, she heard the Doctor's voice, low and lisping, and then Franz's Teutonic tones, which is what her father had said one day when he had been mocking the German. "Listen to the Teutonic tones," he'd said, and he had compared the man to a finely tuned Mercedes-Benz.

When she saw Vernon standing by his pickup at the edge of the clearing she realized he had been watching her for a while. She paused, and when he waved, she went to him and said, "What's wrong?" She had panicked and thought that something terrible might have happened to Raymond. "Nothing wrong," he said. "I'm off today and was passing by and I thought I'd see what a little hippie girl does with her time."

Lizzy did not speak, nor did she acknowledge what seemed to be a mocking flirtation in his voice. She realized how bare her midriff was, and how slight her bathing-suit top must seem, and so she slipped on her shirt and buttoned it up.

"You're so straight," he said, and grinned. He was out of uniform and was wearing jeans and a light blue shirt with short sleeves. The shirt was tucked in. His right forearm was tattooed with a bullet. His hands were big. "Come for a ride," he said.

She shrugged and said that she wasn't dressed to go anywhere.

"Just a drive. I saw Raymond yesterday, at the park. I'll tell you all about him." He grinned.

"Tell me about him here."

He shook his head, motioned at his watch and said he'd
have her back in an hour. "Trust me," he said. "I'm a cop."

Lizzy looked back at her father and Margaret, then she
went around to the passenger door and climbed in. He drove
to town, talking about the house he'd just bought, a bungalow
with two bedrooms and a finished rec room. He said that it
felt good to be a landowner. He hit at his chest once, twice.
Lizzy studied the tattoo on his forearm. She asked him if he
had cigarettes.

"Don't smoke," he said. His right wrist hung over the steering wheel. The air, hot and humid, pushed in through the
open windows. Lizzy felt sweat rolling down between her
breasts. She touched her upper lip. "What about Raymond,"
she said.

Vernon parked on a side street and pointed at a grey house.
"That's it." He shut the engine down. "I'm gonna gut the
kitchen, make myself a nice island and put in cherry cabinets
and a new range. The previous owner was an old woman.
Wanna beer?"

Lizzy shook her head.

"Come on." He climbed out and walked towards the house.
Called back to her, "The beer's cold."

Lizzy watched him disappear inside. She was curious about
Vernon and she wondered if it was because of his relationship
to Alice. Or perhaps it was something murkier, maybe his
connection to Constable Hart. She wondered if Vernon knew
what Hart had done to Raymond. She felt strangely guilty as
she got out and went up the walk. Inside, she smelled old

carpet. They walked through the foyer and went into the kitchen. Vernon took a beer from the fridge and sat down on a stool, looking out at the backyard. "Hey," he said, as if this were exactly what they both wanted. He pushed a second stool her way and she sat as he went to the fridge and pulled out another beer and passed it to her. She was aware of his height and how he could look down the front of her shirt. She shifted slightly and held a hand to her throat and drank, and after she had swallowed she said, "Thank you," and looked about.

The cabinets had been ripped from the walls and the sink was gone and there were wood scraps on the floor. The room smelled mouldy and dusty. There were boards with nails leaning up against one wall. She looked at her bare feet.

"Yeah, I was gonna warn you," Vernon said. "Watch for nails." He motioned at her feet and said that she had really nice arches. He held a finger in the air and closed one eye and moved his hand as if tracing her foot.

"Don't get weird," Lizzy said. She made a face.

"I like feet," Vernon said, and he bent over and touched her foot and said, "There."

"Don't," Lizzy said. She swivelled away from him and in doing so realized that she still had on her bathing-suit bottom beneath her shorts and her bum was still damp. Her bare legs seemed far too long and far too bare. She pressed them together. She asked where Alice was.

"What do you know about Alice?" Vernon smiled.

"You're gonna marry her. That's what she said."

"That a fact. And when did she say this?"

Lizzy saw Vernon's blond eyebrows and the freckles on his nose and brow. He was sweating. The underarms of his shirt were wet. She could smell him, a slight body odour, not bad, but definitely peculiar to him. "At the bar one night. She was there and she came over to talk and said she was getting married to Vernon. That would've been you, right?"

"We're not. Least, not yet. Maybe won't at all. Things change, right?"

"Does she know this?" Lizzy asked. She sensed Vernon's bravado disappearing.

He wiped at his face. "She knows what she wants to know."

"Funny. That's how everybody seems to live. Ears and eyes closed. Don't tell me if it's going to hurt. I don't want to know." She pointed the beer at Vernon. "Bet she'd be really happy to know that I was here in this house."

"She doesn't have to know."

Lizzy grimaced. "You trying to seduce me?"

"I don't know. Is it working?" He said she had the best eyes, really sleepy and wide set, and he stepped forward with his hand up as if to verify something about her face, or perhaps her eyes, and he took her jaw and leaned down and kissed her, roughly and quickly. She put a hand to his chest and stood. Her back was against the wall. When he spoke, his voice was quiet. He said that he was sorry, that he had miscalculated.

Lizzy repeated the word, *miscalculated*, and she nodded. "So did I," she said. And then she talked about Raymond. She said that she was in love with him. He was a better person than she was. She said that she wasn't trying to convince Vernon of her own goodness but sometimes goodness was evident in a person and this was the case with Raymond. She said that last year Raymond had been taken out to an island by Constable Hart and left there, then after nine days he had been rescued by a passing barge. "But you know the story," she said.

Vernon shook his head. He said that Raymond Seymour had capsized his boat and ended up on the island and almost died. Hart had had nothing to do with it. That was just a tall tale and she was gullible if she believed it.

"I believe it," she said. She looked back at the living room and beyond that, the two bedrooms. "I hope you have a good life here. With Alice." She put her beer down on the floor. Said that she'd hitchhike home. Okay? He shrugged. She turned and walked out expecting Vernon to follow her and offer her a ride, but he didn't. She walked past his pickup and up over the hill and down into the town, and just east of the movie theatre a woman in a camper picked her up and drove her home.

Raymond bought Corn Flakes, powdered milk, baby formula, apples, twenty tins of creamed corn, six pounds of bulk wieners, a dozen loaves of bread, eggs, syrup, margarine, camp-stove fuel, four jerry cans of gasoline, ten cartons of cigarettes, and fifteen boxes of .22 shells. He bought toilet paper and disposable diapers. He piled the supplies into the back of his pickup and covered them with a blue tarp, tying it down with pieces of rope he'd found behind the bench seat of his pickup. He drove out of town and through the reserve and on up to Bare Point where he unloaded the supplies and laid them out in the bottom of his boat.

He left in the dark and approached the landing at the back of the park without the aid of a light. As he rounded the point that led past Coney Island, he cut his engine and sat silently on the water. A fire burned on the shore. Figures gathered around the fire and then moved away. The water slapped the hull. He heard voices and saw the light of a police boat off to the left. He raised his engine and locked it into place. He picked up an oar and rowed his way through the channel and on towards the landing. The bow of the boat scraped the sand and he climbed out onto the shore. Two men appeared and pulled the boat up to secure it. Then the supplies were carried up to the camp.

Gary was pleased. He said so. Then he handed Raymond another list and another bundle of money and he told him that he should bring the next shipment in several days, and he shouldn't hang around the park. Gary squatted beside him, his knees cracking. He grunted. "Not the most exciting work, but necessary. You're the guy." He patted Raymond's shoulder, reached into his pocket and pulled out his cigarettes and handed one to Raymond. He stayed squatting and Raymond sat, holding his knees to his chest. They smoked and looked out at the dark lake. Lights glowed over on Coney Island. The flash of light from a police boat. A man calling out, and then silence. Gary put out his cigarette and lit another and he began to talk. It didn't appear that he was addressing Raymond in any way, but more that he had begun to talk to himself, or to some larger crowd. He said that the cowardly had their shenanigans. They weren't real. Weren't grounded. He said that he had great sympathy for the white man, who was limited in his knowledge of how to deal with the Indian, and it wasn't the white man's fault that he was ignorant, but sometimes you had to yell at him in order to get his attention. Like now, with the occupation. You had to shake people up. The Indian was a slave, had always been a slave of the invader, and would never understand that he was a slave. "We have to find again the place where we come from," he said. He looked at Raymond as if his had suddenly become a singular face in the larger crowd, and he said, "And you, Raymond. You need to find that place too. You need to let go of this need for the wider world. That white girl, that life over there." He stood, crushed his cigarette beneath his boot heel, and told Raymond that it was time.

Riding back to Bare Point, a strong westerly came up and carried with it heavy clouds and the smell of rain. The waves were high and walloped the bow, throwing water up over the gunnels and into the bottom of the boat. Raymond turned the stern to the wind and then aimed for shore. In the shelter of the shoreline he coasted, putting along slowly as he bailed water. He was wearing a thin jacket and the water had soaked him through. He began to shiver. The sound of his engine lifted into the air and was quickly caught and thrown elsewhere. When he reached Bare Point he moored the boat on the leeward side of the dock and then he walked up to his pickup and turned the key in the ignition and waited for the heat to blow as he rubbed his hands together, water dripping off of him and gathering at his feet.

He recalled Gary's words, that he needed to find the place where he'd come from. Raymond hadn't understood what he meant. And he hadn't asked.

❧

When he was fourteen, Raymond's uncle Jackson invited him up north for part of the winter. He spent his days checking traps and learning how to set snares. He learned the value of skinning muskrat and sucking marrow from the bones, and he learned to give thanks to the animal he had killed. He was taught that wolves are attracted to caribou intestines, and he learned that snares could also trap fox or coyotes and some-times moose. There were moments, riding the traplines, when he thought of home. He missed Kenora, and he missed his grandmother, and he missed the possibility of walking into town to watch a movie or buy a hamburger. In the evenings he played cards with his uncle and then they sat, without talking, before the stove, and while his uncle smoked, Raymond waited. Or he imagined he was waiting, though he could not have said what it was exactly he was waiting for.

In late December, Raymond and his uncle went out by snowmobile to check the traplines, and they got caught in a snowstorm. The storm blew in around noon, and by mid-afternoon, visibility was zero. Raymond was riding behind his uncle, his face pressed against his parka, and the wind and snow blew up under his hood and against his neck. At some point, the snowmobile stopped and his uncle climbed off, stood in the howling wind, and then leaned towards Raymond and said that they would stay here. He gestured at the ground and fell to his knees and began to dig. Raymond joined him and together they dug a tunnel in the snow and hollowed out a space at the end of the tunnel. This took somewhere near an hour, and by the time they were done, Raymond was sweating. They crawled down through the tunnel into the larger space, which was big enough to sit in. With the rifle that he always carried, Jackson fash-ioned an air hole, stuffing the barrel with a piece of cloth so as not to ruin it, and pushing the barrel up to the surface and wiggling it slightly. He chuckled, as if amused by his own inge-nuity, or as if he was pleased to have arrived at this place. He crawled back through the tunnel and covered the opening with loose snow, packing it, and immediately the sound of the wind disappeared and with it the light. Raymond heard him remove his parka. He told Raymond to do the same, and to use it under his bum. They sat cross-legged, knees touching. Raymond could not see his uncle, but he heard him breathing. His uncle lit a match and in the brief flare Raymond saw his uncle's face and his missing teeth and he saw his own hands. Perhaps his uncle saw fear in Raymond's eyes, because he began to hum something. It wasn't particularly musical, and Raymond didn't recognize any tune, but the sound his uncle made was comforting and it carried him away to a place where there was no danger. Even when his uncle stopped humming, the sound continued, until at some point Raymond realized that the noise was the wail of the wind above them, now audible again. They slept, and woke, and slept some more. His uncle had, in his pack, two chocolate bars, and they ate those slowly. They took snow and ate it, letting it melt in their mouths. When they had to pee, they knelt with their heads bent, and aimed at the walls that surrounded them. The stream of pee produced immediate warmth, and then it dissipated just as quickly.

When he was not sleeping, Raymond listened to the wind and to his uncle breathing and sometimes he asked questions, though his uncle was not given to lengthy answers. When he asked if they were going to die, his uncle laughed. He said that dying or not dying was not the point. He was quiet, and finally he said that he had lived out numerous storms, many worse than this. He asked Raymond if he was afraid to die. Raymond lied and said that he wasn't. His uncle chuckled. He said that fear of something only made you panic. He said that when a wolf was caught in a snare, like the one they caught the other day, it was the panic and fear that killed the wolf, not the snare. He said that he had once found the leg of a wolf beside a snare. The wolf had been caught by his hind leg and gnawed through the muscle and bone and taken its own leg off in order to survive. His uncle said that they might lose a finger or a foot to frostbite, but that was all. At about this point Raymond began to shiver. His whole body shook, and when he tried to speak, his voice rattled along with his jaw. His uncle asked him if he could feel his feet. Raymond wiggled his toes inside his boots and said he could feel them, though they were numb. His uncle told him to hit them together. His hands as well. He moved closer to Raymond and put his arms around him and pushed Raymond's head against his chest. He breathed on the top of his skull and Raymond felt the heat of his uncle's breath and he smelled him, a mix of wood smoke and sweat and grease. He eventually stopped shaking and he fell asleep in his uncle's arms. When he woke he was alone. Light fell in through the open hole and when Raymond climbed up into the sunshine he discovered a lake of snow and in the distance, a single line out on that bright lake, his uncle stood, head raised, talking to the sky.

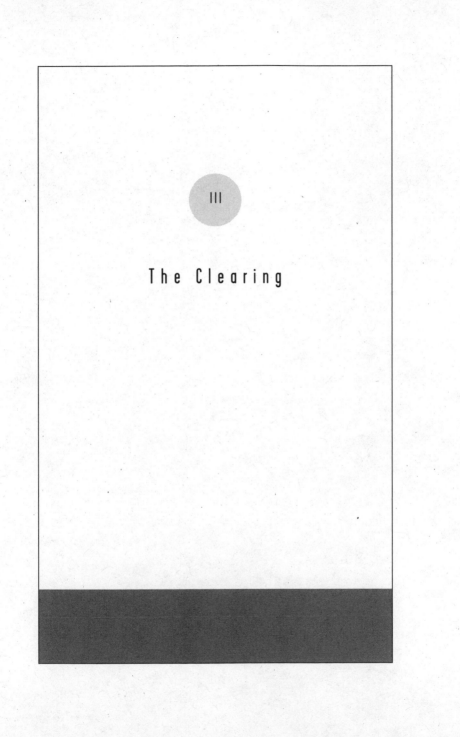

III

The Clearing

In 1964, at the age of ten, Nelson Seymour was taken from his grandmother's house on the reserve near Kenora and placed with a Mennonite family in a small town called Lesser, south of Winnipeg. A white man and a white woman came to the reserve in a blue Ford Galaxy looking for two brothers, Raymond and Nelson, but Nelson was the only one home with his grandmother at the time. He was taken immediately. His grandmother tried to stop them but her pleas were ineffectual. The man was wearing a fedora and he took it off and held it at his hip and he said, "Where is the other boy, Raymond?" The grandmother looked at the floor. Then she lied and said that he was away, up north with his father. The man in the fedora looked around at the bicycles in the yard and the old swing. It was autumn and the leaves were gone from the trees and the wind was sharp and cold. The man looked down at a piece of paper that he held in his hand. "It says here that Raymond Seymour has been attending school. How is that?"

The grandmother turned her gaze to the sky and shrugged and said that the school people were wrong. The man looked at Nelson. "Your brother, Raymond, where is he?"

Nelson glanced at his grandmother, who regarded him and nodded. Nelson imitated her nod, and then began to cry. The man put his hat on and then turned away and walked out towards the car with a weeping Nelson, while the woman gathered up a few of his things. The grandmother called out that Nelson was hers and where were they going with him, but there was no answer.

Later that night, Raymond was back home and his grandmother told him that the government folks had taken Nelson, and she said that she didn't know when he was coming back. She didn't know where he was going, maybe to live with a white family because this is what had happened to Elijah Prince a month earlier. She said that Nelson was strong, stronger than Raymond. Her hands were folded on the table and they were shaking. The next morning she brought Raymond to stay with his aunt Donna, off the reserve about five miles away. Raymond remained there for two months. He did not attend school any more that fall, and no questions were asked, and it would be years later that he'd learn that he should have been taken with his brother, and might have been if the authorities had decided to come back for him.

Within the first month at his new home, Nelson ran away three times, once almost making it back to Kenora before the police picked him up. Another time, in the middle of January, his adoptive father found him walking on Highway 59, just outside Île des Chênes. Driving back to Lesser, his new father said that Nelson should start appreciating what he'd been given. "You have a mother and father who love you, you have a wonderful home, clothes, food, you have three sisters who would do anything for you. Your name is Nelson Koop, you're my son now and I'm your father. No one's going to hurt you. You understand that?"

It had snowed the day before, and the fields were blown over and everywhere there was a pure whiteness that was blinding in the sun. Nelson looked out the passenger window and studied the fields and imagined walking out into the emptiness. After this last escape he did not run again, though he often thought of it. At the beginning of the year he'd been placed in grade five and he'd done very poorly. Halfway through the term, he was sent down to grade four where the boys made fun of him, though they stayed away from him because he was known for having quick, hard fists. On the first day of school a boy named Benjamin Senkiew had hit him and given him a bloody nose. The following day, passing by Senkiew in the hallway, Nelson attacked him and pummelled his face until he was pulled away by the gym teacher. He was suspended for a week and returned to find that he was neither taunted nor talked to and he grew accustomed to the silence and the grudging respect and the hatred that surrounded him.

The fall he turned fourteen he joined the football team and quickly became known for his ruthlessness and his disregard for his own body. He came to be accepted, and for a time he went out with Glenda Ratzlaff, a tall, thin girl, but her father disapproved, and so all he was left with was the recollection of her soft hands sliding up inside his T-shirt as they stood in the cold night behind the curling rink.

As the years passed he relinquished the memories of who he was and where he had come from, though there were times, in the middle of the night, when he woke from a dream in which someone was calling him by the wrong name, and he would sit up and say, "My name is Nelson Seymour."

His new parents had never hidden the fact that he was adopted and that he came from a reserve in Kenora; however, his knowledge, his education, his religion, all of this was steeped in the world of Mennonites and the faith of Mennonites, and in many ways he was more Mennonite than Ojibway. One summer, his family rented a cottage on the Lake of the Woods and as they drove through Kenora the familiarity and smell fell down upon him. One morning, very early, he stepped out onto the dock of the cabin where the family was staying. A fog hovered over the water and the rising sun appeared as a weak lamp through the haze. A loon called and then floated into view and the smell of the pulp-and-paper mill carried across the water. A chasm opened up before him and he experienced a sharp ache in his heart. Later, when he went up to the cabin, Mrs. Koop was making coffee. She was wearing her bathing suit for her early-morning swim and she had fastened a towel around her waist. She turned to look at him as if inviting him to speak, but he didn't tell her what he had seen or felt.

At the age of thirteen he had become a Christian, and was baptized into the Lesser Mennonite Brethren Church. He wore a purple choir robe over a T-shirt and shorts, and the pastor, when he immersed him, held the back of his head firmly. His father was very pleased with his decision and his mother invited relatives and friends for lunch, and after a meal of rice casserole, corn, and Jell-O salad, Nelson played a brief viola concert for the guests who praised him for his virtuosity.

And then, in his last year of high school, after years of being offered other people's ideas of how he should live, he began to make his own choices. He quit school and took a job as a truck driver at the local feed mill; this put money in his pocket. He had a series of girlfriends, of whom the last was Joelle Picard. She was so sure of herself, so easily giving with him, that he began to see himself in a more generous light. And then one night they got drunk together and Joelle teasingly called him an Indian. Nelson leaned into her, took her jaw in his hand, and squeezed until she cried out. As this was happening, he felt he was standing outside of himself, watching someone else twist Joelle's porcelain chin, and he felt a dismay that surprised him. He never saw her again.

The following month he stole a pickup and drove west until it ran out of gas. He hitchhiked home and was picked up by a young couple who wanted to know where he was from. He said Kenora, and the girl, who wore her brown hair in braids, turned and looked at him for a long time and then she grinned and offered him some hashish. "This is great shit," she said. When they dropped him off in Winnipeg, the girl climbed from the car and hugged him, looping her bare arms around his neck. Nelson imagined strangling her boyfriend and living forever with this beautiful girl. The idea did not seem far-fetched.

In early spring, he left his home in Lesser and lived in Winnipeg with Abe, the brother to his adopted father. Abe operated the elevator out of the Bate Building on McDermot. He lived in a one-bedroom apartment on the third floor and he offered Nelson the living-room couch, from where he could hear fights on the sidewalk below, gigantic blow-ups full of cursing and threats and ineffectual swings. One night there was a brawl involving fourteen men. Nelson leaned out the window to watch. The police eventually arrived and confiscated the pipes and crowbars and baseball bats. Drunken men were herded into a paddy wagon and taken away. One man was ferried off in an ambulance.

Abe, claiming Nelson had no muscle on him and probably needed something more manly in his life than a sissy viola, enrolled Nelson in the local gym on Princess where he learned to box in a haphazard fashion. He ran with the other boxers through the streets of downtown Winnipeg and returned to the gym to jump rope. He was not a smooth fighter but he had a dirty streak and it was this meanness that his trainer failed to coax out of him. In the evenings, Nelson walked up Albert Street and passed by the drunks who hung out by the back door of a local hotel. Many times he saw himself standing at the entrance to the bar, on the verge of entering, but then he turned away. He knew that at some point he would travel out to Kenora to look for his family. He was afraid and found all kinds of reasons not to do this until, one afternoon, he hitchhiked east and arrived in the town he had left ten years earlier. There, he asked after his family, and it did not take long to find his brother Raymond living in the cabin near Bare Point. The following week a celebration took place at his grandmother's house. Cousins and uncles and aunts arrived and his grandmother made blueberry pie and there was a feast laid out on the table: macaroni salad, fried fish, duck soup,

Klik, Tang, mashed potatoes, and perogies. Nelson told his cousin Gerald that he had eaten lots of perogies in Lesser, only they were called verenika. Gerald looked at him and said, "That how you got fat?" and he laughed and Nelson saw that Gerald was missing a front tooth. Nelson knew that he was being offered a form of love, but it felt hard and strange and he didn't know what to do with it. He had called his step-mother that day to let her know where he was, and Mrs. Koop had said that she missed him. "We all miss you," she said. "The door is open." He said that he knew that.

In the evening, late, his sister Reenie sang a few gospel songs in a clear, bright voice. Then she strummed her guitar and asked if Hank Williams would suit, and then not waiting for a reply she sang "I'm So Lonesome I Could Cry." When she was finished she said, "We didn't know where you were, Nelson, and they wouldn't tell us. We were just waiting and waiting for you to come home. Ten years. It's amazing, isn't it? Welcome back."

That night, after he and Raymond got back to the cabin, he lay in bed and listened to his brother breathing and he thought about his grandmother never really looking at him and no one saying anything about where he'd been, or even asking where he'd been, and he'd felt arrogant and lost and superior to all these dumb people that were supposed to be his family. He desperately missed the Koops.

He had got a job tending the garbage dump, his brother mowed the grass at the golf course, and in the evenings, after dark, they sat in the silence of the cabin and Nelson talked about boxing and how he enjoyed the feel of his fist hitting another man's face. One night, about a month after Nelson had returned, Raymond told him that he still remembered when he, Nelson, was taken. "I come home from Charlie's — you remember him — and you're just gone. Grandma tells me what happened and I'm thinking you must have turned white as soon as you climbed into the car." They were sitting at the table. A dog barked outside somewhere. Raymond turned to look at his brother, but he could only see his outline in the dim light of the candles. He said, "Grandma took me straight up to Aunt Donna's for a while. She only told me later that they were looking for me too."

"Yeah? That what she said?" Nelson lit a cigarette and in the brief flare Raymond saw his eyes clearly. "Maybe she lied."

"Why would she lie?"

"You jealous? Wishing *you* could have gone on that trip?"

"I didn't know, that's all. I didn't know." Raymond reached for Nelson's cigarettes and then, as if to conceal any emotion, he said, "Maybe Grandma *did* call up the government folks and ask them to take away her Nelson because he was too smart and needed some white people to push some dumbness deep into him. And they succeeded." He grinned.

"Fuck you," Nelson said.

Raymond drank water from the dipper. Nelson wondered why Raymond didn't drink beer, if he didn't like the taste.

"Not that," Raymond said.

"Something else, then? Maybe you're diabetic?" Nelson laughed.

"Not interested, that's all," Raymond said.

"I hated Sundays in my home," Nelson said. "Went to church in the morning and then came home and ate roast beef and corn and potatoes and in the afternoon nothing moved. Stand on the driveway and look out down the road. There was dust and the occasional bike and I thought that life had ended." He said that there was space here as well, but this space was different and more generous. "Christianity, God, that was everything," he said.

"Like Reenie," Raymond said.

"Yeah, I guess. She takes it seriously."

"Seems so."

"I took it seriously. Still do in some ways. It's clapped on my back like a fucking rudder." He got up and took another beer and said that the water was deeper than he had been led to believe.

Raymond looked at him and said that he spoke in riddles and what was that supposed to mean. "If you think you're better than us, what you doing here?"

"I never said that."

"You think it. Talking about this and that and boxing and God and using big words that I've never heard before and letting us know that you play viola, whatever the hell that is, and all the books you've read and the girls you've fucked and what you doing now? Pushing garbage around on a hill."

"Shit. Never said I fucked a bunch of girls. Anyway, boys had to go to St. Pierre and St. Adolphe to get laid. Friendly little Catholic girls."

Raymond was quiet.

"I remember the beginning," Nelson said. "I cried and cried. Finally, they sent Emily down to me at night. That was my older sister. She'd hold my hand and talk and read to me and talk some more. I don't remember any more what she said, but her voice was soft and low and she smelled sweet."

Raymond said that Nelson had been lucky to have someone like Emily Koop holding his hand. He said that he'd stopped eating for a week after Nelson was taken away, and then one day their grandma had come out to Aunt Donna's where he was living and she poured milk down his throat until he choked and threw up. She wasn't mean about it, he said, and she kept repeating that this was for his own good, and then after he'd thrown up a second time she sat him down and made him lick peanut butter off a spoon. She did this several more times until he started eating real food again.

"I didn't know," Nelson said.

"'Course you didn't. How could you? You were gone."

"You did that?" Nelson's voice was low and quiet, his face lifted towards Raymond's.

"I didn't cry at all. Just stopped eating."

"Didn't cry, eh? One tough shit you were." Nelson reached forward and punched Raymond lightly on the side of his head.

"You could teach me how to fight," Raymond said. "Show me how to hold my hands."

Nelson shook his head and said that fighting was a dangerous thing. "Makes you believe you can take on anybody, anywhere. You don't want that." Then he said that the Koops had taught him how to hug. Mrs. Koop was always going on about how he didn't hug properly, how he always kept his arms at his sides like he was a dead animal, and so she made him wrap his arms around her and squeeze. "Here," Nelson said, and he reached for Raymond, grasping at his neck. Raymond slipped away. Laughed and said, "Fuck off."

Nelson went after him, kicked over the chair and lunged at his brother. Caught him around his waist and threw him down on the wood floor. Raymond fell hard and the breath went out of him, but he swung his elbow and hit Nelson in the ribs, just below his heart. Nelson bellowed and pinned Raymond's shoulders to the floor with his knees. Straddled him with his crotch near Raymond's throat. They were both breathing heavily. Nelson was grinning. "Suck mine," he said. Raymond writhed and fought and then stopped moving.

Nelson released his brother, rolled away, and lay on his back looking up at the ceiling. He reached for a cigarette and lit it. There was a long silence, and it seemed that neither one of them wanted, or even knew how, to break it. Then Nelson said, his voice quiet, "Surprise is all. That's how you beat the shit out of someone. Remember that."

They shared the cigarette. Then Raymond talked about high school, about Alice, about the island and how he was left for dead by Alice's policeman uncle. He took a long time to tell his story. He added details he had forgotten, the colour of the sky, the wind at night, the sound of wolves over on the mainland, the hatred in Earl Hart's eyes. He said that he had not been scared of death, and he had thought, by the ninth day, that he would probably die, and then he'd been rescued. He said that being on the island had helped him understand the pointlessness of his own existence. Not that he didn't want to live. No, he did. But he had seen that he was no different from that tree, or that rock, or that bird he'd killed, or that fish leaping out of the water, or those clouds above him.

When Raymond finished talking they sat together in the silence while the candles guttered on the table. Then Nelson said that he had grown up being taught that there was a God who was willing to save anyone who wanted to be saved. "But then I get to wondering what you do with a man like Hart? Can he be saved? Maybe God's just looking down and laughing at the things we do to each other. Maybe he doesn't care much."

"Well, he made the world," Raymond said. "And I guess he should care about it. You don't make something and then turn around and say, 'This is crap, I'm gonna burn it.'"

"You might."

"But you probably wouldn't."

"Know what I think? You don't know shit."

"Fuck you."

"Okay, how many days to make the world?"

"For your God, and your story? Seven."

"Six, asshole. On the seventh day God laid back and got a blow job."

Raymond laughed.

Nelson called himself blasphemous and Raymond said that he had no idea what that was.

"You heard the story about Joseph?" Nelson asked. "Gets sold by his brothers?"

"Joseph who."

"Shit. I'll tell it to you sometime."

One of the candles flickered and went out. Outside, down by the creek, an animal moved and the night drifted.

When Raymond finally showed up at the Retreat it was a Sunday, a week or so later, and Lizzy walked up to him where he stood in his boots and jeans and a red snap-button shirt that was too small on him. He'd grown a moustache and it was minor, somewhat uneven. She noted it, but said nothing. He wore a bandana and his rifle was on a rack in the rear window of the pickup.

"You wanna go away from here," he asked. "A ride maybe?"

She wanted to say yes, but she was confused by the mix of desire and anger she felt. She said, "Just like that? You abandon me and then come back and you think everything's the same? That I'm just gonna hop in your truck and go for a ride?"

He shrugged, and as he did so she wanted to slap him, make him feel something. He said that she could think what she wanted, but he hadn't *abandoned* her. "We married or something?"

She put her hand against his chest and pushed him so that he stumbled backwards. "Or something," she said. She saw them both as teetering on the edge of a cliff and she understood that the wrong words might send one of them tumbling. She didn't want that. She walked around to the passenger door and climbed into the pickup. Raymond got in, shaking his head and smiling.

"I'm not interested in fighting with you," she said, and she slouched in her seat and told him to drive.

They went through town and then west on the 71 towards the Manitoba border. After a while Raymond slowed and took a side road down towards a small lake and he parked at the entrance to a boat ramp, which appeared to be no longer used. He lit a cigarette and threw the match out the window. They hadn't talked much during the drive, but Lizzy had been aware of Raymond's sense of purpose, even in the silence, and how he appeared older. Her anger gradually subsided and what remained was resignation. She sat and looked straight ahead and told Raymond that she felt like a person who had been lost in a desert and then suddenly, before her, he had appeared holding water in his cupped hands. Only the water was quickly disappearing and she wasn't even sure if the water was meant for her. She looked at him. "I missed you," she said.

He said that she told a great story, did she know that? "The desert, the water. Where do you come up with that stuff?" He reached out and touched the back of her head. "I missed you too."

"Really? You're not just saying that because you're supposed to?"

"Am I? Supposed to?" He slid his hand down her neck. "Trust me," he said.

"You're not in trouble, are you?" she asked. "When I was up there, at the park, the police made you out to be criminals.

I don't want you getting hurt." She said that those men, Lionel
and Gary, maybe they were like the Doctor at the Retreat,
who just kept talking until his vision sounded perfect. Maybe
the leaders of the occupation were the same. She said that
adults could be pretty fucked up. "I was worried about you."

He closed his eyes and said that he felt something bad was
going to happen. "You know?" He patted his stomach. "Right
there. Hard to breathe." He said that the feeling had been there
for about a week.

Lizzy put her hand on his stomach. "Maybe it's excitement," she said. "All that power." She punched him lightly
and laughed, but he didn't laugh with her. She slid towards
him and took his face in her hands and kissed him and he let
her do this. She pulled away and studied his face, the darkness she could not gain entry into. She kissed him again, resolute now, desperate even, and then she fell back and said that
he'd changed.

He lifted a hand and let it fall onto his thigh and he said
that he was no longer sure about anything. He said he'd
dreamed recently that he was a small animal on a string. She
laughed. "You silly boy," she said. "It doesn't matter." She put
her head against his chest. "Everything's fine."

Driving back up into Kenora she leaned against the passenger
door. His smell was all over her, in her nose, on her fingers,
her breasts, inside her. She felt a sleepiness brought on by a
feeling of well-being, and her eyes closed briefly, and she may
have slept. Raymond, turning once in a while to look at her,

saw that she did sleep because her fingers jumped lightly, and this allowed him the freedom to observe her. She had taken off her sandals and had tucked her legs up beneath her and her feet lay very close to his thigh. He saw the bones of her feet, their smallness, her naked ankles, and though he had just seen her completely naked, he had not felt then her vulnerability and her hopefulness. Her hair fell dark across her left cheek and obscured her jaw. Her shoulders were thin and her breasts were small and he knew that her spine resembled a column of pebbles laid out in perfect symmetry. Lying back on the grass, he had kissed her shoulders and the small of her back just half an hour earlier.

After making love they had stood in the sunshine and Lizzy had asked about the tarp covering the back of the pickup, what was underneath it. He'd shown her the groceries. He said that the job he'd been given by the leaders of the occupation was to get food and deliver it to the park. He was going to go out there later. He said that the police had closed the park entrance and there was no way of bringing in food and there were children going hungry. He paused, as if uncertain about the words he was using, and then he said that he delivered the food by boat.

She hadn't registered any particular surprise. She'd lifted the tarp and said, "Diapers," and she'd wondered if the sex had made her soft.

About halfway back to Kenora, Lizzy woke and sat up. Her cheek was creased from sleeping against the side of the door. Raymond reached over and touched her face. Perhaps because of the distraction of Lizzy, or perhaps because of his own sense of happiness, Raymond didn't see the vehicle or the flashing lights behind him. Only when the short burp of a siren sounded did he look in his rear-view mirror. He did not understand at first that the police cruiser was asking him to stop. When he finally caught on, he slowed and he muttered, "Shit," and then he said it again as he stopped on the shoulder.

"Who?" Lizzy said, and she turned to look back.

A local constable. And Raymond's hands began to shake as the policeman climbed out of the cruiser. It was Earl Hart.

"Fuck," he said.

Hart approached the driver's side. Raymond sat straight, both hands on the wheel. And then Hart was standing there, leaning in slightly, and he said, "Mr. Seymour." He surveyed the cab, took in the floor, the gun rack, then Lizzy. Rested his gaze on Lizzy for a long while and then he said, "Well, well."

Raymond took out his cigarettes and lit one. His hands were shaking.

"Thought it might be you," Hart said. "Saw the gun in the back window and figured that that was mighty brazen. And I wondered, does this boy have a permit for such a weapon and such, and so I thought I'd make enquiries. Same someone new. Some people have all the luck, eh?" Raymond just looked straight ahead.

"What's your name again?" He was speaking to Lizzy, but he was watching Raymond.

She said her name, first and last.

"Right. Right." He asked if she had ID.

She said she didn't.

"Not on you." He nodded, as if this were to be pondered.

Raymond spoke into the windshield. "I'm not in the wrong."

Hart chuckled. "You've been in the wrong most of your life. I hear you're having a good time up at the park. Pretty big event. Playing warrior. Scaring little children. Must feel like a real man. What's in back?" He straightened up and turned, leaning towards the box and lifting the edge of the tarp. He let the tarp drop. "Setting up a trading post are we? Step out of the vehicle. Both of you."

Lizzy reached for the door handle and Raymond said, "Don't." She turned to look at Raymond who reached for his own door handle and said, "Stay in the truck."

Hart moved back to allow Raymond room, and as he did so, Raymond turned and swung his feet up and kicked out against his door. The door bucked outwards in a wild arc and caught Hart on the chest and waist and crotch. His face showed surprise as the air went out of him, and then he fell.

Lizzy screamed.

Raymond climbed from the pickup and bent over Hart. He tugged Hart's pistol from the holster and heaved the gun into the ditch. Then he walked over to the cruiser and reached inside and switched off the engine and pulled the keys from the ignition and threw them across the road into the ditch on the other side. When he came back to the pickup, Hart was attempting to rise. Raymond stepped around him and climbed in. He leaned out his window and said, "Watch your feet." He pushed the stick shift up into first and drove off.

Lizzy turned to look out the rear window and then back to Raymond and said, "Why? Why? He asked you to get out of the truck, that's all."

"That's right."

"He wasn't going to do anything. Jesus, Raymond." She began to whimper. "Now what?"

"Listen." He looked at her. "Calm down. I'll drop you off at the Retreat later. Okay? He doesn't care about you. He wants to get me. Even more now. You're over there somewhere, so don't worry. You've got to leave me deal with this."

"I'm a witness," Lizzy said. "You didn't do anything wrong." She began to hiccup and this brought on more sounds similar to laughter. Raymond took her hand.

She said that there would be more than just one policeman coming to look for him. Didn't he know that? "You can't assault a cop and just get away with it." Then she said that she wouldn't leave him. That they should go to the police station and turn themselves in and she would be a witness for him. At this, Raymond turned on her and said, "I don't need a witness. No witness. Never had one before, don't need one now."

She sat upright and stared straight ahead as if she was gauging the light that fell across her arm and onto the dashboard where it revealed the dust that lay there. She felt the warmth of the sun on her right arm and imagined that she was sitting with the ease of a young girl out for a ride in the country. The light on the hairs on her arm made them appear more golden than they actually were. Her feet were resting on the dash and her legs were bent and they were at the level of her eyes and the light that fell across her arm and partially across her chest also fell onto her legs. And so she was warmed by the light that came from the sun.

❧

Nelson was at the cabin. He was sitting on the swing and when they pulled up he raised his head and watched them. They went to him and Raymond said he'd hit a cop, Earl Hart, and that Hart would probably be coming after him. He looked over his shoulder, back down the road, and he said that he thought he should pack and leave.

He went to the truck and took three beers from the case in the back. He found a screwdriver in the cab, popped one cap, and gave the bottle to Lizzy. He did the same for Nelson. Then he opened his own beer, drank, and said that there might be a convoy of police cruisers coming down the road any time.

"I don't think so," Nelson said. "You're not that important."

"What'll I do?" Raymond asked. He was leaning towards his brother, who waved a hand and patted the seat beside him and said, "Sit, relax. If he comes, he comes, but he won't come. Isn't that right, Lizzy?"

Lizzy squinted and looked away and thought that she should be back at the Retreat with Fish and William. Down by the pond. Getting ready for dinner. Margaret would be calling for them right about now.

Nelson lit a cigarette and handed it to Raymond. They sat side by side, with Lizzy standing and facing them. Raymond told the story again, as if by retelling it the facts might change, but they didn't, and as he spoke the sun dropped behind the cabin and then below the trees. Then, as if rising from a deep sleep, Raymond sat up straight and said, "We gotta go. Now." And he stood and went into the cabin. When he returned he sat down again and by the time dusk arrived he was well into his fourth beer. He appeared to have shrugged off what had transpired on the highway and the conversation had turned to alcohol and its comforts and dangers. Raymond said that he was not a happy drinker, and that it would be wise for Lizzy to leave before things turned wild. Nelson could drive her home. But no one made any move to rise, and Lizzy understood that she remained outside of the world these two brothers inhabited.

For the next while she tried to convince Raymond that he should turn himself in. She said that she would vouch for him.

Nelson laughed and said, "Vouch for him? Maybe you could write up some sort of warranty promising that he will behave, and that he is in no way dangerous, and that the world would be a better place if we had more boys like Raymond." He raised his beer bottle and pointed it at Lizzy. "Who do you think you are?"

"Leave her the fuck alone," Raymond said.

Lizzy ducked her head and stood. With the sun having set, the air was cooler and she felt the cold on her back. She shivered and went inside. She sat down and rested her elbows on the table and watched the flame bend and waver in the smoky glass of the lamp. She heard Raymond and Nelson talking, their voices rising and falling. She laid her head on her arms, and she must have fallen asleep because when she opened her eyes Raymond was standing beside her. He put his hand on her back and said that he was worried about her. He would drive her home, okay? She stood and studied him and said he couldn't drive, he'd been drinking too much, and besides, Hart would be looking for him. She would walk back by herself. He began to protest, but she waved him away and said it would be safer to walk.

She went outside, past the swing where Nelson still sat. He watched her walk by but he said nothing. She walked down the trail beyond the pickup and into the dark corridor of trees that led to the main road and then down that road. The noises of the night were all around her, the sounds of animals scurrying in the ditches, the call of night birds. At one point, she saw an arc of light from an approaching vehicle. She slipped down into the ditch and crouched there and when the vehicle passed she saw that it was a police cruiser. She watched the tail lights disappear and she considered returning to where she had come from, but the possibility of what she would find there frightened her, and so she turned and continued down the road towards the Retreat.

art arrived from the rear. He had parked a hundred yards down the trail, got out of the cruiser, and worked his way through the bush up towards the cabin. He approached the Seymour boys from the back, as they sat side by side in their piece-of-shit swing, admiring their pitiful rifle. He laid the muzzle of his pistol against the back of Raymond's neck and he said, "Slow, boys. No sudden movements." To Nelson, he said, "Empty the chamber of the rifle and then lay it down on the ground."

Nelson began to turn, but Hart swung his pistol away from Raymond's spinal cord and caught Nelson across the cheekbone. Nelson swore. "Do as I say," Hart said.

Nelson dropped the shells he was holding onto the ground and then laid the gun at his feet. He spoke then, sidelong to his brother, in a voice that revealed no fear, no anger. "This would be Hart, then," he said. He turned and saw the man holding the gun. In the darkness, he looked him up and down, and he laughed.

"Don't do that," Raymond said.

"Let's go." Hart gestured at the cabin, the open door. They walked, the three of them forming a triangle, towards the cabin. Inside, the flame of the lamp fluttered and danced and in that dancing Raymond saw the darkness at the corners of the room. He moved over towards his brother, who was leaning against the far wall. He felt sluggish and weary.

Hart held the pistol at chest level and moved it back and forth, from boy to boy. He asked where the girl was.

"What girl?" Nelson said.

Hart pushed his chin out at Raymond. "You know the one. Liz something. Bird."

"She flew away." This was Nelson again. He wouldn't stand still and he wouldn't shut up and this seemed to make Hart nervous.

Hart looked around, motioned at the bedroom and said, "What's in there?" He stepped backwards and looked into the room and then at the boys. "Regular palace you got here."

Then he said that Raymond had made the wrong decision that afternoon. He said all he had wanted was a show of respect. And now look where he was. "Stuck in a shit-hole cabin, looking down the barrel of a gun." He said that he had come alone. "Wanted to deal with this myself. My way."

He looked at Nelson and asked him his name.

"Geronimo," Nelson said.

Hart nodded. He reached down to his belt and unlatched the handcuffs there and held them in his left hand. He said that he wanted Raymond to put them on. He didn't want any more trouble. Things could go from bad to worse or they could get better. He reached out with the hand that held the cuffs and asked Raymond to move away from the wall, to put his hands behind his back. He said, "Geronimo, you back over towards the door."

Neither of the boys moved. A low groan rose from Raymond's belly and went up his chest and floated out his mouth. It was like the sound of a boat grinding against its mooring, and as the sound erupted, Nelson turned to his brother and saw that Raymond's shoulders were shaking and his chest was heaving.

Nelson stepped towards his brother, who waved him away. Nelson told Hart that his brother wasn't interested in handcuffs. And where would he take his brother, in any case? Back out to that island? He said that this time anywhere his brother went, he would go as well. "Take me," Nelson said, and he hunched towards Hart and held out his wrists. Hart, wary, moved to snap on the cuffs, and as he did so, Nelson swung outwards with his left fist and caught Hart's gun hand, on the meaty part of the palm. The gun fired and the bullet went through the ceiling and the gun landed in a corner of the room. He jabbed with his right hand at Hart's mouth and caught his ear because the man had ducked, then kicked at Nelson's feet. Nelson went over and fell hard on his back and he felt the air go out of him. He heard Raymond cry out, and he saw Hart's boot coming at his head, and he knew the man was quicker than he'd thought and that he could not avoid the blow. He pulled backwards to lessen the impact and Hart's heel caught him across the jaw. The pain stunned him briefly and then he rolled sideways, scrambling around the legs of the table, rocking the lamp, which stayed upright and remained burning, a flickering and unholy light that cast long shadows. Hart chased him, calling him a nasty little motherfucker who had all kinds of suffering coming his way. Then,

as if he were a magician, he produced a club in his right hand
and a knife in his left. Raymond moved in and Nelson told
him to get back. Nelson feinted and dodged, aware of his
brother's voice dropping down on him as if from a great distance. He saw Hart's small forehead and the round nose, the
half-closed eyes, which in turn watched his own. The two men
circled the room, alert to each other's movements and the ini-
tiation of fear; enacting a dance that was age-old and final.
Nelson felt no fear. The purity of this act, the notion that you
could strip down to this one single purpose. Hart jabbed with
the club and then his other arm arced and the knife passed
across Nelson's chest and opened him up, just below the
nipples. His shirt blossomed with blood. He looked down
and saw the blood and he heard his own small grunt and the
larger "Ahhh" of Hart's voice. Raymond made a keening
noise. Hart pounced forward, sure of himself now, driving
the knife towards Nelson's throat, his face full of anticipation,
just as Raymond leapt onto Hart's back, wrapping his arms
around his face. Hart stumbled and bellowed with rage. The
knife fell to the floor and Hart flailed with his club at the
heavy burr stuck to his back. Nelson, seizing the advantage,
reached for the knife just as Hart, still carrying Raymond,
lunged at him. Nelson held the knife out, and Hart, blinded
by Raymond's grasp, fell forward and the blade went deep
into his chest. He gave a slow, long moan.

Raymond stumbled upwards and whispered, his voice
rasping and fearful, "Did you kill him?"

"I don't know. He just fell onto the knife." Nelson looked
at his own chest. Blood had soaked his shirt and pants and

was dripping down onto the floor. He walked to the sink and took a towel and held it to the wound, then tied a T-shirt around his chest. Raymond was standing over Hart. He was stooped slightly, looking down at the body as if he were teetering at the edge of a deep gorge and measuring its depth. "He's breathing," he said. He went down on his knees and touched the knife in the man's chest.

Nelson took a chair and sat down and observed the scene. The back of his brother's head, the policeman's foot twisted to the left, the blood on the floor. He sat, breathing with difficulty. Raymond came over to the table. "Now what?" he asked.

"They'll have tracker dogs and Christ knows what coming after me." He held his palms to the ceiling as if imploring to a beneficent God. "I'm fucked."

"He tried to kill you," Raymond said. "He did. Try."

Nelson said that he would have to pack clothes and food and water. He'd take the .22 and some shells. He said that Raymond should drop him off on the dump road. "I'll hide out for the night and then find some place safer," he said. "Don't worry, I won't get caught." He said that it would be Raymond's job to bring Hart to the hospital. No one would suspect him then. It wasn't the best plan, but it was necessary. "We can't have him dead. If they ask, and they will, tell them you had nothing to do with this. Can you do that?"

"They won't believe me."

"Just do it."

Raymond said that he wanted to help Nelson. "I'll come back for you."

Nelson shook his head. "It's better we separate. Like I said, you did nothing."

They sat and watched Hart breathe, the knife rising and sinking in his chest. Raymond said that he'd thought Nelson was a dead man. "And if you were dead, so was I."

Nelson stood and left the room, returning with a silver-coloured duffle bag into which he put canned goods and .22 shells and a sweater and socks and some fruit and bread. He filled several sealer jars with water, screwed on the lids, and put them in the bag. He called for Bull, and when she appeared he picked her up. She sniffed at his T-shirt and clawed his arm. He took the cat outside and pushed her into the bag. She fought and hissed but he zipped the bag shut and put it into the box of the pickup. When he came back Raymond was again bent over Hart.

"He's barely breathing now," Raymond said.

Together they carried Hart out to the pickup and placed him in the box, laying him down on the tarp that covered the supplies destined for the park. Hart groaned as they laid him out. Raymond climbed into the box and rearranged his position. He pushed toilet-paper rolls under his head as cushioning. He climbed out and they stood, looking down at the body.

Nelson grunted with pain.

Raymond carefully lifted his brother's shirt, unwrapped the T-shirt he had tied around his chest, and studied the wound with the aid of a flashlight. The cut was deep and the wound was oozing blood. Raymond reapplied the T-shirt, tying it tighter this time. He went into the house and came back with a half-full bottle of whisky and handed it to Nelson. Then he got into the cab and turned the ignition.

Nelson sat in the back of the pickup with Hart. His chest hurt. With every corner and every jolt he sucked air between his teeth and closed his eyes. When he opened them again he saw the stars in the black sky. There were multitudes and some he knew were already dead, which was a fact he had picked up in Mr. Zeiroth's science class in grade nine. He knew too that everything inanimate was indifferent to his plight at that moment. The rocks, the trees, the stars themselves. Nothing was eternal. He had been baptized as a young teenager. He had done this willingly, believing in eternity. He had wanted to please his stepfather and he had succeeded, but his own pleasure had eventually dissipated. Nothing lasted. He looked down at Hart's squat body and thought that the man would gladly have killed him. The desire had been there on his face and in his eyes.

At the dirt road that led to the dump, Raymond stopped and Nelson climbed from the back of the pickup. He held the rifle under his arm, lifted the duffle bag from the box, and stood by the open driver's window.

Raymond lit a cigarette and gave the pack to Nelson, who slipped it into his jacket pocket.

"You got fire?" Raymond asked.

Nelson said yes.

"You gonna just disappear?"

Nelson shrugged, then he walked off.

The last thing Raymond saw was the bag swinging back and forth like a poorly lit lamp, and then it too was gone.

In the morning it was raining. Lizzy carried Fish down the path to the kitchen. She ran in bare feet and she carried an umbrella and Fish squealed and laughed and Lizzy felt his hot breath on her neck. She had not slept much, perhaps an hour or two. Images of Raymond on the swing beside his brother. And the police cruiser passing by. And her long walk back to the Retreat, arriving just before dawn. She had crawled into bed beside Fish, who had woken briefly and then fallen back to sleep. Lying beside him, she had registered his breathing and she had heard the movements of Everett and William. And then she had slept and woken to the sound of a waterfall and she had become conscious of the rain. She wondered where Raymond was.

At breakfast she ate across from the Doctor and his wife. Several people had already left the Retreat, Ian and Jill among them. They had had "fantastic" plans to go down to California to work on a collective farm. "A commune on a grander scale," Ian had said, and Jill had held his hand and grinned. Stupid people, Lizzy had thought at the time. But now she saw that stupidity could arrive in many different ways. Lizzy had learned that Emma and Franz were leaving as well, driving down to Toronto and then flying to Berlin and then to Tanzania. Harris was not a part of their plans. He would stay on, as would the Byrds, and they would close the Retreat together with the Doctor and his family.

Lizzy wondered if her father felt a sense of collapse, that all the good intentions at the beginning of the summer had been mislaid. It made her heart ache because she could tell that her father was still convinced that her mother would return before everyone left.

Fish sat beside her and looked forlornly at his scrambled eggs. He asked for syrup.

"No more syrup," Lizzy said. "Just eat."

"But syrup," Fish said, looking up with round, clear eyes.

Everett came in, wheeling Harris. Lizzy, watching, felt that Harris had been humiliated once too often, though he did not seem troubled by the fact that his wife was going to leave soon. She looked away and tended to Fish, who had pushed his plate into the middle of the table. "Here," she said, and put a dollop of strawberry jam on the eggs and guided the plate back under his nose. He began to cry. She gave him a piece of toast and tea. Warily, he dunked the toast into the tea.

Everett parked Harris at the table and fixed him a plate of eggs and toast, a mug of coffee, and placed both before him. He sat down next to Lizzy and said, "There's a policeman talking to Dad. They're standing in the rain. I thought it might be about Mum, but it's not."

Lizzy went to the window and looked out to where her father was leaning into the door of the police car, seemingly oblivious to the rain that fell. William was with him, huddling close, as usual these days. Her father righted himself and sprinted towards the dining hall, William running to keep up. When they came inside, Lewis approached her, concern showing on his face.

Her father drove her to the police station, and during the drive her father talked. He said that she should tell the truth. He didn't know what the truth was, and he certainly didn't know what had happened the night before, but she shouldn't shy from the truth, whatever part of it she might know. His voice was quiet, but he was obviously worried and Lizzy told him that he had nothing to worry about, she hadn't done anything. He said that all of this, this mess, was his own fault. He should have taken the children home once her mother had left. He said he hadn't been paying attention, that he'd been selfish, too much inside his own troubles. When they arrived at the station, Lewis asked if Lizzy wanted him with her during the interview but Lizzy said no, she would do this herself.

The woman who questioned Lizzy was a detective, but she didn't wear a uniform and she didn't have a gun. She wore a skirt and a white blouse with a blue flower embroidered at the back, just below the collar. She spoke slowly and softly, but she never smiled. She wanted to know where Lizzy had been the day before, and who she had been with. She wanted every detail: the times, the places, what was said. There was a tape recorder and it was running.

The woman's name was Thibault. At first Lizzy thought she had said "T. Bone," but later she understood that it was a

French name and she had spelled it in her head. When they'd entered the room, Thibault had indicated one chair and taken the other and then bent to write something on a piece of paper. Lizzy saw that she was going grey. There were strands of hair that were completely white and they sat next to the more plentiful, black hairs, but it was the white hairs that intrigued Lizzy, as if they were a sign of softness.

Thibault looked up and asked, "Do you know why you're here?"

Lizzy swallowed and shook her head.

Thibault nodded. She asked how well Lizzy knew Raymond Seymour.

Lizzy said that she knew him. They were friends. "Why? Did something happen to him? Is he hurt?"

Thibault said, "Tell me what happened yesterday. Where were you?"

Lizzy's hands were shaking. "We were going out for a drive, and then on the way back, a police car pulled us over. It was that policeman. Hart. He was angry and Raymond panicked and knocked him over with the door. Later, he threw his gun in the ditch. He was scared. He didn't take the gun. And then we went to his cabin."

"Raymond Seymour's cabin?"

Lizzy nodded. She asked again if Raymond was hurt.

Thibault looked up from her notebook. "Why would he be hurt?"

"Something happened." She looked around the room. "Why am I here?"

Thibault leaned forward and touched Lizzy's arm. "Constable Hart was hurt. Late last night. There was a fight at the cabin. With a knife. You were there as well."

"No. No. I left the cabin. When the policeman saw me, that was the afternoon."

"You didn't see Constable Hart up at the cabin?"

"No. I did not. Raymond was afraid the policeman might come after him. He didn't like Raymond. Last year he left him on an island to die, so Raymond had reason to be afraid. Raymond wouldn't hurt anyone." She started to cry.

"Really? And yet you say he knocked Constable Hart out and threw his gun into the ditch."

"Over. He knocked him *over* with the pickup door. It was by accident." She wiped at her eyes with the back of her hand. "The man, Constable Hart, he was angry. There was no reason to be."

"How is that?"

"Raymond didn't do anything."

"But he did."

"Before. There was no reason *before* for the policeman to stop us."

"So, he's innocent."

Lizzy didn't want to cry again, because she knew that that would make her seem weak, but she began to cry anyway. She shook her head resolutely and turned away. She saw Raymond's face as he told her to stay in the truck. His eyes had been so cold and certain. She looked at Thibault now and said that she was afraid.

"Of course you are." Then Thibault asked what time she had left the cabin.

"Just after dark."

"You drove home?"

"Walked. I walked."

"And you didn't see Constable Hart after the incident on the highway?"

She shook her head.

There was a long pause during which Thibault wrote in her notebook. Voices, muted and unintelligible, passed by in the hallway.

"Can I see him?" Lizzy asked.

"No, you can't."

Lizzy bit her lip. "Has he asked about me?"

Thibault did not answer. Her pencil moved across the page and then she looked up finally. "Did he have sex with you? Raymond Seymour?"

Lizzy lifted her chin. "Why? Why is that important?"

"Did he?"

Lizzy nodded.

"How many times?"

Lizzy closed her eyes and opened them. Thibault was still there. "Two. Three times."

"Penetration?"

"Isn't that what sex is?" She felt that by saying that Raymond had had sex with her, it was as if she were lifting a stone and revealing what was crawling underneath. The question appeared to make perfect sense to this woman, and for Lizzy, in the confines of the room, each question seemed to require the truth. She was very tired and she had to pee but she felt if she admitted this it would be one more shameful thing. "We both wanted to. We agreed." Her voice sounded to herself slightly panicky.

Thibault nodded, wrote something down again, and Lizzy knew that the word *penetration* was wrong. A leap in logic would be made: if Raymond had penetrated her, he could have penetrated Hart with the knife. This policewoman would not know the difference. She was about to protest, when Thibault spoke.

"Did Nelson Seymour ever try to have sex with you?"

Lizzy felt frightened. "What are you trying to say?"

"Just what I asked."

"No," Lizzy said. "No. Nothing like that."

"Did anybody else in your family spend time with Raymond or Nelson?"

"No, just me," she said, and in saying this, she felt she had breached some high wall that had stood in the distance, a wall that had been impassable but was now behind her, and she knew that Everett was safe. She looked at Thibault and said she had to go to the bathroom. Could she?

"Of course," Thibault said. She led Lizzy into a corridor and together they walked down a flight of stairs, Thibault slightly ahead of her so that the blue flower at the back of her shirt was directly in Lizzy's eyesight. And then across a second hallway and up three steps into a cavernous bathroom that smelled of disinfectant. Lizzy went into one of the stalls and locked the door. She pulled down her jeans and under- wear and she sat, but for the longest time she could not urinate. She sensed Thibault beyond the door of the stall, and she realized that she would hear the pee hitting the water in the bowl and this made peeing impossible. Her stomach hurt. She listened for the rain outside, but she was deep in the core of the building and nothing from the outside world reached her.

And then Thibault said, "Here." Her voice echoed in the tiled bathroom and she turned on one of the taps at the sink, and as the water descended from the faucet, Lizzy began to pee. She went for a long time, aware of the release, aware of her hands on her bare knees.

Her father gathered her up as she came into the main area of the police station. He did not speak, just took her out to the pickup and placed her in the passenger's seat. Then he got in and asked if she was okay.

She nodded and looked out at the grey sky. The rain had stopped.

Her father drove slowly up Main Street and then left onto Second and past the Kenricia Hotel and the movie theatre and then past the prison where Lizzy imagined Raymond would be. She told him what Thibault had told her, that Hart had been stabbed by Raymond and Nelson. She said that she didn't believe it was true. She had been with Raymond in the afternoon, and she'd been up at the cabin afterwards, and she knew that there might be trouble, but not like this. She said that she'd walked home. "Raymond didn't force me to do anything," she said.

"You walked home? All that way in the dark? Why didn't Raymond drive you?" .

Lizzy shook her head. "He asked, but I wouldn't let him. He was in trouble."

Her father had that perplexed, simple look he sometimes took on. "I don't understand how this happened, Lizzy. I believe you, but I don't understand."

She knew that there might be something she could say to comfort her father, but she could not find the words. She turned to look out her window and remembered that when she was younger, for a summer, her father had operated a tractor trailer out of Calgary, hauling scrap metal up to Vancouver, and Lizzy had joined him on several trips. She had loved the night driving, the high headlights of the semi spilling onto the road before them and pushing away the darkness, and at each sharp turn she had imagined animals lying in wait in the middle of the road. But always, there was only the road and the trucks with their running lights passing in the opposite direction, and her father with his big hands on the wheel, staring straight ahead, talking to her, telling her long-winded stories about nothing really, and she had never felt so safe, so special, away from her brothers and her mother, by herself with her father. Now, that feeling of safety was gone, and with it the certainty and comfort. She thought about who she was now and who she had been and she felt longing for what could never be recovered.

The next day, the Doctor called Lizzy into his den. It was after breakfast and she was passing by as he stood on the porch, looking beyond her or perhaps right at her. She did not meet his gaze, and he called her name and then called it again, and when she finally looked up he nodded and said he would like to talk. She hesitated, and then said that there was nothing to talk about. He disagreed. He said that he might be of some help. He knew Raymond, he knew Constable Thibault, and perhaps he could help her. She went up the stairs and stood in his doorway and then entered the coolness of his private room. He closed the door behind him and asked her to sit. She said she would stand; what did he want to say? He sat in his chair and swivelled so that he faced her and he placed his hands in the form of a tent beneath his chin and he said that Constable Thibault had come to visit him. She had concerns. About Lizzy's story, about Lizzy's involvement with Raymond. "If there is something criminal, we must address it," he said.

"Only thing criminal is the police holding Raymond," she said.

The Doctor smiled. "That boy is not for you, Lizzy. You are better than him. You are like a cipher. And this interests me. Perhaps you are more like your mother than you would wish to believe. Both of you are clearly beautiful, but inside there is something veiled and impenetrable."

"I am not my mother."

He laughed. "Of course you are. And why wouldn't you want to be? She is an attractive, smart woman."

"I don't think we should be talking about my mother."

The Doctor said the word *chaos*, and then he repeated it. He said that chaos was necessary because it was the gateway to change. "Funny thing, about chaos, how it arrives unannounced, the result of an assassination, a judge gone wild, a minor insult, someone pissing on someone else's property. Little spark and, *poof*, you've got a maelstrom. This indefinable something, so trifling that we cannot recognize it, upsets the whole earth, princes, armies, the entire world. Pascal. If Cleopatra's nose had been shorter, the whole face of the earth would have been different. We're talking about love, but love, vanity, lust, they alter the shape of the earth. You watch. That occupation at the park, this wild nighttime stabbing of Hart, your imagined love of an outlaw, will change something. Maybe it already has. You, for example. Is he guilty?"

"No. He is *not* guilty." She was quick to respond, as if she had been holding her breath and waiting for the clarity of the question to appear out of the mist of nonsense. Yet, even as she said this, she saw Raymond's boots swinging out and Hart falling back onto the road. She pulled in a quick breath and looked right at the Doctor. "And you," she said. "You pretend to like Raymond, you invite him to dinner, and then suddenly, like everybody else, you turn on him."

The Doctor smiled wistfully. He said that she was at an age where everything was black and white. Right and wrong. There was no middle space where she could sort out the world. Some day she would see things differently, but for now he understood her quandary.

Lizzy wondered if he was jealous. Of her. Of her and Raymond. She moved towards the doorway and said that he knew nothing about her. That he knew nothing about Raymond. Then she turned and left.

E verett took a wool blanket and fashioned holes at the end
of it and looped strings through the holes and tied the
strings to empty tuna tins. He dragged the blanket through
the scat that had been dropped by the deer near the cabin stairs
and then he draped the blanket over his shoulders so that it
resembled a cape. He wheeled the camp's only bicycle up the
road to the main highway and set off. In a satchel he carried a
few tomato sandwiches and some cookies and a sealer jar filled
with fresh water and there were matches and a chocolate bar.
To any onlooker, he would have appeared as a vagabond, or a
wastrel from medieval times, a fender off of disease and pestilence, or the portent of pestilence itself arriving in a great
clatter. He had read, in one of the books from the Doctor's
library, about escape and avoiding detection. A book written
by a former marine who had a great fondness for possible
invasions by marauding armies. Packs of dogs might be set
upon him, and he would avoid detection. The empty tuna tins
were to cover his scent. The scat as well. Watery trails were
advised. Or fast-flowing rivers. There were no rivers but there
was a ditch, almost dry, that sprouted cattails and reeds the
height of his shoulders. He parked the bike in the bush and
walked barefoot through the ditch, carrying his runners. The

sun was warm on his face. He came up out of the ditch and sat and dried his feet with a corner of the blanket and put on his runners. He walked up through the bush and stood at the crest of the rock that looked down upon the dump. Gulls rose and fell with a clamour. The bulldozer sat like a large sleeping animal, blade pressed into the ground. He descended, the cape strung out behind him, the tuna tins banging against the rock.

He had dreamed, the night before, of his mother. She had come to him wearing only a T-shirt and he could see her bare bottom and he had woken with an erection and a panicky sense of his own demise. Staring up into the darkness he had imagined Nelson running, running. He was calling for help. At supper, he'd overheard his father saying that the police believed Nelson had not gone far. That he was hiding in the bush, or that he might be injured or have fallen. "Must be ter-rified," his father had said.

There had been beets on Everett's plate and they bled into the spaghetti. Their juice pooled and he could not eat them. His father talked about the dogs and the manhunt as if it were a story that was taking place at a distance. Everett had watched Lizzy's face, trying to find there some signal, but Lizzy looked blank. And then at night, just after the dream about his mother, he remembered the small cave that Nelson had pointed out to him and he had been certain that this was where Nelson was hiding. In the morning, before anyone else had risen, he crept from the cabin and gathered together the necessities of survival.

They had shot two raccoons and several rats that day Nelson had taken him to the dump. They had walked the perimeter of the fence, Nelson ahead of Everett, his shoulders pushed forward, his step easy, and Everett had attempted to imitate his rolling gait. And then the lair, or a den of a small animal, the opening covered with branches and leaves. Nelson had squeezed in, up to his waist, and then he reappeared and told Everett to have a look. "A hidey-hole," he'd said, and laughed.

Everett, fearful, had turned away.

And this was the place he was looking for now, because of course this was exactly where Nelson would go. But Everett could not remember the location and so he clattered up and down the length of fence, the cape catching in the bush and pulling at his neck and shoulders. Nothing resembled anything. He sat high up on the rocks and ate one of the tomato sandwiches and the cookies and he drank some water from the sealer jar. The jar smelled of rubber and the water was warm. The blanket was itchy and so he removed it and laid it at his feet.

A vehicle appeared below; a car pulling a trailer that was piled high with junk. A man got out of the car and removed the lock on the gate and swung the gate open and then climbed back into his car and drove down into the dump. The man backed the trailer up and got out of the car and this time he left his car door open. The radio was on in the car and the music floated up to where Everett sat. He watched the man off-load the junk and then get in the car and drive away. Another vehicle arrived, this time an old pickup with a wood-slatted box. A young boy climbed up into the box and pushed a stove off into the dump. It fell with a rattle and turned over once, teetered, and then rolled down into the hole at the centre of the dump.

A cat appeared out of the bottom of the dump, scrambling away from the falling stove. It looked like Bull. All black. The boy scrambled into the cab of his pickup and reemerged holding a rifle. He bolted a shell into the chamber, raised the rifle, and fired. The cracking sound fell upwards and the cat jumped sideways, ran in a circle, and fled through a hole under the fence. Everett stood and watched Bull disappear into the trees. Down below, the boy called out, "Hey." He was looking up at Everett, holding his hand like a visor to his forehead.

Everett lifted his hand and then lowered it. The boy watched him, then shouted, "Goddamn cat, eh?" and he waved and climbed into his pickup and drove off.

When he was gone, Everett retrieved his cape and climbed down to the spot where Bull had disappeared. For an hour he walked the area, calling out sweetly for Bull to come. "Here, Bull," he said, and at some point he began to call Nelson's name, softly at first and then more loudly. Down below, at the dump, vehicles came and went. When they arrived, Everett hid in the bush, and when they were gone, he resumed his search, but it had become a half-hearted search now. The existence of Bull had at first invigorated Everett, but then his enthusiasm had faded. As the day slipped away, he grew tired.

He climbed over the hill and lay down on the rock in the last of the afternoon sun. He resolved that he would go home and return the next day. He rose and gathered his things. As he descended the hill his foot caught on something and he stumbled and almost fell. He looked down at the opening that Nelson had shown him. He regarded it, then he said Nelson's name. It came out a whisper. He said Nelson's name again. He went down on his hands and knees and called into the opening. The smell of earth and grass. The opening was larger than he had remembered. He said, "Nelson, it's me, Everett. Are you there? Are you hurt? Can you hear me?"

There was no answer, just the sound of the wind coming up the hill from the dump. The air was cooler now. Everett studied the dirt and grass around the opening, hoping to find evidence of Nelson, but any evidence was in short supply. He pondered the possibilities. Perhaps Nelson had left his cat here at the dump and he had run off. Perhaps the cat had escaped from the cabin and come all the way here.

Everett knew he should put his head inside the hole, but he did not. Finally, he took the rest of the tomato sandwiches and the sealer jar of water and the chocolate bar from his bag. He laid these things at the opening, then pushed at them slightly so they disappeared into the darkness. He stood and he gathered up his satchel and cape and he set off down the hill. It was only when he had found his bike in the bush and wheeled it up onto the gravel road that he turned to look back, but by then it was dusk and the shapes of things were hard to make out. Everything, the sky and the land and the trees, had become one.

L ate that night, in the Hall, Lewis found Margaret holding and rocking Billy. He had come in to make a cup of coffee and she'd been sitting by the fireplace, singing softly. The scene was incongruous because Billy was such a large boy. Lewis paused, and then Margaret spoke. "It's me," she said, and Lewis came forward out of the shadows and said, "I know."

"He couldn't sleep," Margaret said. "And I enjoy the fire." She motioned at a chair for him to sit.

He said he wanted coffee, would she like some? She shook her head. He went into the kitchen and put the water on to boil and he measured some coffee into a filter. When he returned Margaret had laid Billy down on a blanket at her feet. Lewis sat across from her. A candle flickered on the table.

Lewis said that that morning, when the police arrived with the dogs, he'd suddenly seen that Lizzy was involved in some kind of trouble. He couldn't sleep, because, if he did, something more calamitous might take place. "I haven't kept track of my children."

"Don't be so hard on yourself," Margaret said. "You're doing the best you can."

Lewis smiled at this sentiment, which was so wrong-headed

and clichéd. He shook his head and said, "Funny thing, they didn't use dogs when Fish got lost. I'm guessing a policeman who gets knifed by an Ojibway teenager is more important than a four-year-old boy."

Margaret said that nothing was more important than Fish. He should know that. "You do such a good job with your children. I marvel. You know that I wanted more children, but Amos didn't." She said that she'd always wanted a daughter. She'd imagined sitting like this late at night and talking to her girl, talking about things that boys had no interest in. "I look at you, Lewis, and I get envious, all those babies, all those bodies to push up against." She lifted her hands to her head and pushed her fingers through her short hair, which she'd cut the day before, chopped it off so all that was left were shaggy tufts. Her long, slender neck was more pronounced, and she wore a necklace of black leather from which a silver cross hung. She leaned forward and said that Amos was too fond of himself. He didn't have room for more children. Her voice slipped to a whisper and she said that Amos liked to sit in her lap like a child sometimes, at night, when they were alone.

Her large hands were on her thighs, spread out. She said, "Oh my," and she sat back. "I know you won't tell anybody this." She shook her head. "Even if you did tell someone, they wouldn't believe you."

"Who would I tell?" he said. He was amazed by this confession. When he compared Margaret to Norma, he imagined that he had chosen badly. He told Margaret this.

She laughed. "So, you're saying you'd marry me if you had the chance."

"Maybe something like that. You aren't greedy."

"Aren't I?" She was quiet. Then she asked if he had something to tell her as well. She said that she was a great repository for men's desires. For their sadness, their stories. She said she'd have gotten rich as a prostitute. "Do you have something to share with me?"

Lewis said no, he had nothing. And as he admitted this he felt embarrassed in some way, as if to not have some secret to share with Margaret was an admission that he was a failure.

Billy shuddered at her feet like a large dog suffering night dreams. She asked if he was lonely and he said that he might be, but that wasn't the worst thing, was it? He said that he had tried to call Norma in Chicago, earlier that day, to let her know what was going on with Lizzy and Raymond, but there had been no answer at her sister's house. "She would want to know about all this," he said. His voice did not match the certainty of his words. Then he said that Norma had written the day before. She wasn't coming back to the Retreat after all. He still hadn't told the children.

Margaret said, "Oh, Lewis," and then she asked him if he wanted her to hold him. She could do that for him, no kissing or anything, she would just hold him. He could put his head against her chest.

He shook his head. He said that he was worried about the children. He wanted to check on them. She nodded as he stood, she did not appear to be hurt by his choice. As he turned to leave, she seemed to have descended into another place, as if she had already dismissed him.

He walked through the clearing and stopped at the children's cabin. He went inside and just stood and listened for a moment, then went over to William. He was breathing evenly. Everett was the restless child, sheet twisted around his knees. His legs were dark with hair. Lewis had not noticed until this moment that Everett had become a little man. He listened to him breathe. Slow and easy. All was well. Lewis experienced a tug of relief, a buoyancy that didn't arrive just because his boys were sleeping peacefully, but in recognition that he had said no to Margaret, that unlike the Doctor he did not need to sit in her lap. He walked over to Lizzy's bed. A double bed that dipped in the middle so that she appeared to be sinking. He leaned forward.

"Dad. What you doing?"

"You're awake."

"Hnn-hmmm." She rolled over so that she was on her back. In the dimness he saw her hair falling across the pillow. "Why are you snooping?"

"Just checking," Lewis said. "Good night."

"Good night, Dad."

He stood outside on the stairs for the longest time. He looked out onto the clearing and the thicket of trees beyond. A soft wind pushed against his face and his bare arms and brought with it the smell of rain. He stood like a sentry, as if some higher order had demanded that he defend this entrance. Only when it began to rain, lightly at first and then with an increasing intensity that turned into a downpour, did he step down into the clearing and make his way to his own bed.

On the second day, Everett brought bananas and a Coke and a carrot muffin that the Doctor's wife had made. He left his bike on the rocks and climbed up above the dump and approached the opening to the cave with seeming recklessness, and with the certainty of someone who wanted not to appear afraid, though he was still, and would remain fearful of what could not be verified. The food he'd left for Nelson was gone: the tomato sandwiches and the chocolate bar. A torn wrapper remained, and the sealer jar was still unopened. He spoke into the hole and said that he had come back. He asked Nelson to talk. "I know you're there," he said. "You ate the food I brought. I don't know if you are sick or well, or if you need me to bring you medicine. I cannot come inside, so please come out. I am alone. There are no police. I haven't told anyone about this place. If you don't want to talk, or you can't talk, leave me some sign that it *is* you. I'll come back tomorrow, and if it is you, leave one banana untouched. Then I'll know." He paused, looked around him as if there were possible humiliation in being observed speaking into a hole. He sat and waited for a sign of Bull, or the magical appearance of Nelson. The dump was closed for the day; an eerie quiet hung over the area. Fires burned in several spots. There was no wind and the smoke rose directly into the sky and it seemed contrary, as if the plumes of smoke were threads dropped from the sky.

Everett rode home in the late afternoon with aching legs, tired and hungry. A police car passed him going the other way, and then another. He stood at the side of the road and watched the cruisers disappear over the hill. He imagined a man trapped in a tree with dogs baying at his feet.

The following morning, early, his father asked him where he was going and he told him that he went up to Bare Point to fish.

His father looked at him and smiled and said, "You never liked fishing in your life, Ev."

"I grew to like it," he said.

"Oh, really, when was that? And where's the fishing rod?"

"I have one there. It's one I found."

"How come you never bring back fish for supper."

Everett shrugged. He said that they were too small too eat. He held his hands apart to indicate the size.

"Big enough," his father said.

Everett climbed on his bike and rode off, looking back to see if his father was watching him. He was.

He rode slowly, smelling the air. By now he had given up any attempt to disguise himself. Gone were the blanket and the tuna tins. Gone the precautionary trek through the watery ditch. It had rained earlier, a light drizzle and the roads were damp. The wildflowers in the ditch gave off a scent that mixed with the smell of barely wet dust on the road. Swallows rose and fell. There was a falcon high above. He saw two deer in the ditch. They lifted their heads and observed him, tails twitching. He had, in his satchel, two rings of smoked sausage. A vehicle approached him from behind. He pulled to the shoulder and hopped off his bike. A purple Ford pickup, beat up, with a very old man inside. The pickup slowed and stopped and then sat there, engine ticking. Broad lettering, "CM," was painted on the passenger door. The old man rolled down his window, called out, "Want a ride?" Then, not waiting for a response, he descended from the pickup and came around to Everett and hefted the bicycle into the box.

"Climb in," he said.

Everett looked at the man and thought that anyone this old must be harmless. He climbed into the truck.

The old man got back in, ground the stick shift forward, revved the engine, let out the clutch, and the pickup jumped forward. He wheezed, "Only got third and fourth. Lost first and second in the war." He laughed. "Where you going so early?"

"Fishing," Everett said. "Up at Bare Point."

The old man said that he used to fish for a living but there was no living to be had in fishing these days. He said he was now a collector of garbage. "Amazing the good shit people throw out. The other day I found a set of dinner plates like brand new. Gave them to my wife for her birthday. Another time I recovered a motorcycle in working order. A Norton. Perhaps it was stolen, perhaps not. I wasn't asking. People look at me as a saviour. I salvage what is lost and forsaken. I retool it and sell it. Or give it away. Children these days are lost and forsaken. Do you have children?"

Everett shook his head.

"You're old enough. Sixteen?"

"Almost," Everett said.

"I had a child when I was sixteen. And a boy who died when *he* was sixteen. My wife broke apart and all the king's horses couldn't fix her." He paused and glanced at Everett. "Where do you live?"

Everett said that he lived at the Retreat.

"What's that?" The hole of the old man's ear was covered by grey wires of hair.

Everett repeated his answer.

The old man nodded. He said he knew the place. It was a den for the iniquitous and indolent. This is what he had heard from a faithful source. His wife. He laughed again. He pulled a pack of cigarettes from his front pocket and worked one of them free while he drove. He lit the cigarette with a book of matches held in his left hand. He did a little trick with his fingers, twisting the match around the back of the book and holding the head of it against the flint pad with his thumb and flicking lightly until the match ignited. He held the book up like a single candle to the tip of the cigarette. He exhaled and this breath extinguished the match. His hands were dark with grease and oil. His fingernails were long. He asked Everett where his fishing rod had gone.

"What do you mean?"

"You fish with your hands?" He showed Everett a scarred palm.

"Oh," Everett said. "It's at the point."

The old man said that it could get stolen that way. "Never know who's going to take what doesn't belong to them. You hear the one about the police dog?" He didn't wait for an answer, just kept going. "An Ojibway fellow named Jack drives into town on a really hot day and he's got his dog with him, so he leaves his dog under the shade of a tree. Jack goes into the bar for a cold beer. Twenty minutes later, a policeman comes in and asks who owns the dog under the tree. Jack says it's his dog. The policeman says, 'Your dog's in heat.' Jack says no way his dog's in heat 'cause he's under the tree. The policeman says, 'No, you don't understand, your dog needs to be bred.' Jack shakes his head. 'No way he needs bread. He's not hungry 'cause I fed him fish this morning.' And the policeman gets mad now and says, 'Look, your dog wants to have sex.' Jack looks up and says, 'Go ahead, I always wanted a police dog.'"

The old man squeezed his eyes closed and chuckled and then opened his eyes wide and said, "The other day the police show up at my place with dogs and guns, looking for something, and they rattled my goat something bad. Made his milk go sour. You believe that?"

"I'm not sure."

"Of course you're not. You're too young to be sure. Here we are." He pulled up to the point and got out and off-loaded the bicycle. Patted the seat and said, "Good luck with the fish." The truck rolled away in a cloud of blue smoke and Everett watched it go. Then he climbed back on his bike and returned the way he had come, arriving at the dump mid-morning, just as the rain began to fall once again. He climbed up to the hole and found the bananas untouched.

He did not know what to do. In fact, he did not know why he was acting in this manner, riding his bike up here every morning to deliver food to a ghost. At first, when he had heard of Nelson's escape, he had imagined that he could help him. But this idea seemed far-fetched now. Yet he still felt something, anger perhaps, or sorrow, though he would not have been able to identify it as sorrow. He stood and surveyed the dump. The rain fell more strongly and lightning dropped from the dark clouds in the distance and thunder rolled in and surrounded him and then more lightning and rain came down, furiously, and with no other purpose it seemed than to soak him through. He did not know that he was crying until he swiped at his face and found there warmth that could not have come from the rain. Finally he stopped crying, pulled the rings of sausage from the satchel, and laid them in the shelter of the entrance to the hole.

Nelson had left his brother at the side of the road and walked in the ditch for a while and then come up out of the water and climbed the hill above the dump and descended to the fence on the south side. He had put his duffle bag and rifle through an opening in the fence, and then gone through as well. He picked up the gun and the bag and heard the mewling of Bull. He slid down through the garbage and came to rest at the centre of the pit. Small fires smouldered within the dump and it might have been an undersized campground suddenly abandoned, or the remains of a bombed-out village. A rat passed by his feet and he swore and kicked out in vain. Stumbled and fell and scrambled to his feet, panicking. He stood, breathing quickly, aware of the fresh blood at his chest. He stooped, opened the bag, and pulled out his cat. She clawed at his arm, trying to escape. He let her go and she fell, landed on her feet, ran a bit, and then jumped onto the lid of a large white box. A freezer. An older model, with rounded corners and a lock handle. Nelson stepped over a pile of twisted steel rods and studied the freezer. He pulled at the handle and opened the lid. The staleness of dead air. In the darkness he could not see what the freezer held, if anything. He leaned forward and peered into the maw, swept his hand back and forth and found it empty. He dropped his bag down inside and took his rifle and leaned it against the container. Then he kicked his way through the garbage, looking for a blanket or something soft to lie down on as a bed. He found a child's mattress, plasticized, and he took this and dragged it back to the freezer, moved the duffle bag, and settled the mattress at the bottom. He eyed the lock handle on the freezer. He took the rifle and ejected the shells from the chamber and put them in the back pocket of his jeans. Then he lowered the lid of the freezer and he held the rifle aloft and brought the stock down hard on the handle of the freezer. He felt the shock of the blow and severe pain in his chest. The lock was still intact. He attempted this one more time, but the pain was even greater and he had begun to bleed again. He held the rifle under his arm, retrieved the shells from his pocket, and re-inserted them in the chamber. He moved back, levered the action on the rifle, held it to his shoulder, aimed at the handle on the freezer, and fired. The bullet entered the lock mechanism, blew it apart, and exited from the rear of the freezer. He aimed then at one side of the freezer, squeezed the trigger, and a bullet went through the other end of the freezer. He now had his breathing holes. The sound of the two shots had lifted into the air and echoed up the far rocks and then come back at him. He did not know if anyone had heard the shots but he imagined it was possible. The first shot had sent Bull over to the fence and up the hill. He called for the cat, but she did not come. He placed the rifle alongside the plastic mattress and then he surveyed the place to which he'd come, and he climbed down into the freezer and pulled the lid shut.

He must have fallen into an immediate and deep sleep, because when he opened his eyes he saw only darkness and he did not know where he was until he heard what he thought was the sound of a fire burning and he smelled the plastic mattress beneath him. He shifted, and in doing so almost fainted from pain. He touched his chest and his palm came away sticky. When he lifted the freezer lid slightly he saw a grey light, which might have been dusk or dawn. He breathed slowly and fished around for his duffle bag and reached inside for the water. He drank sloppily, the water spilling over his mouth and down onto his neck and shoulders. He peeled a banana with some difficulty, took two bites and then fell asleep again. He dreamed of sliding down a muddy hill into a hole that contained mad dogs. The dogs brayed and slavered and wept as he dangled by one hand from a root just above them. He woke and the tumult of his dream became hollers and yapping in the world beyond his coffin. Two pricks of light entered the freezer through the bullet holes at his feet and head. He sat up, breathing hard, trying to ascertain the proximity of what he knew were the hunters. He lifted the lid slightly and saw only the hillside of garbage and the fence, and beyond the fence, rocks and trees. A gull flapped and settled nearby. He closed the lid, heard vaguely a whistle and a cry, and then the wailing of the dogs diminished and finally disappeared.

In his delirium he saw himself holding Hart. They were out in deep water and Hart could not swim and so Nelson had to keep him afloat, only he was failing to do so. He woke from this dream and felt the pain in his chest. His mouth was dry. His head hot. He was shaking and he knew that he had a fever. He reached for the bottle of whisky and opened it and drank and then he poured some of it onto the wound and he cried out in pain. Then he lost consciousness. When he woke, Bull was sitting on his chest, licking at the edges of the cloth that bound his wound. He did not know how the cat had entered the freezer. He had a half-formed recollection of having heard a scratching sound earlier, but this was all. Bull was purring and her tongue, when it touched his skin, was rough. Nelson could not see the cat but he could feel her and he reached out and stroked her back as she settled onto his chest.

"Hey," he said. "You hungry?" He felt for the bag and he found a piece of bread and he broke it and offered it to Bull, who did not want it, and so he put a piece in his own mouth and held it there. Chewed slowly. When Bull scratched to be let out, he lifted the lid and let the cat escape.

At night, a group of teenagers arrived and set up their vans and cars along the entrance to the dump. They opened their van doors and played music that floated down into the dump to where Nelson lay. Pink Floyd and Bob Dylan and Aerosmith. Nelson heard the songs and imagined that he was back in Lesser at a bush party where boys swam in the river and then stood shirtless by the fire. He lifted the lid of his freezer and peered out into the night. Kids appeared as stick people cavorting before a mammoth fire that lit up their faces and the sides of the vehicles. They seemed apparitions floating across the dark sky. They drank beer and threw the bottles down into the dump, several bottles landing within reach of

Nelson's spot. Girls laughed and swore and a boy called out for someone to show her tits. Voices, soft and irregular, came down into the pit and seemed to walk past Nelson's hiding place. He heard the voices but he could not make out what was said. A girl and a boy. And then the voices were above him and the freezer rocked slightly. One of them, perhaps the girl, was sitting on the freezer lid. Murmurings and then silence and then the girl said, "Okay. Okay, Main?" Nelson understood that Main was about to fuck this girl on the lid of the freezer. The girl's voice was ambiguous, clamouring. The boy was silent. "Okay," the girl said again and then she said, "Oh," and again she said this and then she called out, "Main, a cat," and the freezer moved abruptly and the girl said, "A fucking cat. Fuck, Main, it scared me."

"Aww, come here," Main said.

"It was black. A black fucking cat." Her voice fell away and fell away some more and then it was gone. Main was still there. He was sitting on the lid of the freezer. He was smoking and kicking with his booted heels at the side of the freezer. And then he called out, "Nicole," and he called again, and then the freezer shifted and Main was gone, and the din of the party returned.

For a long time Nelson lay and listened and he wondered if Bull was safe. He fell asleep and woke to silence and he lifted the lid and found himself at the edge of another day, the third or fourth in the freezer, he did not know for sure. The kids had left. Their fire burned dimly by the fence. He tried to imagine leaving this place. He pictured climbing up out of the dump and walking down to the road and finding a ride north. The possibility of not being caught was far-fetched and so he imagined building himself a house in the bush. Passing the winter. And then the summer. And the winter after that. At some point he would be found. He had not meant to hurt the man. The man had meant to hurt him. And he had accidentally hurt the man. Perhaps Raymond would suggest this. Perhaps he already had.

His jars of water were empty and his food was gone. He thought that he might manage to crawl out and find some source of water. He tried to climb from the freezer and fell back with the pain and passed out. He woke to a terrible smell and realized he had shit himself. He lay in his own urine and shit and he wept. He was cold. The temperature had dropped and the cold had entered the freezer and crept up around his feet and legs and then to his torso. There was the stench of his own excrement and urine and at some point he realized the wound on his chest was infected and was giving off the smell of rotten meat. He attempted to pour more whisky on it but he was too weak and he spilled the alcohol onto the floor of the freezer, where it pooled at his hips.

A brief and violent thunderstorm passed overhead and he lifted the lid of the freezer and held out the empty sealer jar to the sky. The effort required was immense, and when he drew the jar back inside, it held only a small amount of water and he drank this. He imagined, in his feverish state, that he would be drowned. He slept for long stretches and once, when he woke, he lifted the lid and saw that night had fallen once more. He slept again and he dreamed and in his dreams he quoted whole passages from Ephesians and the Psalms. He saw Raymond as a young boy standing alone in an empty space. He woke and opened his eyes and his mouth was moving and he was reciting a verse from Isaiah, something he had learned at the age of twelve, at the dining-room table, before he went off to bed. "My help cometh from the Lord, who made Heaven and Earth."

He heard a vehicle arrive at the edge of the dump and a door opened and the sound of whistling fell down onto his ears. And at the same time the cat came to him, meowing and scratching on the roof of his house. He imagined that the cat would attract the attention of the person whistling, and so he attempted to draw the cat into the freezer with him. But the cat thought it was a game and stuck her paw into the tiny crack and evaded his hand, scratching him lightly.

His vision blurred and he pulled at the cat's paw. He knew, if he caught her, he would break her neck, but she escaped. She left and came back and scratched and meowed. Nelson fell back against the plastic mattress and cursed the cat. He understood that if he was going to survive, he had to leave this place. Later, after he heard the vehicle pull away, he gathered the strength to climb and fall out of the freezer. He landed on a piece of iron, grunted, and then he stood uncertainly. The light of day blinded him. He shielded his eyes and surveyed his land; the sunlight reflected off his possessions and the cat appeared. She slipped sideways, up towards the fence, and Nelson tumbled after her. He could not walk, so he pulled himself up the hill on hands and knees, up into a world in which sacrifice and providence had already occurred. Up he crawled, past a spokeless bicycle wheel, an endless length of rubber hose, broken stained-glass windows, half a pulpit, empty tar barrels, insulation, plaster and lath, cereal boxes, carved wooden beams, a library of tattered and burned books, and finally a pair of boots. The boots were well-worn but they were still in fine shape, and when he touched one of them, the boot moved and he touched it again. He found the boot to be solid with a foot inside and his eye travelled upwards and he saw a leg and a torso and above that was a head of an old man and the man gazed down at him and Nelson lowered his head and began to tremble.

The old man spoke. "You forsaken son of a bitch," he said. Then he crouched beside Nelson and he held Nelson's jaw and looked into his eyes and he said, "Should be dead." They pondered each other as if they were meeting on the path to hell. The old man said, "Seymour, I guess." He stood and looked about and then he squatted again and said, "You wanna stay here, in this situation? 'Cause if you do, you'll die. Christ, you're already dead. Look at you." He had very few teeth. He rocked on his haunches and lit a cigarette. Nelson was on his back and from his perspective the old man's method of extracting and lighting the cigarette was convoluted, all upside down, but rather miraculous. The exhaled smoke appeared to descend rather than ascend. When he had finished his cigarette, the man punched the butt into the dirt near his feet and he told Nelson that he could help him, or he could leave him. The man frowned, or perhaps he smiled, because the sound he offered was one of high spirits.

"You smell like shit," the old man said, and this appeared to decide things. He leaned forward and said, "Come." He lifted him up and put his hands under Nelson's arms and stood him upright, like a tree that had been cut down and was about to be replanted, and they faltered at the bottom of the pit, and then the old man led Nelson up towards a purple truck that seemed impossibly old, just as the man seemed impossibly old, a mere spectre.

Thursday morning, Lizzy woke early from a dream in which Thibault was asking her to remove her clothes; she had stripped naked and when she looked up Raymond was standing before her. She lay in bed and thought of the interview, and how she had answered Thibault's questions so willingly, and she felt worried that she had been too free with her answers. She believed that Raymond would have been asked some of the same questions and she wondered how he would have responded.

The night before, late, she had gone to her father's cabin and found him sitting in a chair by the window. When she entered, he looked up and for a moment he appeared surprised, as if he had been expecting someone else. Lizzy had stood by the door, and when her father spoke, she came and sat near him.

"You can't sleep," he said. "What's going on?"

She said that she was worried about Raymond in prison. She had heard from Harris that the occupation was still going on, so maybe some people from there would help him. She couldn't stop thinking about him. "Don't you think about Mum all the time?"

"She wrote a letter," her father said. "It came the other day. She hasn't forgotten you."

"Yeah?"

Her father said that her mother had decided it would be best if she didn't come back to the Retreat. She would meet them back in Calgary.

"Did she say that, 'I'll meet you back in Calgary,' or are you just hoping?"

"Not those exact words, Lizzy. But she will. Of course." He paused, and then his voice slid away, and for a time Lizzy did not hear his words, just the sound of his voice. And then he said something about her missing her mother, and Lizzy turned to him. He said that when two people who love each other share a room, and then one person leaves, that person is missed. He said that this is what had happened with her mother. "Her smell, her voice, the air that you shared. All of this is gone. And it makes you terribly sad." He paused, and Lizzy waited, wishing for more, but he had nothing more to say.

❧

Mid-morning, the sky grew dark and a thunderstorm passed overhead, pummelling the Retreat. From the shelter of her cabin, Lizzy watched the trees bend as the rain obscured the clearing, and then the storm passed as quickly as it had arrived. Everett had left earlier by bicycle and had still not returned and she wondered if he had managed to find shelter.

Vernon came to the Retreat at noon to see Lizzy, and when word arrived that he was waiting for her in the Hall, she at first refused to see him, but then her father convinced her to talk to him. He said that this Vernon had some news about Raymond. She found Vernon and walked with him to the other side of the clearing. The grass was damp and the leaves were still dripping water, but the sun had come out and the air was humid and hot. Lizzy faced Vernon and asked him to take off his sunglasses, she hated talking to someone when she couldn't see his eyes. He removed the glasses and held them slightly aloft, as if this was only a temporary thing. His freckles appeared paler and smaller and his nose lifted as if sniffing her. He pulled at his ear. "Raymond ran," he said. "He took off and I'm wondering if he's shown up here. I suppose he will. He doesn't have many places to go and I don't think you want to be harbouring a criminal. Has he been here?"

Lizzy imagined Raymond running down a road and then into the bush. "No. He hasn't been here. Look around." She lifted a hand, offering him the whole area.

Vernon grimaced and shifted his weight and as he did so his face appeared helpless and lost. "I trusted him, and the stupid shit just took off."

Lizzy was aware of biting her lower lip. She hated Vernon at that moment. "Don't call him names," she said. "*You* let him run."

Vernon watched her carefully, or this seemed to be the case, because his glasses were on again and Lizzy could not see his eyes. He said that the other day, at his house, he had not meant to frighten her. "That wasn't my intention." Then he nodded and turned and left.

Later that afternoon, she and her brothers and Harris went to the pond. Everett, who had come back wet and bedraggled just after lunch, pushed Harris in his wheelchair. William, in order to hide the bare spot on his head, had taken to wearing a baseball cap, and looking down at him now Lizzy was conscious of his vulnerability. When Fish had asked Lizzy, the day before, what time their mother was coming back, William had looked up quickly, bewilderment on his face. Lizzy had said that their mother would meet them back home in Calgary, and William had looked away and his eyes had closed and then opened, as if he believed that Lizzy was making this up.

At the pond, the water was cold and William and Fish came up from their swim, shivering, lips blue. Lizzy wrapped them in towels and held them to her chest, one under each arm, until she too felt the chill of their bodies. Everett sat off to the side, pushing sand up onto his bare feet. The sun ascended and it grew warmer. Harris fell asleep, his chin resting on his chest. Lizzy imagined that Raymond might eventually come to her, and she did not know what she would say and do when he did.

She turned to Fish and held his head in her hands, pulled him close, and pressed her mouth to his small, cool ear and whispered that she loved him. She rolled back towards William and did the same to him, but he stiffened and pushed her away. Still, he'd heard her words. She lifted her head and listened to the sweeping of the leaves in the warm wind, which sounded to her like the distant cry of an animal, slack-jawed, hunting at the edge of the clearing.

There had been the light, the haze of the thin clouds, and the sun pushing through and falling onto the ground. And the smell in the air that Wednesday morning had been the clean brisk smell of fall as Raymond and Vernon left the courthouse in Kenora where the judge had set Raymond's bail at ten thousand dollars. The judge said that the severity of the attack on Constable Hart, to which Raymond had confessed, warranted a large bail, and whether it was self-defence or not was yet to be determined. He warned him that his brother was still a wanted man, and whether he was guilty or not, Nelson had fled the scene. "You'd do well not to hide any information about your brother, Mr. Seymour."

Raymond had been conscious of the uniformed policemen in the room and he'd wondered briefly if his brother Marcel might be willing to be his lawyer. He didn't understand how any of this worked. He'd spent a number of nights in prison and the experience had left him frightened. The first night he'd been woken by a banging on his cell wall and his neighbour chanting. Then a voice had called out that he was a fucking hero, a cop killer, and someone else had cheered and soon everyone was joining in and Raymond had covered his ears, wondering about Hart. In the morning he asked one of the guards if Hart was dead, and the guard looked at him and said, "You wishing, Seymour?" That afternoon, in the exercise area outside, a man came up beside Raymond and said, "Bassett wants you."

Raymond looked at the man, who had a pair of dice tattooed on his left temple. He had heard of Bassett, that he was a prisoner to be wary of.

The man had whispered something incomprehensible, and then said, "If Bassett tells you to eat shit, you eat it. You understand?" He turned and walked away. Raymond looked about, trying to determine which one Bassett might be, but he found nothing in the expressions of any of the men around him. That night he slept poorly, and at some point he heard someone call out and then he heard the sound of crying. The next morning, a guard stood by his cell door and said, "You a faggot, Seymour?" Then he said that today was court day and that the judge was waiting on him.

Vernon had taken him by cruiser to the courthouse. As he drove, he talked at the windshield. He said that Hart had been released from the hospital, and for that Raymond should be thankful.

The courtroom was tiny and Raymond's boots echoed on the hard floor. The judge told him to look him in the eyes when he was talking to him, and when Raymond looked up, he saw the darkness of the judge's face and he found no pity there. On the way back to the prison, Vernon said, "Why are you lying, Seymour? You aren't capable of violence. Least I didn't figure that." He looked in the rear-view mirror and said,

"If you know your brother's whereabouts, you better say. They're going to find out anyway, so there's no point trying to protect him." Raymond was silent. Vernon shook his head, sighed, patted his front pocket, and said that he needed cigarettes. He slowed the vehicle and pulled in at the Shell station on Second Street. Through the window Raymond saw the marquee on the Paramount. *Chinatown* was showing. He shifted and said, "You wouldn't let me use the washroom, would you, Vernon?"

"No way, Seymour, not on my watch."

"Look at me, Vernon. You're twice my size. Anyway, I don't *want* to run."

Vernon shook his head and got out and walked into the service area where he stood for a time, talking to the girl at the counter. The girl was laughing. She ducked her head shyly and then looked up and smiled and Vernon leaned forward onto the counter and then glanced back at his cruiser. A woman walked by in high black boots. The traffic passed. Vernon came outside, lit a cigarette, and stood eyeing the cruiser and then looking back at the girl. Finally, he walked to the cruiser, opened the rear door, and told Raymond to get out. When Raymond was standing alongside the cruiser, Vernon made a big show of unlocking his handcuffs. "Go take your crap," he said, and he pushed Raymond forward. They walked, Raymond ahead of Vernon, past the front window and the girl inside, who was watching. The door to the bathroom was along the outside east wall of the building. A single toilet with no window. Raymond turned on the tap and let the water run for a long time, and then he bent forward and drank. When he straightened, he saw himself in the mirror and began to shake. He closed his eyes and he talked to himself. He said that it was okay and then he said his own name and, again, that it was okay. Opening the bathroom door, he saw Vernon standing over by the cruiser, talking on his radio. Then he stepped outside and ran.

Just after sunset, he walked out of the bush, stood on the highway about eight miles from Kenora, faced the oncoming traffic, and put out his thumb. A young man heading up to Sioux Narrows picked him up. The man said he framed houses for his uncle and that he'd put a nail through his palm with a power nailer just that morning and then driven himself to the hospital. He held up his left hand, which was wrapped in thick gauze. As they approached the entrance to the Rushing River Campground, Raymond pointed and asked the man to stop and let him off.

"You camping up here?" the man asked.

Raymond said that he was visiting some friends who were camping.

"You have a nice night then, eh?" the man said.

"Sure. You bet. Thanks." Raymond got out and stood for a moment on the shoulder and heard the sound of the rapids. He walked into the campground and up to the north beach where he sat on a picnic table and looked out across the water to the campfires on the other side of the channel. Children's voices drifted through the air.

He looked down at his boots and considered the many possible roads that would have led him to this particular place in his life, but he couldn't get a firm grasp of any of the roads. The day before, he'd heard someone in the jail say that the occupation of the park might be ending, that the protestors would be giving up their weapons and walking out of the park. He did not understand how something that important could be ended so quickly, with so little excitement, and he wondered if he had been mistaken to be a part of it. He did not know what purpose it had served. Maybe Nelson had been right when he'd said that Raymond was too trusting. Even when they were younger and still lived together, Nelson was the one who had been sure of himself. Raymond had admired his brother's confidence, and though he had tried to be like Nelson, he always felt he had failed.

That night Raymond built a fire with leftover wood gathered from abandoned campsites. The campground was half empty. He slept and he dreamed of his grandmother, who was burning grass in a small glass bowl, and she was washing herself with the smoke, and she looked right at him and her mouth moved, but he could not hear what she said. And then Nelson was in his dream and he was bleeding from his chest and holding out his arms and Raymond, though he was fearful of the blood, held his brother. He woke, breathless, and he saw the darkness and the stars above him, and he knew that he was in the kind of trouble there would be no escape from.

He could not sleep again and he built up the fire and watched the sun come up. He dozed off and woke later to a thunderstorm that forced him to find shelter in the nearby showers. When the sun had reappeared, he walked back out to the highway and caught a ride with someone from Minnesota who was running a truck full of sausage up to Winnipeg. He got out of the truck on the highway west of Kenora, and, keeping off the roads, he wound his way through the bush towards the Retreat.

By late afternoon he was sitting in the trees above the pond. He could see Fish and William swim and then run back in towards Lizzy, who towelled them dry. He saw Everett and the man in the wheelchair and he saw a tail of smoke rising from the kitchen at the Retreat. He had never seen Lizzy in a bathing suit. She appeared to be smaller, as if she'd been diminished by the last few days. He listened for her voice, but he could not hear her when she spoke and at some point Lizzy was holding her brothers and whispering in their ears. Raymond's heart ached, and he imagined stepping down towards the pond to be with them.

A while later, they stood and gathered their towels and walked up the trail towards the clearing, Everett walking backwards and pulling the wheelchair over the rough path, and then they were gone and there was the sound of a bell, which meant that they would soon be going to the building where they ate. He remembered the first time he'd come for a meal at the Retreat. It had been the year before, and the group had stood around the table and held hands and sung and he'd not known what to do with his mouth, and so he'd looked down at the plate in front of him. The act of holding hands had surprised him, and the singing had been full and strong, and the food had been good. He realized he was hungry. He sat and waited. The sun dropped in the sky and then set. The air grew colder. The stars appeared. And still, he waited.

That night, Lizzy woke to a persistent sound, a voice or a tapping sound, a soft knocking, as if the wind were moving and banging a loose door. She saw the shadows of the beds across the room and the shapes of her brothers as they slept. She sat up, swung her feet off the bed, found her jeans, and put them on. Bending over, she felt for her runners and slipped them on over her bare feet. She went to the door and stepped outside onto the front stairs.

She saw Raymond at the edge of the clearing. He came forward and as he did so she went down the stairs. She said his name, "Ray," and he held her as she said his name again and again. Then she pushed away and looked at him and led him to the empty cabin Franz used to stay in. Inside, it smelled of must and the air was thick. In the darkness she fumbled with the windows and opened the one that faced the bush to the west. A soft breeze blew in. Raymond moved back the curtain on the front window slightly, peered out, and said, "There's a light on in one of the cabins."

"The Doctor's," Lizzy said. "Don't worry, his light is always on late at night." They sat on the bed in the darkness and she held his hand and said that Vernon was looking for him. He was definitely not safe here.

He said that he wasn't going to stay long. He'd just wanted to see her.

"Tell me what happened. Are you in the clear? This is bad, Raymond, really bad." She had trouble catching her breath.

He was silent for a moment, and then he said, "Hart would have killed Nelson and me. He pulled a knife on Nelson and I jumped him and he fell and the next thing he's got a knife in his chest. It was self-defence, but for sure one of us will be blamed. Or both." He said that he didn't know where Nelson was now. "He wanted me to leave him at the dump. That he'd figure out where to go from there. He could be anywhere by now." Then he said that he had taken Hart to the hospital and turned himself in and he had confessed to stabbing Hart. "That's the story I gave. And now it's the truth."

"Jesus, Raymond."

Raymond took out a cigarette and lit it. The match flared and Lizzy panicked and said, "Someone'll see." She went to the window and lifted a corner of the curtain. The Doctor's light was out, the clearing was dark. She stepped back, breathless, and whispered, "You have to go. Now."

His face was revealed briefly by the glow from the cigarette. He said that he had nowhere to go. He said that he had never been in a place like this prison before. It scared him. Maybe he'd run up north. Before morning, he said, he would start walking.

Lizzy was still standing by the window and she felt that the space between her and Raymond, the distance from the window to the bed, had become a vast chasm. She did not really know if he was telling the truth. He seemed different from the boy she had gotten to know that summer. She wanted to go to him but she didn't know how to cross that wide space. She lifted a hand, then let it drop. "I'm afraid for you, Raymond. I'm really afraid."

He grunted, as if in agreement, and then he began to speak and it was as if the darkness in the room and the darkness outside had freed him. He said that when he was nine his brother Nelson had been taken away. "There was a man and there was a woman, and they came to my grandma's house looking for Nelson and me. Only I wasn't home. So they just took Nelson." He said that for the longest time he had waited for Nelson to come back. And then at some point he began to forget about his brother. Not all day, or every day, but there were times, like when he was playing, or when he was in school, when he'd suddenly realize he hadn't been thinking about Nelson being gone, or coming back, and he'd felt guilty because Nelson had been the one to be taken away. But then the guilt went away as well, and life became usual. There were times when his grandmother would tell stories about Nelson, and she'd laugh then, and he would wonder if someone would have been telling stories about him if he had been the one taken. He said, "It's like Nelson has lived a bigger life than me. You know? But I always feel like there's something I have to make up to him." He was quiet, and then he said, "Nobody stopped them."

Raymond fell silent. Lizzy, still standing by the window, did not move. She understood that what he was telling her had always been real, but now, as he spoke the words, it had become truer: because she was there, and because, even though he could not see her, he knew that she was listening.

She heard him exhale. He said that he was tired. And hungry. He was going to sleep for a bit, and then maybe they could get him some food from the kitchen. And then he would go.

In the darkness she heard him cross one boot over the other and very soon she heard the sound of his steady breathing. She stood, alert to the sounds coming from the open window. The wind in the trees, and faintly, from the highway, the sound of a truck gearing down. She stood there watching while Raymond slept. He was on his back and his breath caught with each intake so that he startled, but not enough to wake himself.

She felt alone, but with this came a strange elation, as if she herself were safe from danger. She did not know, nor would she ever truly know, Raymond Seymour. She had explored his body as if it were some sacred site, but that was just skin and blood and bones. The shell of the body. She didn't know what he believed, not really, she didn't know how he saw the world, or how he saw her. About all of this, she did not know. Just as she did not know that in the autumn to follow, she would despair the heartlessness of the world and her inability to consume her own sadness. That, with the passing of time, what was precise and unbearable would eventually dim and gather a layer of longing, and as she would grow older and try to recall the details of the events of this summer, she would fail, and she would always lament that failure.

She went to Raymond now and lay down beside him, hoping he would wake, but he did not. She wanted to hear his voice, and she wanted to tell him that he should go soon, before it got light. She whispered, "You are good. You know that?" Then she lay there, judging the time and the sound of the night, and she fell asleep with her face pressed against him.

When Raymond woke, he saw the dim light of the early morning. He worked his way free of Lizzy, stood above her, and then went to the door, opened it, and surveyed the empty clearing. He saw the pale light from the Doctor's window, paused, and then stepped outside and down the stairs and over to the side of the cabin facing the bush and peed. As he made his way towards the entrance to the cabin he heard a voice and looked up and saw the Doctor at the edge of the trees. The Doctor's voice was clear and it broke the silence. "Come over here, Raymond." Raymond took a few more steps into the clearing. Then he saw, by the trail that led to the main road, that Vernon was walking towards him. Raymond turned to look behind him and perhaps it might have appeared that he was going to run. He did not hear the shot, because the bullet hit him before the sound arrived. He put his hand up to his throat and sat down carefully in the clearing. One leg was straight out in front of him and the other was bent off to the side. He sat slouched forward, one hand at his throat. He pulled his hand away and saw the blood. When he tried to say something, the blood bubbled out of his throat. He looked about. A haze had settled over the clearing. The treeline, the sky, all was wavering. He saw the Doctor off to the side and he saw Vernon approaching him. And there was Hart behind Vernon, cradling a rifle in one arm. Vernon's mouth was moving but Raymond couldn't hear him. Raymond cocked his head quizzically and tried to tell him that he was shot, but Vernon knew. He was kneeling before him and looking at the wound, as one would inspect a hole in a fence. Vernon shook his head. "You stupid prick," he said. He saw Vernon's face up close, and it seemed confused, as if on the verge of weeping. He saw Vernon shake him. He didn't feel anything but he knew Vernon was shaking him because Vernon's arms were moving and he knew his own shoulders and head were moving. Vernon was wearing a red vest. He held Raymond's wrist and with the other hand he pushed against Raymond's throat as if to stopper something there. He stood and stepped backwards. The front of Raymond's shirt was full of blood. He saw the blood and it was like a vast hole and his head fell towards the hole onto his chest. The lunge and flicker of his brother floating in a white boat, a herd of deer turning to look backwards, birds disappearing into a black cloud. He lifted his head briefly, and then it dropped one last time.

Behind him, the cabin door opened and Lizzy appeared. She ran down the stairs, missed a step, and stumbled. She was calling, though Raymond could neither hear nor see her. She came into the clearing and as she did so, she stopped. Her mouth opened and she let out a silent howl.

The sun had climbed just above the treeline and it fell into the clearing where Raymond sat. One leg was stretched out before him as if he were hurtling over something. His chin had dropped to his chest. Raymond's shadow was slight. His body had tilted a little. And then Lizzy was upon him, saying his name, touching his head and shoulders and chest, her hands bloody now, the long wail of her "Nooo" lifting into the sky. From a distance, the two of them might have appeared as children at play, one who is impatient and imploring, and the other who has sat down and refused to budge.

When they were young and still living together with
their grandmother, Nelson understood that Raymond
wanted to be just like him. Raymond copied his movements,
his speech; he tried on his clothes and boots and even took to
saying that his name was Nelson, not Raymond. Sometimes,
to humour his brother, Nelson played along and they would
spend the day talking to each other as if they were the other
person. And then one day Nelson grew tired of the game and
he pinned Raymond to the ground and began taunting him.
Raymond struggled uselessly and cried out that Nelson
should let him win. "I'm you," he said. "Then free yourself,"
Nelson said, and he held him down and aimed a fist at
Raymond's ribs. "Who are you then?" he mocked, and he did
not release Raymond until he admitted that he was a little
prick, and that his name was Raymond.

That fall, while in prison, Nelson thought often of his
brother, whom he had always pictured as the lucky one, with
family nearby and his grandmother's love; he had never lost
who he was. Nelson had arrived at the medium-security
prison in the middle of September, after a stay in the hospital and a brief trial at which he was found guilty of attempted
murder of a police officer. On the second day after his arrival

at the prison, out in the exercise yard, a wiry boy who spoke French set upon him for what appeared to be no good reason. Nelson, surprised at first, moved backwards, his arms in the air as if grasping for the rung of a ladder that did not exist. The boy held a makeshift knife made from the sharpened handle of a spoon, and he said words that Nelson did not understand, though the sounds were musical and distracting. Nelson's astonishment was eclipsed by the cold arrival of reason and he quickly dismissed the boy with a flurry of fists. Before the guards arrived, he pushed the boy's head against the cement of the yard and whispered in his ear that the next time he would beat his brains to froggy pulp.

Throughout those early days in prison, he fought his way up the pecking order and he grew to understand the place in which he found himself, and he came to feel a kind of comfort. Sometimes in the evening, before he slept, he played dice with Yuri, his cellmate, a thirty-one-year-old Slav who had permanently crippled a friend over a gambling debt. The cell smelled faintly of urine. The cement floor was cold. Outside, an early winter bore against limestone walls; inside, the whistle of wind through the air shafts. One night Nelson won a pair of shoes, a carton of cigarettes, Yuri's wife for a night, things real and things not, and by the end of the evening he gave it all back, even the false wife, aware of Yuri's past and that he didn't want to be maimed in his sleep. Yuri said that his previous cellmate, the man Nelson had replaced, had hung himself one night. Fashioned a noose from a bedsheet. He woke in the morning to the smell of piss and shit and the sight of the man's bare feet, purple and swaying.

That night Raymond came to Nelson in a dream and he sat down and began to speak. His face was turned away from Nelson and so all Nelson saw was his silhouette. He said that he had chickens to slaughter and would Nelson help him. He held up his hands, which were spotted with blood, and wiped them on the shirt he wore, and Nelson saw that it was his own, a favourite snap-button cowboy shirt, checked orange and white. Then Raymond laughed and his laughter was easy and good and he said that there was nothing to be afraid of, he was in good hands. "Look at me," Nelson said, and he called Raymond a stupid shit, getting himself killed. Nelson woke, heard the weeping of a prisoner two cells over, and he covered his ears and stared up into the darkness.

One day, a man in a suit appeared, bearing in his briefcase a survey with myriad questions. He wore a fedora and he was runty and pale and he interviewed Nelson in the visitors' lounge while a guard stood nearby. He held a pencil and took notes and he asked Nelson where he'd been born, and did he watch TV as a young boy, and when did he leave home, and how many brothers and sisters did he have? At some point, the man held up a flashcard and on the card was a paragraph, and he read the sentences out loud and asked Nelson if there were words that he did not understand. One word, *sublime*, was complicated, and Nelson wasn't sure about it, but he did not want to admit this. "You can go fuck yourself," he said. The man did not flinch. He bent towards his notebook and scribbled something and then he looked up and asked if Nelson believed in God, or if he was an atheist. He said the word *atheist* and he rolled his eyes slightly and Nelson thought that he might be retarded. He said that this was none of the man's business. And then the man asked what he wanted to do with his life, and Nelson looked at the man, and he leaned forward, and he said that he would live, and he would live well. "In spite of shits like you, with the hat and the milky hands and a nub for a dick."

At night, in the darkness of his cell, Nelson lay on his cot and imagined his ultimate release and retribution. He would kill Hart. He saw no reason not to. He had nothing but time, and time augmented his passion for revenge. There was only absence: of God, of family, of Raymond. Still, he understood conformity and submission – his training in this had been arduous and complete – and he learned to curry favour with the guards and with those prisoners who held the power. One day, in the dining room after lunch, Ernest, an enormous man and a prisoner with power, cornered him and said that he wanted Nelson to take care of a young man called Soot. Ernest said that he only wanted a message sent; he did not want Soot dead. "That's pointless," he said. "Something more meaningful would be fine." He pushed a thick finger against Nelson's sternum.

In the morning, Nelson caught Soot alone in the shower. Came up behind him, twisted his left arm behind his back, and pulled it from its socket. Then he walked away, barely winded, as Soot howled and writhed on the wet floor, his penis shrivelled and blue. Ernest tried to reward him with hashish and a month's supply of cigarettes. Or sex, if he liked.

Nelson shook his head and said he wasn't interested in any of that. He wanted to be left alone; that would be payment enough. Ernest peered at him, eyes black and lidless, and then, before dismissing him, he whispered that he had met men like Nelson before, men who appeared to have no fear, no shame, no thing to lose. He said that this kind of man was very useful to him. "Might this be you?" he asked, but Nelson did not respond.

One night, he dreamed of the dump and of the dogs tracking him, and he woke abruptly and sat up. A light burned dimly down the long corridor beyond the cell door. A voice, high-pitched and anguished, called out. He lit a candle and the flame wavered and danced, and in that muted weightlessness he saw his past spool and jump. He saw a white-enamel chamber pot in the corner of his room; his breath steaming as his bare knees shook. The back seat of the Ford Falcon, covered in plastic, smelling of the poly that sealed the windows in his grandmother's house, and the heads, oblong and monstrous, of the man and the woman who had taken him away. The pale, thin arm of his stepsister and the passing glimpse of her sex as she changed in the bush at the edge of a gigantic brown lake. The anthracite in the coal bin and his shovel feeding the fire; the taste of carbon still there in the morning as he bent to his porridge and heard the drone of his stepfather's voice spilling Matthew into the room, his thoughts roaming, roaming. Dorothy Stoez's mouth and the taste of her tongue, the texture of her nipples, the tumbling nonsense words — they had met in an outhouse behind the school, surrounded by the stench of ammonia, seeking love.

His grandmother's thick grey socks with the red stripes. Reenie singing, her eyes closed, her bracelets jangling. He saw Raymond, flat on the ground beneath him, crying, twisting, little cocksucker.

And he saw him dead. He did not know if Raymond had been surprised, if death always burst through the door like an unexpected visitor, if there was enough time to protest and call out, "Hey, you're taking the wrong person." And he saw Raymond wearing his jeans, his shoes, his shirt. No animosity this time, just the consolation of becoming each other. The long summer day rose and fell and the light seeped from the sky and darkness came, and to keep back the darkness they built a fire, their shadows indistinct against the wall of night that looked down on them.

ACKNOWLEDGEMENTS

The line spoken by Lionel on page 167, beginning "And we won't get any demands met. . . ," is taken from an interview with Lyle Ironstand and Louis Cameron that originally appeared in *Paper Tomahawks: From Red Tape to Red Power* by James Burke.

The author wishes to thank Blaine Klippenstein and Jerry Tom. He also wishes to express his gratitude to his editor, Ellen Seligman.